REPARATION

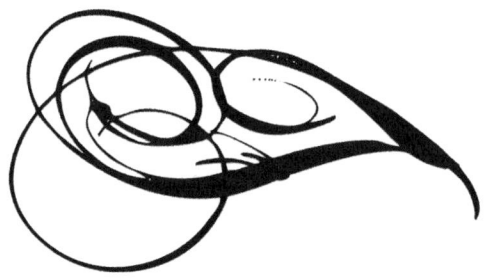

STYLO FANTÔME

Reparation
Published by BattleAxe Productions
Copyright © 2014
Stylo Fantôme

Editing Aides:
Barbara Shane Hoover
Leticia Sidon

Cover Design:
Najla Qamber Designs
http://najlaqamberdesigns.com/
Copyright © 2014

Formatting by Champagne Formats

This book is licensed for your personal enjoyment only. It is the copyrighted property of the author, and may not be reproduced, copied, re-sold, or re-distributed. If you're reading this book and did not purchase it, or it was not purchased for your use only, then this copy must be destroyed. Please purchase a copy for yourself from a licensed seller. Thank you for respecting the hard work of this author.

ISBN-13: 978-1505579925
ISBN-10: 1505579929

Dedication

For the street team ladies.

For fans.

For Jameson.

For my own sociopathic tendencies.

For dirty words and dirtier sex.

For not being afraid.

1

"SOMETHING IS WRONG."

"I am aware of this."

"She's acting weird."

"I am aware of this, as well," Jameson sipped at his coffee, his eyes scanning the newspaper he was holding.

"Something happened, in Paris," Ang continued pestering him.

"Yes, I think it might have something to do with you showing up with her sister in tow," Jameson commented, flipping a page.

"Well … yeah, but not just that. Something else. Something is *wrong*," Ang stressed.

"I am aware of *all of this*. I'm the one who goes home with her at night, you know," Jameson reminded him. Ang grumbled, but didn't say anything.

He's becoming immune to me. Hmmm, I'll have to try harder.

"I may have fucked things up in Paris, but you fucked things up in her brain," Ang finally retaliated. Jameson chuckled, turned another newspaper page.

"She seems to have gotten over that. In fact, she doesn't seem to be angry at me *at all*, anymore. So really, I'm not sure why I'm here.

I've been benefiting from your little mistake every day since I got home," Jameson said. Ang leaned over the table.

"You've been benefiting from me ever since you two started having sex – *I'm the one who got to sleep with her for five years, you know*," Ang said in a mocking voice. Jameson finally glanced at him.

"*Angier*, it's hard to call dibs on her sexual prowess when *I was there first*," he reminded him.

"Get fucked, *Satan*."

"I have been – *every day*."

"I hope you enjoy all the hard work I put into her, I —,"

"Can we *please* stop talking about her as if she is a car that both of you like to have sex with, *thank you*," Sanders finally interrupted. Both men looked over at him.

Ang had called Sanders, asked to meet with him, to talk about Tate. Of course, Sanders had told Jameson. Jameson was not about to let either of them have any conversations about her without him, so he had invited himself to their little lunch meeting. Ang hadn't been too happy, but Jameson had to give it to him. Tate was Ang's main concern, so for her, he would tolerate being in the devil's presence.

"What is it, exactly, you would like me to do?" Jameson asked, sighing heavily. Ang leaned back in his chair.

"She doesn't listen to me anymore," he started.

"You two go out, *all the time*," Jameson pointed out. It was a fact that did not make him happy.

"Yeah, but she doesn't really talk anymore. We used to talk about everything. Now, it's all ... *fluff*," Ang tried to explain.

"What is fluff?" Sanders asked. Ang shrugged.

"You know, shit. Stuff. Nothing serious. She's fun, and she flirts, and she always wants to be doing something, and it's driving me nuts. I tried to talk to her about that day, in our hotel room, and she just acted like I hadn't even said anything. I get the feeling if I brought up her hospital stay, the same thing would happen," he told them.

REPARATION

"So, what? You want me to ask her to relive some of the most emotionally painful moments in her life?" Jameson clarified. Ang snorted.

"Fuck off. I just want her to not be a robot anymore."

Jameson blinked. It was a good description. A sexy robot, pre-programmed to say all the things she thought everyone wanted to hear. He glanced at Sanders, who was staring into his salad. Of the three of them, Sanders was probably the closest to her, emotionally. If anyone knew what was going on, it would be him.

"Sanders," Jameson started. "Do *you* know what is going on with her?"

"No. I mean, she'll talk about those things with me. She doesn't act like a robot, at least not around me. But yes, she has been a little odd, ever since we got back. It's like she is trying to forget everything," Sanders agreed.

"Do we want her to remember? I thought our goal was to get her to move one," Jameson pointed out.

"That's not my goal," Ang said. Jameson snorted.

"I don't give a shit what your goals are."

"I —,"

"We want her to *feel*, sir. I think she is numbing herself, but that is just my opinion."

"Well then. I guess it's up to me to make her *feel* something. If she wants to pretend like there's no history, then I'll remind her. Gentlemen," Jameson dismissed himself, standing up abruptly. He threw some money on the table and walked away.

Always making me work, baby girl.

Paris *had not* ended well, for any of them. Sometime between storming out of Ang's hotel room and Jameson holding her, Tate had changed. A slight shift to the left. Or backwards. He couldn't quite tell. Either direction, it had been enough to throw him completely off guard, and he still felt like he hadn't gotten back on his feet yet.

She was mad at Ang. She felt betrayed by Ang. She was hurt that he had kept his relationship with Ellie a secret, and she was *pissed* that he had a relationship with her sister, *period*. Ellie and Tate had never exactly been friends. Ang was sleeping with a sworn enemy of sorts. It didn't matter that Ellie and Tate had made peace – it still wasn't okay, in Tate's eyes.

She didn't want to stay in Paris. Jameson wasn't surprised. She didn't want to stay in Europe at all. *That* surprised him – he had figured they would at least head back to Marbella, but she wanted to go home, back to Boston. He reminded her that he still had two weeks left in their little game. Two weeks to convince her to stay with him. She had informed him that it wasn't necessary. She wanted him to come home *with her*.

He was absolutely fucking shocked.

It was too easy. Jameson knew that – Tate loved to rail against him. She never caved to anything easily, and she never gave up when it came to their little games. He couldn't figure out her angle. But since it worked so well in his favor, he acquiesced to her demands. He chartered a plane, and two days later, they flew out of Paris. On his birthday.

Happy fucking birthday.

Sanders wasn't very much help, either. It was like they were conspiring against him. Jameson knew Tate didn't believe him when he said he hadn't known that Ang was bringing Ellie. But he wasn't positive Sanders believed him, either, and *that* was a problem. Tatum trusted anything that came out of Sanders' mouth. Neither of them were speaking about it to him, though, and once again – she was still sleeping with Jameson at night, still pretending like everything was

REPARATION

okay between them, so he didn't have incentive to make a fuss over it or to even really care.

Except you do care. You care so much, you can't even see your way around her anymore.

She didn't talk to Ang or Ellie during their remaining days in Paris, but on the plane ride home, there was a very tearful reunion of sorts. Ang tried to apologize, and Tate accepted, crying the whole time. Ellie cried and apologized, and Tate cried some more. Ang even shed a few tears. There were so many goddamn tears, Jameson thought he was gonna drown before they could even get back to America.

But despite the tears, there was something that rang ... *false*, about the whole scene. He couldn't put his finger on it. Tate had been *so angry*, and then to just be ... over it? And not just over it, but smiling and laughing like she hadn't been mad at all. Like she had never been mad in her whole life. Highly suspicious.

Technically, she didn't have a place to live in Boston anymore. Before going to Europe, she had been staying with her "friend", the first baseman for the Boston Red Sox, Nick Castille. Jameson vetoed that idea before she could even say anything. She couldn't move back in with her old roommate, Rusty – the girl had found a new roommate. She didn't want to live with her sister, and Jameson didn't want her living with Ang.

He informed her that she would living with *him*, in a condo he had recently purchased in the financial district. Jameson had braced himself for an argument, was prepared to drag her there, kicking and screaming, but it wasn't necessary. Tate had simply agreed. He kept waiting for her to argue, to kick up a fight, but the moment they got there, she simply wheeled all her luggage into his room, demanded to know which part of the walk-in closet would be hers.

Something is most definitely fucking wrong with this woman.

He wanted to shake her. Ask her what the fuck was going on,

what her silly little game was, now. But it was hard. He didn't want to slip back into having to fight for every smile from her. He had worked so hard to get back to a good place with her, and in their own kind of fucked up way, things were *really* good.

After picking out her section of the closet, Tate had pressed him against a wall and gone down on him, all while Ang and Ellie were sitting in the living room, oohing and aahing over his designer furniture. For the next two weeks, it was like old times between them. She had no qualms about fucking his brains out, anywhere and everywhere. As dirty and filthy as he could dish it out.

So who was he to ask her to snap the fuck out of it? If this was all a game, it was one he liked, *very much*.

"Tate?" Jameson called out, opening the door to the condo. He didn't see her anywhere, but he could hear music floating out from the bedroom. He opened the door wide and nodded, gesturing for the four large men behind him to enter the room. They all trailed in, carrying boxes and tape and plastic wrap. Jameson left them to it.

"Tatum," he said her name again, walking down the hallway.

"In here!" she called back. His bedroom door was wide open, and he followed the music to the closet.

She was standing in front of her clothes, bumping her hips from side to side, following the beat. She was only wearing a lacy pair of booty shorts and a shelf bra. Her hair was a messy pile on her head. She was pouting her bottom lip out, trying to decide what to wear.

"What are you doing?" he asked, taking his gloves off as he walked towards her. She glanced at him.

"Getting dressed. What is this restaurant like? Heels? Stockings?" Tate asked, running her hand along some hangers.

REPARATION

"We're not going out to eat," Jameson told her. She finally turned to face him.

"We're not? You said —," Tate started.

"I know what I said. Plans change sometimes," he snapped. She blinked at him in surprise, then smiled. He had been hoping to stir up a fight, but it looked like he was stirring up something else.

"Ooohhh, have a bad day?" she purred, pressing herself against him. Her body shivered when it came in contact with his cold clothing. Boston was still in the grip of winter – Jameson missed Marbella more than he would've thought possible.

"No. Actually, I had a very *interesting* day," he replied, running his hands up and down her arms.

"How so?" she asked, sliding her arms around his waist. He dragged his hands up to her neck and held them there, then started walking backwards, forcing her to follow.

"I had lunch," he replied.

"I assumed you had lunch every day. I didn't realize it was such a novel experience," she snorted.

"I do have lunch every day. Today, I had lunch with Sanders," Jameson continued, stopping them when he got near the bed. Her arms got stiff around him.

"Sanders? How is he? I haven't seen him in a couple days," she asked, but he could see something in her eyes. Maybe wariness? *Nervousness*. What was she nervous about?

"Lunch with Sanders, and *Angier*," his voice got quiet.

Tate laughed and pulled away from him, climbed up onto the bed. When she was standing, she turned towards him and began to lightly bounce on the mattress. He had trouble not staring at her breasts.

"That must have been really interesting. Did anyone get stabbed?" she asked. He shook his head.

"No. It wasn't so bad," he replied.

"What did you guys talk about?" she questioned, a practiced air of innocence surrounding her voice. Too bad he already knew there wasn't anything innocent about Tatum O'Shea.

"*You*," he replied honestly. Her eyes got wide and she stopped bouncing.

"Really? And what did you say about me?" she asked. He smiled and ran a hand up the back of her leg, then dragged his nails back down.

"Well, *Angier* informed me that I have been benefiting from his sexual teachings," he told her. She snorted as he moved his hand up her leg again.

"*Fucker*. I was already kinda freaky before he came along," she said.

"'*Kinda freaky*'?" Jameson laughed.

"What did *you* say?" she pressed.

"I told him that there wouldn't have even been a you without me, so he could shut the fuck up," he replied, really digging his nails in as he worked them back down her calf. She sucked air through her teeth.

"Bold statement, Mr. Kane. Doesn't sound like a very fun lunch," she told him. He shrugged.

"Something good came out of it. I made a decision," he started. He stopped touching her and took a step back. Out of kicking range.

"About what?" Tate asked, putting her hands on her hips.

He let his eyes wander over her body for a moment, committed it to memory. She was probably going to get angry. In the old days, when Tate got angry, it meant kinky sex. In Europe, it meant he wasn't allowed to touch her with a ten-foot-pole. Nowadays ... he was prepared to be sleeping in a dog house for a very long time.

For someone who didn't want a relationship, this is all very relationship-like ...

"We're moving," he informed her. Her eyebrows shot up.

REPARATION

"Moving? Jameson, we've only been here two weeks. Half my shit is still in suitcases," she pointed out.

"Good, then it shouldn't take you long to pack. Which you should be doing. Right now," he instructed.

"Huh?"

"We're moving *tonight*," he explained.

"*Tonight*? Jesus, what, was there a fire sale on mansions somewhere around here?" she joked.

"I already own a mansion somewhere around here," Jameson said softly. She stopped moving. Stopped blinking. It almost looked like she stopped breathing.

Ah, not a robot after all.

"You're going back to Weston?" Tate asked, her voice soft and low. He shook his head.

"*We're* going back to Weston," he corrected her. She shook her head.

"No. I'm not going back there," she said.

"Oh, yes, you are."

"No, I'm not."

"I'm sorry, did you think this was a debate? I didn't *ask you* if you were going, I *told you* that you were going," he said calmly. She glared down at him.

"I'm not going into that fucking house, and that is fucking final," she snapped.

"You *are* going into that house, and *that* is final. I don't care if I have to fucking carry you," he replied.

"Why? What's wrong with this place? I like this place. You must like it, *you* bought it," she pointed out. He shrugged.

"I like the Weston house better. Sanders misses it, he's already started opening it up," Jameson explained.

"No. No, I'm not going there. You can't make me," her voice was getting louder.

"Oh, yes I can."

"Why can't I just stay here?" she asked.

"Because I want you there."

"You don't get to tell me what to do, Kane."

"Oh, yes I do."

"*Stop it!* Why? Why do I have to be there, in that house?" she demanded. He decided to risk it, and he stepped closer to her.

"Because," he started, his voice soft. Gentling the blow. "*It's our home,* baby girl. And it's time to go."

Houston, we have ignition. Prepare for blast off.

"That is *not* our home!" Tate yelled, a blush creeping across her chest. "That is *your* torture chamber! So fuck off, and go back to your fucking mansion in the country!"

"It's not much of a torture chamber without someone to torture," Jameson pointed out. She looked shocked.

"*Fuck you,* then you shouldn't have let Pet get away from it," she hissed.

Always about Petrushka. This is why I hate having girlfriends – it's the "ex" part that's a bitch.

"She didn't '*get away*', I kicked her out."

"That's your version of what happened."

"It's the *only* version of what happened."

"I am not about to go and sleep in the same bed you fucked her in, I am not some —,"

Play time is over.

Jameson grabbed her ankles and yanked her legs out from underneath her. Tate shrieked as she went down flat on her back. She had barely made contact with the mattress before he was jerking her forward, still holding her ankles, dragging her to him. He leaned over her, forcing her legs to part around him.

"We have been over this, so I am *never* going to say this again, understand? *I did not fuck her,*" he growled. Tate glared up at him.

"I'm still not going into that house," she growled right back.

"Oh, you'll go. You'll go if I have to drag you there by your fucking hair," he warned her.

"You'd probably love that," she snapped.

"So would you."

She sighed and some of the tension went out of her body. She rolled her head to the side and looked out the open doors. The moving men were visible at the end of the hall, boxing up odds and ends. Jameson stared down at her. *Detachment*. That's what was wrong with her. Tate had a way of detaching herself. Like she was present, could say all the right things, but she wasn't really there – she was somewhere he couldn't reach.

He *hated* that.

"I don't want to go there," she whispered.

"Why?" he demanded.

"I don't like it there," she answered.

"You used to love it there," he reminded her.

"'*Used to*' being the operative term," she pointed out.

"So what's changed? You keep claiming that everything is fine. Apparently, it's not fine at all. Apparently it's all completely fucked," he called her out. She turned back towards him.

"That was a *really* interesting lunch you had, wasn't it," she breathed.

Busted.

"They're concerned about you," Jameson said softly.

"But you're not," Tate finished his statement. He shooks his head.

"Don't be fucking stupid. I'm here. I'm doing this, *for you*. Stop asking questions you know the answers to. Now get the fuck up, and get dressed," he ordered.

She sat up abruptly and he had to lean away. He had barely stood up when she pushed herself up as well, sliding against almost every inch of him. He stared down at her, waiting for her to argue, to whine, to try to bribe. The last one was fairly effective – he wasn't as immune to her charms as he liked to pretend.

"Fine. Fine, I'll go to that fucking hell house," she said in a quiet voice.

"Good. We're leaving, *now*," he snapped. She raised an eyebrow.

"So impatient," she clucked her tongue at him.

"You should know that by now," he replied. She sighed and stepped around him, slowly made her way towards the door.

"When they pack my clothes," she started, "make sure they don't steal any of the expensive underwear."

Then she disappeared down the hall. From where he was standing, Jameson couldn't see to the end of it, but he heard one moving man wolf-whistle. Another cat-called. Then the front door slowly creaked open, before slamming shut. Jameson chuckled to himself.

So feisty.

Goddammit.

Tatum sat in the back of the Bentley, chewing on her nail, trying not to show how nervous she was about where they were going. She hadn't been to the Weston house in a month. She hadn't actually been inside it since October, almost three months ago. She willed away the memories. Tried to think of happier times.

She glanced at Jameson out of the corner of her eye. He was leaning back in his seat, staring out the window. As if he knew she was staring, he reached over and rested a hand on her knee. But it wasn't to comfort. His nails bit into her skin and she sighed, resting her head back. His fingers dragged up higher, disappeared under the bottom of his overcoat. She had made it onto the elevator, wearing nothing but her bra and panties, when he'd casually stepped in behind her. By the time they got to the lobby, he had wrestled her into his overcoat. It was a peacoat, but it was large enough on her that it stopped above the knees.

"Scared, baby girl?" he whispered, still not looking at her. Tate concentrated on the roof of the car.

"No," she replied.

She was fucking terrified. Over the past two weeks, Tate had perfected acting like she didn't care. Didn't care that Jameson was a sociopath who liked to cause her mental anguish, just to get off. Didn't care that Ang had slept with the person responsible for making her feel worthless, responsible for ripping her life in half. Didn't care that Ellie had stolen one of the last pieces of Tate's life that still felt safe, still felt right.

She spent so much time pretending like she didn't care, she'd almost forgotten what it felt like to actually care, about anything. Only Sanders grounded her, and she had to keep him at arms length. He was too clever, too close to her; he would figure out what she was plotting. And she would not be derailed, not this time. The house *did* scare her – she was worried she would take one look at it, and break down. Go back in time. Be stuck in that room. On that floor, looking up at him, just wanting him to see her. And she *would not* be that girl again.

For the last seven years, Tate had thought she was a bad girl. Not a bad person, but most definitely very naughty. She liked to have sex, she liked to have fun, she liked to do whatever she wanted. But she'd had an epiphany while she was in France. She was actually a *good* girl. She liked people, wanted to make people happy. She loved her friends, would do anything for them. She would never have done anything to hurt them, and whenever she accidentally did, she felt bad. She apologized. She did her best to make amends.

Tate felt like a sucker. All those years, running from her good girl image, and here she was, still the best fucking girl on the block.

Didn't matter how many dicks a girl sucked, she was still good if she always said please and thank you. No more. She was *over it*. Over being so goddamn nice all the time. Jameson was the devil. Ang was disrespectful. Ellie was a bitch. When did it get to be Tatum's turn?

Yes, but what are you after you've alienated everyone, hmmm? What kind of creature then?

Tate shook those thoughts away. She was going to do whatever it took to get some fucking closure. What had Jameson said in Paris? What sugary sweet lie had he spun? *Seven years?* It was time to end it. Then she would just walk away. Start life, for real. Maybe a little later than most people, but hey, better late than never. Maybe she'd go back to school. Maybe she'd become a nice, normal girl, finally. Maybe she'd take Nick up on his offer and move to Arizona. Who knew?

She certainly didn't.

"We are almost there. Are you alright?" Sanders called out. She smiled up at the ceiling.

You know you'll lose him. Is it worth it?

"*I'm good*," she whispered.

"Excuse me?"

"Let's get this over with," Tate growled, leaning her head forward.

They were pulling down the driveway. Jameson's house sat far back on his property – estate would be a more appropriate word – and a pebble filled circular drive led them to the large brick building. The driveway was long, and though there was none right then, she figured that when it did snow, it must have been a bitch getting the driveway plowed.

Well, for anyone else, it would've been a bitch. For Jameson Kane, all he had to do was snap his fingers and people probably cleared the snow away with their tongues.

Not me. Not anymore.

"Patience there, tiger. Wouldn't want you getting sick again,"

REPARATION

Jameson teased her. Tate glared at the back of Sanders' head, watched his neck turn pink with a blush.

"You don't have to tell him *everything*, Sandy," she grumbled. Sanders had brought her back in December, tried to cook dinner for her while Jameson was out of the country. She had barely made it onto the porch before she lost her cookies over the railing.

"Yes, he does. Unload the bags, will you Sanders?" Jameson asked, opening the door and stepping out before the car had rolled to a complete stop. Tate slid across the seat and got out behind him, refusing to take his hand.

She took a deep breath and started stomping forward. She walked up the steps and barreled through the front door, coming to a stop in the hall. There. Like ripping off a band aid. She stood in the entry way, staring at the stairs. Now if she could just get her feet to move forward, she would really be winning.

"Are you alright?" Sanders' soft voice asked again, and she turned her head to find him standing behind her.

"As I'll ever be. I can take that," she started, reaching for a suitcase that had been packed for her. Sanders breezed past her, heading up the stairs.

"It's fucking freezing in here," Jameson grumbled, walking up next to her. She glanced at him.

"Only because you're used to it always being so hot – you kept it like a furnace in here," she snapped.

Like a crematorium.

"Well, you've always insisted that I'm the devil. Wouldn't want to break from character. C'mon, let's get a fire lit, and I'll have Sanders …" he rambled on, heading towards his library.

Tate couldn't move. She couldn't go in there. Her ghost was trapped in that room. She and Jameson had easily spent more time in that room than any other room in the house – including his bedroom. When he was at home, he worked out of the library, used it as an office. At night, he stayed in there, close to the fire. Reading. Drinking. Talking with her. Touching her. *She could not go in there.*

"No," she said, her voice louder than she'd intended. He stopped just outside the library door, turned towards her.

"Excuse me?" he asked. She licked her lips and closed the front door behind her.

"I don't want to go in there. You have a million rooms here, why don't you actually go see some of them. Have you ever even been in the study upstairs?" she asked, trying to think of any excuse at all, without giving away her fear. Jameson narrowed his eyes.

"I don't give a fuck about my other rooms. I like *this* room," he replied.

"That's stupid," she rolled her eyes.

"*You're* stupid, but you don't hear me bitching about it every two seconds," he pointed out.

"Yes, you do."

"Shut up."

"Or let's go to the conservatory," she started to offer. "I wonder if my geraniums are still alive. Did you hire —,"

"*Tatum*, cut the bullshit. Why don't you want to go in there?" Jameson demanded.

She took a deep breath. Stared him in the eye. Jameson hadn't seemed to have caught onto it yet, but she had a very powerful weapon against him. *Sex.* He simply couldn't resist it, and he was easily distracted by it. His one weakness, if it could be called that. It was very handy for Tate, because she used it to forget. When she was lost in his heat and his skin and his fire, she could forget she wanted to hurt him, the way he had hurt her. Forget that she wanted to destroy a small piece of his heart, the way he had done to hers.

Tate moved her hands to the buttons on the jacket she was wearing. Popped the top one open. Jameson cocked up an eyebrow. She worked the second one open, then trailed her fingers down to the

REPARATION

third button. By the time she got to the bottom button, both his eyebrows were raised, and he had a decidedly mean glint in his eye.

Good, I need something to sting extra hard tonight.

"Because it's *boring*," Tate breathed the word as she let his jacket fall to the ground. "Always in the library. You're so vanilla, *Kane*. A million rooms, and you only ever want to fuck me in one." She clucked her tongue at him as she kicked the coat away from her feet.

"I get the very distinct impression you're trying to distract me," he said. She smiled and took slow steps towards the stairs.

"Is it working?" she asked, reaching up to let her hair down.

"So far," he replied, his eyes following her as she started up the stairs.

"Good."

They didn't make it to his bedroom. They didn't even make it to a guest bedroom. It would've happened right in the hallway, if Sanders hadn't been somewhere in the house. As it was, Jameson pinned her against the wall in a linen closet, and he was sure to make it sting.

Tate sat outside, bundled up in an old sweater that used to belong to Sanders. It was a bright, shiny day out – and totally freezing. She wore a thick pair of wool socks over her knee socks and had tucked herself into a lounge chair. She sat next to the pool, which had been covered, and took out her cell phone.

"I was just thinking about you," Nick said when he answered.

"Psychic," she joked, pulling her knees up to her chest.

"How're things?" he asked.

Tate had kept him mostly in the dark about everything that had happened. He just knew that she was back in Boston, and that she and Jameson were "*friends*"; she never elaborated on what kind of friends, and thankfully he never asked. By the time she got back to Boston, he had already moved into his house in Arizona. Spring training didn't start till mid-February, but he liked settling in first.

"Good, things are good. Just kinda hanging out," she responded.

"No job?" he asked.

"No, no job."

"What about school? You mentioned once —,"

"No, *Dad*, no school either," Tate said sarcastically.

"Well, I worry about you. When you don't keep busy, you either vegetate, or get into trouble. And if you're going to get into trouble, I'd like to at least be there," he told her. She snorted.

"I'm not getting into trouble, *or 'vegetating'*, I promise. Sandy and I went up to New York the other weekend, he took me to the Natural History Museum, all that good stuff," she assured him of her innocence. Nick would be the last person alive who would buy it, by the time she was through.

"You and Sanders alone together for a weekend, huh," he said. She smiled.

"Ooohhh, sounds like jealousy," Tate teased.

"No, no, not at all. Sanders is a very fine man. When you marry him, can I walk you down the aisle?" he asked.

"Of course. Now if we can just convince Jameson to walk with Sandy, it'll be perfect," she joked.

"Is there any way we could not invite Jameson?" Nick asked.

"Jameson isn't the kind of man you don't invite places – he just invites himself, anyway," she assured him.

"Not exactly surprising. So, when are you going to come visit me?" Nick asked.

They had talked several times about her coming out there. Nick thought it was a great idea. Tate thought it was horrible. She was in a bad place, a bad state of mind. She didn't want him to see her like that, and she didn't want him to become a casualty on her path to

REPARATION

becoming a bitch.

"I don't know, Nick. When does training end?" she asked, for the millionth time.

"End of March. Tatum, it would be really nice to see you, before I have to go on the road," he said in a soft voice. She hated his soft voice. It could make her do almost anything.

"I'll try, I promise. Maybe in a couple weeks, before training really gets under way," she offered.

"That would be nice. I mean, there's no pressure. I just want to see you. I'm not asking for anything else," Nick told her.

"I know that. Thank you."

Sometimes, Nick felt like the only person who wasn't asking her for something, or expecting her to be anything. It was nice.

"Though I wouldn't stop you if you suddenly felt like getting naked and climbing into bed with me," he threw out there, and she burst out laughing.

"Good to know, good to know," Tate tried to contain herself. Then she saw Jameson prowling through the conservatory, and her laughter dried up.

"So. End of March?" Nick asked. She nodded, watching Jameson.

"I'll try," was all she offered.

"That's all I ever ask. I gotta go. Take care of yourself," he instructed her. She nodded again as Jameson finally walked out of the house.

"*I never do*," she replied, then hung up the phone.

Jameson was slowly making his way towards her, his hands in pants pockets. She sighed as she watched him. He was wearing a suit, this one with a vest. It killed her. She wanted to lick the fabric, he looked so good. He had everything tailored, so everything fit him like a glove. She loved it. She always loved the way he looked; he always took her breath away a little.

Sometimes, he made it very hard for her to hate him.

"Talking with your *boyfriend?*" he asked snidely as he approached her.

And sometimes, he made it very easy.

"He's lonely. Can I go visit him?" Tate asked. Jameson snorted.

"Abso-fuckin'-lutely not," he replied, standing right over her.

"Scared you'll lose me?" she laughed. He laughed as well.

"I couldn't get rid of you if I tried. No, but I don't want to have to fly to Arizona, of all the god forsaken places, to rescue you from some ridiculous situation you will no doubt get yourself into," he answered, taking his hands out of his pockets and opening his jacket.

"All true. But still. Can I go see him?"

"*No.*"

"It's very hard for me to be a good girlfriend to him, when you're always interfering," Tate teased. Jameson glared at her.

"It must be even harder for you to be a good girlfriend to him when *I'm* the one who's always inside you," he responded. She shrugged.

"What are you doing home?" she asked, cutting through the flirting. Or was it teasing? Bullying? It was all the same to her.

"It occured to me that maybe you would be uncomfortable here, all alone," Jameson said.

"Sanders is here," Tate reminded him. He rolled his eyes.

"Sometimes that's almost like one and the same. I only had one consultation this afternoon, so I rescheduled it and came home," he explained.

"For me?" she asked. He nodded.

"For you."

Sometimes he could almost be sweet. Sure, he was the devil incarnate, but in his own weird way, he would try to be sweet. She tried to encourage those moments, figured they would lure him into a false sense of security.

"That's very nice of you," she said, reaching up and grabbing

REPARATION

onto his hand. He frowned, but allowed her to link their fingers.

"I also had something else," he went on.

Uh oh.

She let go of his hand.

"What?" she asked, instantly wary. He lowered himself so he was sitting on the lounger across from her.

"I have to go out of town," Jameson started. Her breath caught in her throat. "Just to Los Angeles. I've been trying to sell off my piece of a film company, and it needs my personal attention. I'll be back in a couple days, five at the most."

Los Angeles. L.A. didn't scare her, Tate didn't have any bad memories associated with that city. She had been nervous that he was going to say New York, or worse, Berlin. L.A. she could handle. It was actually a good thing. Ang hadn't been over to Jameson's house, but maybe now he could be convinced to come over if the devil wasn't home.

"Oh, that's it?" she feigned nonchalance. "That's fine. Are you taking Sandy?"

"I was planning on it, but I don't have to," Jameson offered. She waved her hand.

"No, it's cool. I'll just bug him if we're here alone. When you're not here, it's basically me just following him around all day," she laughed. Jameson didn't. He looked suspicious.

"I didn't think you would take this so well," he told her. She managed to shrug.

"Why? You've been to L.A. before, remember? Maybe this time, instead of two women, you should try for a full on orgy," she joked. Still no laughter.

"And I certainly didn't think you would be okay with *that*," he added. Tate was surprised. Was he actually worried about how she would feel?

"Why wouldn't I be?" she asked.

"Well, last time I attempted to sleep with another woman, I had to pull you off of a certain slutty maid after —," he started. She held up her hand

"That was completely different. I don't care if you fuck other women, I just don't want to be a part of it. Besides, she was a bitch who didn't know her place. I was there first," Tate said. He finally smiled.

"Staking a claim on me? Sexy. But I'm kind of disappointed, does this mean no threesomes in our future?" he asked, pouting his lower lip out. She resisted the urge to nibble on it.

"Sure, we can have a threesome," she nodded as she laid back on the lounger, putting her hands under her head.

"Really?" he asked, his voice full of surprise. She nodded her head again.

"Of course. I've got, like, a dozen guys I can name, right now, that I would love to be in a threesome with you. I know you don't like Ang, but we've kind of had this long standing thing that if I was ever gonna try DP, he had to be one of the P's," Tate explained. Jameson's foot hooked under her lounger and suddenly she was being shoved over. She rolled onto the grass, snorting and laughing.

"I find it disgusting right now that *Angier* and I have fucked the same person. I certainly don't ever want to be doing it at the same time as him," Jameson said, standing up and straightening his suit.

"So you're saying there's a chance with another guy?" she asked, propping her knees up. She watched him as he sighed, then stared off into the horizon.

"If you were serious – which you aren't – I would do it. But only after I got to do every sick, deviant, fetish thing I could ever possibly want to do with you, first," he told her.

"That could take years!" she laughed up at him.

"Yes, but my needs come first, Tate," he reminded her, then turned and walked away.

2

TATUM WASN'T SURE IF SHE'D ever actually been alone in Jameson's house before – she was pretty sure Sanders had always been there, at least. Without anyone there, it was big and drafty and kinda scary. She went to sleep in Jameson's bed, spooning his pillow. She felt like a baby.

She had worried about what to do for transportation, or how she would even get Ang out there, but it turned out Sanders and Jameson had been holding out on her. The Bentley wasn't the only car. There was a Jaguar S Type that never saw the light of day. Sanders preferred the Bentley, and Jameson hardly every drove himself. It was all hers, she was told. Tate decided not to point out that it would have made life a lot simpler, in the old days, if she'd had access to her *own fucking car*. Like, say, a certain night … when she had wanted to leave … but didn't have a ride … so she drank herself retarded and stole a car anyway. Yeah. Not cute. One more point to the devil.

She had a lot of catching up to do.

She had to plead and beg for a couple of days, but she finally got Ang to agree to come out. She didn't even have to give him a ride, as it turned out. *Ellie* loaned him her car. *Barf*. But Tate smiled and hugged him at the door, pretended like she didn't care. Not even one little bit.

"See, it's not so bad," Tate pointed out, ushering him inside. Ang frowned while he looked around.

"It's worse."

She had dinner delivered and they ate in the kitchen. That room had taken her a while to get used to, as well. She had some good memories in it, most of them burned into the island. But there were some bad memories, too. Ukrainian-Danish monsters, stomping around Tatum's land.

"It's a lot, but you get used to it," she commented as they walked out of the kitchen and he took in the huge hall.

"Maybe *you* get used to it – you grew up somewhere like this, I bet. I grew up in a shoe box," he said.

"This is the sitting room," she started giving him a tour.

"What do you do in a sitting room?" Ang asked, glancing in the large room. Two sofas faced each other over a large, flat coffee table, and a gigantic fireplace stood on the far wall.

"I have no fucking clue. On the other side is the living room," she turned back to look behind them.

"My whole apartment could fit in here," Ang breathed, walking into the room. Turning to the pristine couches. There was a bar at the back of the room and a door in the far corner. She led him through it.

"Holy shit!" he exclaimed, and she smiled, not turning on the lights in the conservatory. The lights around the pool and pool house were on, casting an orange glow into the room.

"I love this part of the house. In the summer, Ang, you would die. It gets so warm in here, almost like a sauna, and it looks right over the pool," she explained, walking the length of the room.

"It smells amazing in here. Who takes care of all these? I gave you that bamboo once, and you killed it," he reminded her.

"It's one of Sanders' hobbies. Jameson and I aren't allowed to touch anything. One time we overturned a table of American Beauties. He was able to save them, but he didn't speak to us for about two days," she told him.

"And how did you two manage to overturn an entire table full of roses?" Ang asked, an eyebrow cocked up. She snorted.

"Shut up."

"*Slut.*"

"You love it."

She led him upstairs. She gestured to Sanders' old room, but didn't go inside. No one went in there, it was like an unspoken rule. Across from the main house was a guest house – a home still bigger than most average Americans'. Sanders was staying there.

She showed Ang the upstairs study, a den, a game room. Several very posh guests rooms. She showed him a bathroom so big, her old apartment could have fit inside it. They both laughed at the fact that their homes could fit inside just two rooms in Jameson's home. *Rich people.* Then they circled back to the main hall, worked their way towards the door at the very end.

"What's left?" Ang asked. Tate chewed on her bottom lip.

"*My* room," she replied, and swung the door open. She went inside, but Ang stayed in the doorway, looking around.

"Your room, huh. Looks more like Satan lives here," he commented, his eyes wandering over the dark decor. The heavy, oak furniture. The huge, black bedspread. She rolled her eyes.

"You scared of the devil, Angy wangy?" she teased, walking further into the room. He snorted and followed her inside.

"So this is where it happens," he sighed, striding up to the bed.

"What?" she asked, standing next to him.

"The magic," he deadpanned, and she cracked up.

"Sometimes. C'mon, look at this," she said, and led him into the walk-in closet.

"If you're trying to impress me, it won't work. My sexual favors can't be bought," he told her, fingering one of Jameson's blazers. Tate pulled the jacket down.

"Yes, they can. Try it on," she offered, holding the jacket out. He looked like he was going to be sick.

"I'm sure you miss him, but I am not about to dress up like him and ride around on you while you wear a saddle, or whatever sick fetish you richies are into," he said loudly. She burst out laughing.

"Ang. This is Dolce & Gabbana. It cost over $2,000. Have you ever worn an article of clothing that cost that much? C'mon, put it on, and we'll go get high, and then he can bitch about that time *Angier* made his two-grand-jacket smell like weed," she suggested.

Ang put it on.

"I'm taller than him," he commented, staring at his wrists where they jutted out of the cuffs.

"Duh. Haven't you noticed?" she asked, walking around, straightening out the material. She smoothed her hands over his shoulders, let her touch linger.

"I mean, yeah, I guess. He's just …" he let his voice trail off.

"Larger than life?" she filled in for him. He nodded again.

"Don't tell him I said that."

"Won't breathe a word."

"Good. At least I've got something on him," he commented, pushing up the sleeves.

"At least two and a half inches. He's like six-two," she told him, coming back to his front.

"Short stuff."

"You've got more on him than that," she teased, winking at him. He nodded.

"Damn straight, and don't you forget it. Now where's the weed?" Ang asked.

They moved into the make-shift office Jameson had created out of a balcony. She opened the windows before pulling up two chairs for them. She produced a joint and they tucked in, Tate spreading a blanket across both of them. They sat in silence for a while.

"It's so peaceful here," she finally sighed. Ang nodded, taking a deep pull.

"Surprisingly. I thought hell would be a lot scarier," he managed to squeak out before exhaling the smoke.

"A person can get used to hell," she replied softly.

"What?" he asked, turning towards her. She shook her head, taking a drag.

"It's not so bad, huh? Nice house, nice grounds," she commented, passing it back to him.

"Heh, nice grounds. *Groooouuunds*," he drew out the word before leaning forward and grinding the butt out against the window sill. "I'm happy if you're happy, kitty cat. Are you happy?"

"Most of the time," Tate breathed, closing her eyes.

You don't want to do this. Don't be this person.

"What do you mean? Are you really okay?" he asked, and when she opened her eyes, he was looking at her. She wondered why he hadn't thought to ask that question *before* he had started fucking her sister.

"Yeah, I'm good. Just cold, let's get out of here," she said, pushing the blanket away and standing up.

After she secured the huge windows, she led him back into the bedroom. She showed him the sideboard where Jameson kept most of his every day things – a lot of cuff links, tie pins, watches, things of that nature. Everything plated in gold and diamond and platinum. While Ang guffawed over all the stuff, Tate made her way over to the bed. Knelt on top of it and crawled towards Jameson's side.

"Holy fuck, Tate, this table holds more money than I'll ever see in my life. I don't know whether to be impressed, or disgusted," Ang called out from behind her. She pulled a box out of Jameson's night stand and then turned back to Ang.

"Look at this," she offered, knee walking back towards him. He met her at the edge of the bed and she opened the box. "This is a Jacob and Co. watch."

"It's awesome," he said, taking the box into his hands and looking over the timepiece.

"It's worth over $300,000."

"*Fuck!*" he exclaimed, and dropped the box. It bounced on the mattress and rolled, the lid snapping shut. She laughed and picked it up, sat it on the pillows.

"I know, right? Who would spend that kind of money on a watch?" she asked.

"Why the fuck would you even let me touch that? That watch is worth more than *I* am," he laughed as well, but he looked a little shaky.

"I think it's funny. All this stuff, it's silly," she said, reaching out and playing with the button on the blazer he was wearing. He was taller than Jameson, but leaner. The blazer was pretty loose on him.

"It's fucking stupid. A watch!? Why? How often does he wear it?" Ang asked. Tate shrugged, unbuttoning the jacket and pushing it open.

"Not often. Once in Spain. You should see the shit he keeps in the safe," she said, plucking at his shirt. He began absent mindedly batting at her hands while he glanced around the room.

"You're shitting me. Please tell me it's behind a huge portrait of like his dog or something," he chuckled. She hooked her fingers inside his belt.

"No. It's in the closet," she replied.

"Tate, what are you doing?" he asked, finally clueing into the fact that she was touching him. She smiled up at him. Ang liked to pretend he liked being poor, turned up his nose at rich people, but really, he was fascinated by it, and even better, *distracted by it*. It was one of the things that had attracted him to Tate, she knew. It was

REPARATION

probably part of what drew him to her sister.

Bitch.

"What? I feel like I haven't touched you in a long time," she said, pulling him close and wrapping her arms around his waist. She pressed the side of her face to his chest and he sighed, wrapping his arms around her shoulders.

"Are you really okay? You kinda scare me, sometimes," he mumbled. She ignored the sadness in his voice and worked her hands up his back. He felt so different from Jameson.

"I'm okay, Ang. I'm happy here. Everything is great," she whispered, massaging her fingers back down his spine. He shivered under her touch.

"You can always come live with me," he said softly. She laughed low in her throat and pulled away a little, running her hands up and down his sides.

"Do you think your *girlfriend* would appreciate that?" she asked, watching him from under hooded eyelids. He ran his hands under her hair, lifting it away from her shoulders and piling it all on the back of her head.

"I don't think she'd care, but more importantly, *I* don't care. You've been my best friend for a million years," he replied. She smiled, running her teeth over her bottom lip while she pressed herself against him.

"Sometimes a little more than a friend," her voice was soft. He laughed, scratching his fingers over her scalp.

"Most of the time. God, we used to have fun," his voice fell into a murmur as his eyes wandered over her face.

Please, don't hate me after this. I have to get my soul back.

"Used to?" she asked, her voice soft as she ran her hands along his body.

"Tater tot, we haven't had fun since Satan came to town," Ang chuckled, his hands moving to the back of her neck.

"Hmmm, he's not in town right now," Tate reminded him. He narrowed his eyes.

"No, he's not, and I doubt he would appreciate me seducing his succubus in his lair," he told her.

"I doubt he'd care. Besides, succubi are supposed to sleep with lots of people," she pointed out.

"Succubi? Is that how you pluralize it?"

"Succubuses sounds weird."

"Like a slutty bus."

"Slutty *buses*."

"Wait," he stopped. "Did you just imply that you want to sleep with me?"

"Ang. If I laid it on any thicker, I'd be staked out on the mattress," she said bluntly.

"I thought it was '*against the rules*', or some bullshit," he said, glancing around the room, like he was checking for hidden cameras, or waiting for Jameson to pounce out of the shadows and eat him.

"That was before; besides, since when have you cared about what upsets Jameson?" she evaded answering him.

"I don't. But I don't want to piss off Ellie, either. She's not exactly as free a thinker as you and I," he laughed.

I'm counting on that.

"That's not fair. She wouldn't know you if it wasn't for me – she owes me a finders fee," Tate mock pouted, sticking out her bottom lip. He pinched it between his thumb and finger.

"What's going on with you, babydoll? Satan not giving it to you good enough?" he questioned. She tilted her head down, drawing his thumb into her mouth and sucking on it. He hissed air through his teeth. She let him go and he dragged his thumb down her chin.

"How about you stop worrying about him for tonight. I know I have," she said in a husky voice.

Like that would even be possible.

REPARATION

She knew she had him. The temptation to put something over on Jameson was too great for him. She knew Ang very well, knew how to get to him. They hadn't slept together in a long time – since August. They had quit cold turkey, and he hadn't had a say in the matter. In fact, he'd been pretty angry about it for a while. Here was his chance to strike back. Fuck Tate, in Jameson's bed. In *Satan's home*. Much too hard to resist. She closed her eyes as his head lowered towards hers.

Please, please don't hate me.

"*It's haaaard out here, for a BITCH!*"

His pocket started blaring Lily Allen. Talk about a mood breaker. They stared at each other, in the darkness of the bedroom. The only light was coming from the closet and the windows. The chorus to the song repeated itself, and she realized it was his phone. He licked his lips.

"Ellie," he said, then pulled away, walking into the closet to take the call.

Moment gone, plan ruined. She huffed and fell backwards onto the bed. She tried to ignore how elated she actually felt; she wouldn't have another chance like that one for a while. It would've been perfect. Fuck Ang in Jameson's bed, piss off all three of them. Originally, she wanted to do it in the library. She hadn't even gone into it yet, so if Jameson found out she had not only gone in there with Ang, but slept with him in there, *game over*. But she couldn't make herself go in there yet. The bed was a close second.

"How's the little woman?" Tate asked, staring up at the ceiling as Ang walked back into the room.

"Okay, she has a cold," he said, standing in front of her legs. He reached down and grabbed her by the arm, pulling her upright.

"Does she pee when she sneezes?"

"What? No. What the fuck was all this about?" he demanded. He had taken off the jacket and was holding his car keys in his hand.

"What do you mean?" she asked, standing up and straightening out her shirt.

"This, Tatum. What the fuck is going on with you?" he asked. She laughed.

"Ang, since when have we needed a reason to have sex? One time we did it to celebrate Election Day. I wanted to do it because you're here," she told him. He narrowed his eyes.

"Since when has Jameson not been enough for you?" he countered.

"Hard for him to fulfill needs when he's thousands of miles away," she replied, and lead him out of the room.

"Is that what this was about? You're lonely?" he asked as they made their way down the stairs. She took quick breaths.

Yes. I'm always lonely. So lonely.

"Ang, it was just fun. I'm a little stoned, you're sexy, it's been a while. It didn't happen, big whoop. Next time I'll just take my top off, maybe then you won't hesitate," she managed to joke.

"If you whip out your boobs next time, I promise to fuck you until you won't be able to look at Satan the same," he joked. She snorted.

Yeah, good luck with that.

"If Ellie could hear you now," she sighed, opening the front door.

"Yeah, it wouldn't be pretty. Seriously, you okay out here? You can come stay with me, or her, until they come home," he offered. She shook her head, almost shaking with the amount of tension running through her body. She just wanted him gone.

"No, I'm good. Besides, someone has to water Sanders' plants. He'd kill me and bury me in there if I let one of them die," she said. Ang nodded.

"Okay. Take it easy, kitty cat. Call me if you need anything. *Anything*," he urged, then leaned down and gave her a quick kiss.

"Good night!" she called out after him.

Tate had barely swung the door shut when she fell to her knees.

REPARATION

She crawled forward, pressed her back to the door and pulled her knees up. She tried to get her breathing under control while she wrapped her arms around her legs. Holy shit. *Holy shit*, what had she almost done? Ang had no clue, he thought she was being weird, but all sexy and cheeky. *Stupid man*. He didn't know.

And Jameson. Jesus, if he even knew how far it had gone right then, he would've been pissed. If she'd actually gone through with it? Slept with Ang? *God*. He would hate her. Ellie would hate her. And Ang would hate her, as soon as he found out it was all on purpose. Most of the time, it all sounded like a great idea.

But sometimes, when she was alone, and she couldn't stop the crying, it just sounded like she was the worst person she'd ever met.

Well, next to Jameson …

Tate stood in the doorway a couple days later, watching as Sanders unloaded the car. Jameson was sitting in the backseat, talking on his cell phone. She smiled and held out her arms when Sanders finally made his way up to the porch.

"What did you do?" he demanded, and she laughed.

"What? What!? I'm alive, I didn't kill any of your plants, and I cleaned up the meatball explosion in the kitchen," she defended herself.

"I had this strange feeling while we were gone, and you sounded odd whenever I called," he said, looking her over.

"No, nothing strange here. Just bored most of the time," she replied. Jameson finally got out of the car and strode up onto the porch. Sanders gave her one more Look, and then headed inside.

"God, what a fucking nightmare. Sanders was ridiculous, he worried about you the whole time," Jameson grumbled, pushing his way past her. She shut the door after everyone was inside.

"Sweet to know someone worried about me," she laughed, following him up the stairs. Sanders left Jameson's luggage in front of his room, then headed back downstairs.

"If I wasted my time worrying about you, I would never get anything done," he responded, pulling his tie off and walking to the edge of the bed. Tate kicked the door shut behind her.

"See. Sweetness. You're just full of it," she teased. He glanced at her while he slid his jacket off, let it fall onto the bed.

"You're in an awfully good mood," he said suspiciously, unbuttoning his shirt sleeves. Tate shrugged.

"I spent a week alone. It was quiet. Peaceful. Nice. I didn't have to listen to you bitch the whole time," she taunted him, smiling as she said it. He narrowed his eyes, then walked past her into the closet.

"Starting awfully early, baby girl. At least let me —, what is this? Why is this on the floor?" Jameson asked. Tate held her breath and crept to the door into the closet. The blazer Ang had worn was crumpled up on the floor, where he had left it. Tate had never picked it up.

"What?" she asked, feigning ignorance. He picked the blazer up and shook it out.

"Why is this on the floor?" he asked, holding it up. He made a face. "Jesus, is that *weed*? Were you getting stoned in my jacket?"

"Oh, no. Ang was over, and we —," she started to explain, as if it were an every day occurrence. Jameson turned towards her, his eyes wide.

"*Angier* was here? In my house?" he asked.

"Yeah, I invited him over one night. We were bored, I gave him a tour. Thought it would be funny for him to try on the jacket," she explained. His eyes got wider.

"You let him wear my clothing?" Jameson sounded shocked. She had blown his mind. Jameson was very sensitive about his things.

"Yeah. It looked good on him, though he's a lot taller," she said, looking down and picking at her nails. Jameson walked over to her, his movements slow and deliberate.

"You brought *Angier* to my house, let him wear *my clothing*, and then you proceeded to get high," he laid everything out. She glanced at him and nodded before going back to her nails. She couldn't look at him for too long. His eyes were blazing, and it was always a look that set her skin on edge. Made her itch to be touched. Hurt.

"Yeah, in the sun room," she finished.

"You smoked in my room," his voice was soft. She had trouble hiding her smile.

"Well, not *in* in your room, we were —," she started.

He grabbed her by the throat and she went onto her toes, her fingers flying to his hand. He stared down his nose at her, and he looked equal parts pissed-the-fuck-off and *really* turned on. It was an odd look, one that she had only ever seen on Jameson. A look that made her heart rate double.

"What's your game, baby girl? You knew all those things would make me very unhappy, so why did you do them?" he asked, his voice still soft. Tate sighed.

"We were having fun. Maybe, just maybe for ten minutes, I wasn't thinking about *you*, Jameson," she replied. His fingers got tighter and he walked her backwards, out of the closet.

"Doubtful. *Fun*, huh. What else did you do?" he asked, backing her up to the side of the bed.

"Hard to remember. Gets a little fuzzy after the joint," she replied. He stepped up so he was almost touching her.

"A little fuzzy, hmmm. Tatum, you're being far too obvious to have actually fucked him, so you can stop trying to make me jealous. I'm not jealous. I'm *angry*," he growled through clenched teeth. She flicked her eyes to the bed, then back to him.

"You're so sure? You're *positive*?" she whispered. His gaze went to where she had just looked and then came back to hers. He cocked his head to the side.

"Positive enough. Why are you trying to make me mad? What has gotten into you?" he asked, and she managed to squeak out a laugh.

"I think the question should be *who*."

He shoved her and she fell onto the mattress. She tried to scramble backwards, but he grabbed her ankle and pulled her back into place before he crawled on top of her. He straddled her thighs and sat back on his heels, working the buttons of his shirt open.

"I thought you'd at least give me a chance to relax when I first got home. That's not a short flight," he told her. She snorted and wiggled around, trying to scoot out of the sweater she was wearing.

"It's been five days," she reminded him. He let his shirt fall backwards to the ground and then peeled off his undershirt.

"Five days, huh," he mumbled, leaning down close to chew on the side of her neck. "Guess that means you didn't fuck *Angier*."

"Not for lack of trying," she laughed. He believed it was a joke.

"Shut your fucking mouth, Tate. It's only good for one thing, anyway."

"Thank you. I had a very good teacher."

He propped himself up over her, stared at her for a moment. It was dark in the bedroom, but she could see light from the closet glinting off his eyes, giving him a cold, steely look. Not much different than usual. She had expected her comment to make him mad. She was wrong.

"If it upsets you that much that they're together," he started, his voice quiet, "then just ask him to stop. He would, for you."

Busted.

"I wasn't —," she started to cover up when he pressed his hand down flat on her chest.

"*Don't lie.* All you do is lie anymore, baby girl. It gets tiring. You want to break them up – the question is, why are you trying to do

REPARATION

it in a way you know would piss *me* off?" Jameson asked. Tate held her breath. Apparently she wasn't as unobvious as she liked to think.

"Would it really piss you off?" she asked back.

"If you fucked *Angier* in our bed? *Yes*, it would piss me off," he assured her.

"So what, if I fuck him, you're gonna kick me out?" she pressed, her breathing getting fast. He chuckled.

"Tate, you can lie to yourself all you like – *I* have already accepted the fact that there is very little you could do to make me stop wanting you," he told her, pressing down harder on her breast bone before dragging his hand down her body. Her eyelids fluttered shut.

Wanting. Not caring. Big difference, baby girl.

"Leaves me a lot of scope, Mr. Kane. I haven't slept with Ang in a long time, could be kind of fun," she whispered.

"Only if you like seeing me mad," he whispered back. She finally chuckled as well, squirming as he started undoing the button on her shorts.

"I *love* seeing you mad."

"Tatum. You have never seen me *really* mad."

Scary fucking thought.

His hand dived under her shorts then, and she forgot what they were talking about; his fingers always had the ability to make her forget everything. Scratching her, squeezing her, choking her, inside of her. Very talented, those fingers.

"*Ooohhh, wow,*" she breathed out, her shoulders lifting off the mattress.

"Tell me why you're trying to break them up," Jameson demanded, pressing two fingers inside of her.

"Because," Tate panted. "I'm angry at them."

"Why? Why do you care who *Angier* fucks?"

"I don't care. I care that *she's* fucking him," she replied, her head tossing from side to side as his fingers worked quicker.

"*Why?*"

"She stole my life away from me, my future. She doesn't get to steal my best friend, too," Tate replied, a little surprised at herself for blurting it out so plainly. Those damn fingers. He stopped moving and she groaned.

"Seems to me the life you have now isn't so bad. Maybe she did you a favor," he pointed out, dragging sticky wet fingers up her body. She managed a laugh.

"You would see it that way. I see it as more of a *burden*," she teased him. Jameson glared, then pressed his two fingers into her mouth. She moaned, leaning her head forward to work her lips all the way to his knuckles.

"*Fucking Tatum*. Didn't I tell you? No more games," he growled at her, pulling his hand away and then yanking her shorts down.

"Jameson, you and I have never stopped playing games," she pointed out, hurrying to pull off her bra.

"Such a bitch."

"You bring it out of me."

"*Shut up.*"

He yanked her legs up, hooking her knees over his shoulders. Her hands went into his hair. Once upon a time, he had treated going down on her like it was some monumental thing, some amazing gift he was bestowing upon her. It was pretty goddamn amazing, but he wasn't so stingy anymore.

She wouldn't say it out loud, would barely even whisper it inside her own head, but she had actually realized, he was a pretty giving man.

Even scarier fucking thought.

When she'd had a big enough orgasm that she thought she was going to pass out, he finally let her go. While her head was spinning, he crawled back up her body, kissing his way to her throat.

"You're very good at that," she panted. She felt his smile against

REPARATION

her pulse, his fangs against her skin.

"I know."

"Did Petrushka teach you how to use your mouth?" she asked bluntly. Jameson snorted.

"No. By the time I got with Pet, I had learned all my tricks," he replied, leaning away from her enough to unbuckle his pants. Tate helped, using her feet to work them down his legs.

"All of them, hmmm? So I guess there's nothing new to learn from me," she sighed. He laid all of his weight on her.

"Tatum, I think I learn something new from you every single day."

Nice words scar so bad.

3

"IF YOU WON'T TALK TO them," Sanders started the next day, walking into the kitchen. "Will you talk to me?"

"What do you want to talk about?" Tate asked, holding out a spoon covered in brownie batter. She held it in front of his face until he took a taste.

"Paris. Last fall. Why you're trying to break up Mr. Hollingsworth and Mrs. Carmichael," he said. She blinked in surprise.

"Jameson told you about all that?" she asked, dumping the brownie mix into a pan.

"I asked if he had talked to you. He mentioned it. May I ask why you're doing this?" Sanders pressed again. She sighed, opening the oven and sliding the pan inside.

"Because. I'm upset. I'm tired of feeling like people walk all over me. I shouldn't have to ask them to not be together – *they should've known better*," she tried to explain. He shook his head.

"Sometimes, it is possible for a person to have no control over the people he likes," he pointed out, staring at her very hard. She frowned.

"Jameson and I are completely different, he never —,"

REPARATION

"I was talking about *me and you*, Tatum."

Well, isn't he just full of surprises.

"What are you saying, Sandy? You don't want to be my friend, but you just can't help it?" she laughed. He nodded, and her laughter dried up pretty quickly.

"When I first met you, I did not like you. I never liked any of the women Jameson brought home. But you wouldn't leave me alone. You talked to me. I grew accustomed to you. And then I started to appreciate you. I looked foward to us spending time together. Now, I'm not even sure how it happened, but I feel like I *need* to be in your presence. I did not want, nor did I ask, to love you. It just happened. Would you hold that against me?" Sanders stated.

Tate was completely blown away. Sanders loved her? Of course, she knew that he liked her. That they were friends. He had called her his best friend, once. Very touching. But people also referred to their dogs as their best friend – Tatum felt like a spaniel about half the time. But he loved her. Sanders loving anybody was shocking enough, but her ... she didn't know what to do with that information.

Except feel like the goddamn devil – I am completely unworthy of him.

"Sanders," she breathed. "I think I hate myself."

"No you don't. You're just confused. Talk to him, talk to Mr. Hollingsworth," he urged. She shook her head.

"I can't. I just ... I feel like this is something I need to do. It's all I think about. Sometimes, I stay awake all night, because I can't stop thinking about ruining things for everyone," she whispered, glancing at the doorway. Jameson was somewhere in the house.

"You're being overdramatic. Maybe you should see a therapist," Sanders suggested. She snorted.

"Fuck that."

"What Jameson did was wrong, but he has apologized. You claim to have forgiven him, but you haven't. If you are going to keep holding it against him, then I personally feel you should not be with him. What Mr. Hollingsworth did was wrong, he should not have kept his relationship a secret – he should have discussed his feelings with you before anything started. But it is not the end of the world. For your sake, for everyone's sake, just talk to people," he urged.

She stared at the counter top. Of course she should talk to everyone else. The thought ran through her brain a million times. Every time Tate was with Jameson, it was on the tip of her tongue. If anyone would understand an uncontrollable urge to hurt people, it would be Jameson. But she couldn't talk to him – she wanted to hurt him, too.

She wanted blood.

"I get it. I really do. And I'll snap out of it, I promise. No more sneaking Ang into the house, no more dirty tricks while you guys are gone," she promised. She hated lying to Sanders, so she kept her options open without being specific. He sighed.

"I honestly think you'd —," he started to say, but then Jameson walked into the room.

"Think she'd what, Sanders?" he asked, moving to stand between them. Tate shrugged and put the brownie spoon in her mouth.

"I think if she keeps eating sweets the way she has been, her weight is going to balloon out of control," Sanders replied, then marched out of the room. Tate stared after him.

Was that … did he just … was that a dig!? Did Sanders just snap at me, in Sanders-speak!? Good for you, Sandy.

"Am I getting fat!?" she exclaimed, turning to look down at her ass.

No matter what was going on in her life, she always tried to make it a point to exercise, in some fashion, at least twice a week. In Spain, she had jogged up and down the marina. In Weston, she used a small gym that Jameson had put into a spare room. She couldn't be getting fat! She turned in a circle, trying to judge.

"Your ass is perfect, he's being rude. You've upset him. What were guys talking about?" Jameson asked, leaning against the island.

"Ang," she replied. Jameson hung his head.

"Fuck, I just cannot get away from that guy."

"You're the one who blabbed all of our pillow talk to Sandy. Do you throw in the dirty stuff, too?" Tate asked, licking the spoon clean.

"Only if he's been very good. Let's get out of here," Jameson suddenly said.

"But I just put brownies in," Tate told him, gesturing to the oven. He moved to stand in front of her and ran his finger along the inside of the bowl she'd used to make the batter.

"So. Set a timer, Sanders will take them out. Let's go get lunch," he suggested, licking his finger. She followed the movement with her eyes and he smiled.

"You take him for granted," she warned him. He barked out a laugh.

"You are always so wrong. C'mon, *fat ass*, let's go," he urged, roughly squeezing her butt before walking past her.

"I am not —," she started to argue when he hooked a finger into her apron and yanked her backwards.

"*I wasn't asking, Tate.*"

They went to lunch in Weston, which surprised her. He was either at home, or in Boston. She couldn't remember him ever doing anything in Weston, but he drove them straight to a restaurant and walked right in, like he had been going there for years. He had ordered before she even sat down, and she had to wait for the waiter to come back before she could put in her own order.

Being alone with him in public was the worst for her. She couldn't seduce him in a restaurant, during the middle of the day. Well, she could, but it would be a little awkward, while he was stuffing his face and a family of four sat behind them. So she was subjected to his company. And sometimes, Satan was very pleasant company, indeed. It almost made her feel guilty about her plans.

Almost.

Because she loved it so much, he had taken the Jaguar, and then surprised her by cruising around with her for a while afterwards. It was freezing, but the sun was out, so he opened the sun roof. She leaned her seat back, enjoying the breeze.

"Tate," Jameson started, his voice heavy. She groaned.

"No more talking. I feel like everyone keeps wanting to have *'talks'* with me. I am a big girl. I make my own decisions, retarded as they may be, *thank you*," she said quickly.

"I wasn't going to have *'a talk'*. I was going to ask how much convincing it would take to get some road head," he replied. She burst out laughing and glanced over at him.

"Jesus, Jameson, are you always fully erect?" she chuckled. He smiled.

"Not quite always."

"Not quite, huh. What about when you're at work? What could possibly get you excited there?" she questioned.

"Well, we did hire a new secretary. She is particularly edible," he said. She stopped laughing.

"Oh really. Fuck her yet?" she asked, trying to sound breezy.

"Despite what you may think, I don't just fuck every woman who steps in front of me. I do let some of them get away," he assured her.

"What about this one?" she kept on.

"*No,* I haven't fucked her."

"*Yet.*"

"Yet," he agreed.

"Well, don't hold back on my account. I would hate for you to be uncomfortable at work," she managed to joke.

Tate wasn't sure how to really feel about it. She was going to dump Jameson like a bad habit, as soon as the perfect opportunity presented itself. She shouldn't care who he slept with, really. But still …

"You and I both know you wouldn't like that to happen, so I have restrained myself. *For you,* I would like to point out. I want brownie points," he said. She snorted.

"You're still in the red on brownie points. And really, I don't mind," she assured him.

"Yes, you do."

"I don't."

"Tatum."

"*Jameson.*"

"Stop it."

"*You* stop it."

"Okay, how about I bring her home. You could cook us dinner, and I could fuck her on the table afterwards," he suggested, his tone biting. The picture he was painting, the idea of him fucking someone else in their – *correction, his* – house, made her want to throw up. But Tate figured being flippant would be more beneficial to her cause. She took a deep breath.

"Alright. But I'm a shit cook, you should probably just skip to the fucking," she warned him. He barked out a laugh.

"Baby girl, why can't you just admit, out loud, that you don't like sharing me," he said in a soft voice.

"Because it's not true. You're the one who doesn't like to share his toys," she reminded him. He nodded.

"There's only certain people I don't like to share with, and I'm okay with that fact," he agreed.

"Maybe I'm not," she countered.

"You want to sleep with other guys? Go for it. I never said you couldn't," he told her.

"Really? I seem to recall a sharp pair of scissors telling me otherwise."

Jameson was quiet after that, and after a couple minutes, he pulled the car into a turn around area. They were deep in the country, surrounded by frosty fields. Boston was in the middle of a cold snap, and temperatures had been in the low-twenties. As he turned the engine off, Tate wrapped her sleeves around her fists and turned to look at him.

"I don't care if you sleep with other men. I *do* care if you fuck them and then rub it in my face; try to make me feel like shit about it. It doesn't work – it just pisses me off and makes *you* look like a stupid whore," he told her bluntly.

My, my, Satan makes a daytime appearance.

"I have a game," Tate started, undoing her seatbelt.

"What?" he growled, eyeing her warily as she moved her seat back.

"How about we both tell the truth," she suggested, pulling her hair up into a ponytail.

"I never lie, so this will be pretty easy for me. You, on the other hand, haven't been acquainted with the truth in quite a while," he called her out. She rolled her eyes.

"*Yes*, it would bother me if you had sex with your secretary," she stated. His eyebrows went up.

"I already know that, though I'm surprised you admitted it out loud," he replied. She crossed her eyes at him.

"It is one thing for you to sex up some random chick in a far away place. It is another thing for you to find some new fantastic lover that's better than me right here at home. As you once said, I'm not done playing with you yet," she explained.

"I'm flattered."

"So. Now you admit something, too," she urged.

"Like what?" he asked. She took off her scarf, threw it into the backseat.

"Like the idea of me having sex with someone else makes your blood boil," she filled in for him. Jameson snorted.

"Tatum, I couldn't care —,"

"He almost kissed me."

"Excuse me?"

"Ang. In the bedroom. He almost kissed me. I was kneeling on your bed. He had his arms around me," she painted a picture. Rage rippled across Jameson's features.

"Why are you telling me this?" he demanded.

"To point out how mad you are right now," she replied.

"That's because I don't like *Angier*. A stranger is completely different," he snapped.

"Oh really? So another man, some stranger, touching me, doesn't bother you," she clarified, and slowly shrugged off her jacket.

"Not in the least," he replied. She smiled.

"Another man fucking me doesn't bother you. So if I were to go downtown, and rent a hotel room for a weekend, and just sow some wild oats, you would be cool with that?" she clarified, putting her jacket into the backseat.

"Completely."

"Ooohhh, I know what I'm doing next weekend. I'm going to get a room, and then I'm going to put on the tiniest skirt I own, and then I'm going to go bar hopping. I am going to find some devastatingly sexy guy. Fuck it, maybe I won't even need him to take me back to the room," Tate said, shivering as she described it.

"You do love a good alley-fuck."

"Don't I, though? Or a car. Cars are good. If he has a car, I'll just climb into the backseat and let him bend me over the console. Been a long time since I've had good car sex," she sighed.

"You could be having it right now."

"And ruin the fantasy? No, I'll wait. I'm very glad to know you're okay with all this, it's so exciting! If it's really good, then maybe I'll take him back to the hotel room, and let him touch every inch of my body, put his dick in any orifice he wants. Maybe, if I'm very lucky,

I'll get some new bruises to bring home," Tate said. Jameson's hand went into her hair and pulled, yanking her towards him.

"Sex is one thing. If I see a bruise, we have a problem," he hissed.

"That's stupid. So I can have sex, just not *good* sex?" she asked. He glared at her.

"You can have perfectly good sex without someone leaving a mark on you. *I* get to leave marks – not other men," he told her.

"Maybe you can have good sex that way, but not me. No, if I'm gonna go out and get nailed, then I'm gonna get *fucking hammered* by some guy. Like, can't walk right the next day," she laughed.

"I think it's time for you to shut the fuck up," Jameson informed her. She shook her head.

"But it's just getting good, and not like you care, *right*? I hope whoever it is isn't shy, cause I love going down on a guy in public. Just right there in some dark night club. I'll just slip onto my knees – men seem to love that, don't they? – and press him against a wall, then take every inch of his —," her voice got softer and softer, all while his fist pulled harder and harder.

"*Tatum*," Jameson interrupted, his voice sharp.

"Hmmm?" she purred, trailing a finger up his chest.

"You are not getting a hotel room this weekend."

"I'm not?"

"And you are not going bar hopping."

"Boring."

"And you are most certainly not making every '*orifice*' available to some random guy."

"And why is that?" she asked.

"Because," Jameson answered, his free hand undoing his belt buckle.

"Because why?"

"*Because*. If another man ever touches you, I will fucking kill him," he replied simply. Tate smiled broadly.

REPARATION

"*I win,*" she whispered.

"It's going to be awfully hard to gloat with your mouth full of dick."

"I'll manage."

"*Bitch.*"

She was about to make a witty remark, but then he was forcing her head into his lap and she was a little busy.

If he doesn't want you fucking anyone else, that means he's jealous. And if he's jealous, that means he cares. And if he cares, then maybe he really never lied. And if he never lied, then you don't have to ruin everything. And if you don't have to ruin everything, then maybe you can admit out loud that you have most definitely, certainly, positively, absolutely, irrevocably sold your soul to Satan.

4

TATE COULD HANDLE ANGRY JAMESON. She could handle mean Jameson. She could handle funny, smart, sexy, witty, foul mouthed Jameson. But there were two versions she had had trouble with, sadistic Jameson, and nice Jameson. Sadistic Jameson had only ever truly come out twice – when he had tricked her into visiting her parents, and big time when he had brought Petrushka home. He could push her around and call her all the names he wanted, but fucking with her mind or her heart, *that* was not okay.

Nice Jameson, though, he was the worst. She didn't trust him. He hadn't come out till so late in the game – she hadn't thought he even existed. When she was always expecting him to be bad, it was shocking to see good. It was like she was constantly waiting for the other shoe to drop, the other hand to swing. Hovering in a state of permanent wincing.

She hated it, and anymore, nice Jameson was around more than any of the others combined. Her conscience was being ripped in half. She would find herself staring at him, moon-eyed, practically worshiping every word that fell from his mouth, and then she would slap herself.

He brought Pet to America. He brought Ellie to Paris. Who's he gonna bring home next? Do you really wanna be here to find out?

It was torture. Sanders wasn't helping, always looking at her sideways, pulling her aside to *chat*, to *assure* her that Jameson's intentions were noble and pure. Bullshit. Jameson and nobility didn't dine at the same table, and he had probably been born with a dirty heart, so purity was out of the question.

Kinda like me …

She was so fucked. She just wondered when she would finally throw in the towel and really admit it to herself.

"What are you doing?" Sanders asked as he walked into the library. Jameson didn't look away from his task.

"Trying to find the best place for this," he replied.

Several people were standing in his library, all wearing white gloves. They were from a museum – Jameson had hired them to move and hang his original Mark Rothko painting. He had inherited it from his father, and for a long time, it had stayed at the house in Pennsylvania. When Jameson sold the house, he had the painting moved to the lobby of his offices in New York. He had never thought much about it, other than it was a good investment. But when he opened his firm in Boston, on a whim, he had the painting brought there and placed in his own personal office.

Tatum loved the piece, though she had only ever been in his office that one time, when he had basically propositioned her. She had commented once that she was a fan of Rothko's work, and was impressed that he had one. Very little truly impressed Tatum O'Shea.

She wouldn't go in his library. Too many memories associated with it. He didn't understand women, understand their stupid brains – all the memories were *good* memories, nothing bad had happened to her in there. It wasn't like he was trying to force her into Sanders' old room. *No one* went into that room. He was going to have the whole thing gutted and ripped apart. Have it turned into a fucking yoga studio for her.

Jameson liked his library, and he liked spending time in it. He didn't, however, like sitting in there and having to listen to her and Sanders galavanting around the house all day. Laughing in the conservatory, whispering in the kitchen, tumbling down the stairs. Well, really, that last one was just Tate. Still. He was ready to strangle somebody. She was there to entertain *him*, not Sanders, and she couldn't do that if she wasn't in the room.

So. He was going to bribe her, with her favorite piece of art.

I wonder if Angier has this much trouble with her.

"If I may – move the couch to the center of the room, move those bookshelves, hang the painting there. It will be a focal point," Sanders said quickly, gesturing to the wall opposite the fireplace. Jameson blinked and looked around the room.

"The couch will cut the room in half," he replied, turning around. The library was long, narrow. There was a lot of open space between the two walls. In the old days, Tate's preferred spot was stretched out on the floor. She had never used the couch and it had never occured to him to move it.

"Yes. You will need to buy a coffee table. Why are you bringing the painting here?" Sanders asked. Jameson nodded at the museum people and they began rearranging his furniture.

"Because it's one of her favorites. I thought it would entice her to come in here," Jameson explained, walking out of the room and heading into the kitchen.

"You could just ask her," Sanders suggested. Jameson laughed.

"Don't you think I've tried?"

"No, I don't. I think you've told her. I think you've commanded. But I highly doubt you've ever asked," Sanders said.

Well then.

"Sometimes, I think you two are working against me," Jameson grumbled.

"I would never, I assure you," Sanders responded.

"She seems to be lightening up, doesn't she?" Jameson asked.

It had been two weeks since they had gone to lunch together. Since he had admitted he hated the idea of another man touching her. After she made him come down her throat, she had pulled him into the backseat. Went into graphic detail, again, about all the things she was willing to let other men do to her. It drove him insane. He had wanted to commit murder *and* fuck her as hard as he could. He settled for the latter.

There had been a lot of talk of them fucking other people. A lot of cursing, and biting, and scratching. Plenty of choking. The Jag was not big; he was pretty sure he still had a charley horse from their exertions. But for all that, she seemed … mellower. Like it had calmed something in her. Like some of her anxiety had been abated, though he couldn't figure out how. Had she really been concerned about him having sex with someone else? Or was it something else, something she hadn't ever told him? Something that maybe still bothered her?

It made him nervous. And Jameson Kane didn't get nervous very often.

Why so nervous? Afraid you'll lose her? You'd have to admit you want to keep her, first.

There had been some light talk in Spain. Heavier in Paris. He wasn't a man of much feeling or emotion, but once in a great while, it bubbled to the surface. Tate had a knack for bringing it out of him. At any given time, if someone asked him how he would feel if Tate walked out the door and never looked back, he would probably say "*fine*"; but if they happened to catch him at a truly honest moment, the answer would be *"fucking terrified"*. He didn't want her to go away, *ever*. They fit together and that was that. He didn't delve into it, he didn't question it. He just went with it.

God, if she would just do the fucking same.

"Maybe. Slightly. Some of her anger is gone. But there is still no trust. She is waiting for you to strike," Sanders answered, his eyes sliding away to look out the kitchen door.

"She told you this?" Jameson was surprised. Sanders shook his head.

"No, I just know it," he said.

"How?"

"Because I listen. I pay attention. *I know her,*" Sanders replied.

Ouch.

"Maybe we just know her in different ways. You fulfill her emotionally and I fulfill her sexually. Maybe this is just how it works for us. Maybe we've been in a threesome this whole time," Jameson suggested.

"Sometimes, sir, you make me ill," Sanders almost snapped, not keeping the disgust out of his voice. Jameson smiled.

"Glad to know I've still got the touch. I listen to her, Sanders. I pay attention. But I can only go so far – she's knows what I am. What else can I do?" Jameson asked. Sanders finally turned to look at him again.

"You could try *asking her* what's wrong," he stressed. Jameson groaned and put his head into his hands.

"All I wanted was sex. Just a little freaky sex, every now and then. When the fuck did it get so complicated?" he grumbled.

"When you met your match, sir."

"Sanders?"

"Yes?"

"Shut up."

"Of course."

REPARATION

They stood in silence for a minute. One of the things Jameson loved about Sanders, they could be in complete silence. For long periods of time, sometimes for a whole day. And Sanders never minded Jameson's blunt, crass nature. It was heaven. If only he could train Tatum to be the same way.

"Where is she?" Jameson asked, lifting his head. She had left that morning, but he hadn't bothered to ask her what she was doing; she had left him half dead in the shower, completely weak in the knees. The woman could probably suck a golf ball through fifty feet of garden hose. It was outstanding.

"I believe she went to see Mr. Hollingsworth," Sanders answered.

"*Fuuuuuuuck.*"

"I advised her not to do anything rash," Sanders offered. Jameson snorted.

"And how did she respond?" he asked. Sanders was quiet for a while, and Jameson looked at him pointedly.

"She … she blew a raspberry. All over my face," he replied. Jameson laughed.

"Poor Sanders. Still in love with her?" he chuckled. The other man turned slightly pink.

"I have lots of purell," was all he said before walking out of the kitchen.

Tate was very nervous. She fiddled with the silverware at her table as she looked around the restaurant. It was evening, lots of couples were sitting around her, having romantic dinners. *Perfect.* She glanced at the front door and went back to fiddling.

She felt like her brain was cracking apart. Jameson's words, Sanders' words, all ricocheting off her neurons and brain waves. Driving her crazy. Or making her sane. She couldn't tell which anymore. She wanted to make everyone pay. But she wanted to be normal. But she wanted to hate everyone. But she didn't want to hate herself.

It was all too much.

"Tater tot! Sorry I'm late," Ang called out, hurrying between the tables. Tate managed a smile, sitting up straighter. Tried to put on her best adoring look.

Sex hadn't worked, and now she knew for a fact that it would never work – Jameson had basically said that he wouldn't care. But love. Love was a different ball game. Jameson had told her that, a long time ago.

"... I don't really care about being the other man, as long as I'm **the** *man. Can't be that, if you go off and fall in love with your best friend. ..."*

Tate would convince Ang that she was in love with him. They had danced in and out of the friend zone for years – she was very confident that the temptation to call her his own, to win her from Jameson, would be enough to make Ang leave Ellie. Dump her, for Tatum. History, repeating itself. And Jameson hated sharing his toys, hated Ang, hated love. He had fought to win back his fuck-toy, but he wouldn't fight for her affections.

She had to believe that.

"No big deal. How are you? Haven't seen you in forever," she laughed, leaning over to kiss him on the cheek.

"Yeah, well, ever since you pulled your weird, satanic, seduction act on me, I've been afraid for my soul," Ang explained.

You don't know how close you are to the truth, Ang. Run far, far away from me.

"Oh shut up, you loved it," she teased before they were interrupted by a waiter.

REPARATION

They chatted. They flirted. She made a lot of very direct eye contact. Felt a lot like throwing up. *Really* wanted to drink. But she kept on smiling. Kept laying it on thick. Ang would have no clue what hit him.

"So I gotta ask," he started, after their plates had been taken away. Tate leaned across the table, smiling big. "What the hell is going on?"

Apparently he has a big fucking clue. You're as subtle as a baseball bat to the head, you dumb bitch.

"What do you mean?" Tate asked, trying to feign innocence.

"You're wearing your titty-mcgee shirt, flirting like it's an Olympic sport, and smiling like some creepy doll. What the fuck is going on?" Ang demanded. She swallowed thickly, shaking her head.

"Nothing, I don't know what —,"

"We have met, you know. Sometimes I think you don't realize that. I know you, bitch. I know what's normal, and what's not normal. And the way you've been acting lately, I'm pretty sure you couldn't even spell '*normal*' if I asked you to," he stated.

Something snapped. She almost thought she could hear it, her sanity breaking. Echoing between her ears.

"You obviously don't know me that well," she said in a loud voice. Ang's eyebrows shot up.

"Excuse me? Tate, I've known you for almost six years. We practically see each other every day. I'd say I know you pretty well," he countered.

"But not well enough to know when I'm *pissed the fuck off*."

"You're pissed off?" he clarified.

"Yes."

"About what?"

"I'm pissed that you're a complete asshole," she blurted out.

See. There's that filter problem again. Maybe you should see a doctor about it.

"*Me!?*" he exclaimed, pointing at himself. She nodded.

"Yes. A huge asshole. And that makes me mad. Like, so mad ... I can't ... I want ... you ..." she began breathing hard, waving her hand as she searched for words.

"What did I do!? Is this cause I wouldn't fuck you!?" he demanded. Several tables turned to look at them.

She had gone too far. Couldn't pull back now. She had finally hit the bottom of the rabbit hole.

One sip makes you big, and one makes you small. One makes you sane, and one makes you crazy. Time to make a choice.

"No, no, that's not it," she replied, nervously running her hands through her hair. Cold hearted revenge had been on the menu, not frank honesty. She wasn't quite ready for this meal.

"Then what the fuck did I do!?" he threw his hands up. She took a deep breath. Tried to imagine Sanders' voice, telling her what to do. Telling her to just say everything.

"You. Ellie. I am not okay with this," Tate breathed quickly.

"You're still upset about *that!?*" Ang all but shouted.

"Yes."

"But ... when we were on the plane! You cried! You said it was okay!" he reminded her, a bewildered look in his eye. She nodded.

"I know. I lied."

"Why!?"

"Because, I wanted to hurt you back," she mumbled, looking down at the table. He leaned forward.

"I'm sorry. Wait. Back up. Please explain exactly, *what the fuck,* you're talking about," he told her. She took another deep breath.

Just say it. Get rid of the poison. Word-vomit it up.

"I was so mad at you. I felt ... lied to, and betrayed. Why her!? I mean, I know, I can't tell you who to sleep with and who not to, and the heart wants what it wants, all that bullshit, and I can't stop you, but *why her!?* You knew how I felt about her, but you did it anyway. I couldn't ... I couldn't believe it. Not from you. I always thought you were better than me, better than him," she laid it all out.

"*Do not* compare me to him," Ang's voice was hard.

"I'm not. But in *that* moment, you didn't seem a whole lot better," she whispered.

"Jesus, Tate, we've been back for a month, and you've been keeping this bottled up? The whole time? The three of us have been to dinner, for god's sake," he pointed out. She cringed.

Yeah, and I wore a low-cut top and you stared at my tits and I thought her head was going to explode. Stupid boy.

"Sorry. Sanders has been bugging me to talk to you. I just … I had it my head … I wanted …" she let her voice trail off. It should have been enough, finally admitting out loud that she was upset. But her guilt was suddenly making itself known, knocking at the door to her conscience.

Helloooooo, you're a vile, evil bitch, and you owe it to him to tell him! Remember that swimming pool, hmmm!?

"Sanders knows about this, but I don't!? You talk to that fucking weirdo about our shit?" Ang snapped. She cut her eyes to him.

"*Do not talk about him like that*. Sanders is the best goddamn person I've ever met, in my entire life, and neither of us are even worthy of knowing him. Call him another fucking name, and I'll stab you with this fork," she threatened him, holding up said fork.

"Christ, you have gone crazy."

"Keep talking shit, and I'll show you crazy."

Ang burst out laughing, and she eventually followed suit. Stab him with a fork!? Up until a month ago, she had never so much as hit anybody. Now she was brandishing flatware as weaponry.

I have gone crazy.

"I shouldn't have said that, Sanders is awesome. I'm just mad. You used to tell *me* all your secrets," Ang sighed. She nodded.

"I know. I always tell you *everything*, hence why you should've known that fucking my sister would probably piss me off. You're my best friend with whom I've had sex with on multiple occasions. I've hated her for most of my life. What kind of sad, daytime soap opera were you trying to recreate?" she asked.

"A lame one. I don't know what to say, Tate. I didn't know it was still bothering you, that it even bothered you *this much*," he told her. She took a deep breath. Being a bad girl hadn't worked; maybe she should shoot for sainthood and be completely honest.

"I know. I hid it really well, because I wanted ... I wanted ..." she kept trying to start.

"If it's something even you're nervous to say, then I am really scared," he commented.

"I wanted to break you up. I wanted you to have sex with me, so I could rub it in her face. I was mad at Jameson, too, so I figured doing it in his bed would be like killing two birds with one stone. Tonight, I was going to convince you that I was in love with you, so you'd leave Ellie for me and Jameson would let me go. And then I was going to dump you. I wanted to make *all of you* regret fucking with me," she explained quickly.

There. That wasn't so bad. And you only kinda-sorta sounded like the worst person ever.

"That is so fucked up," Ang breathed. She nodded.

"I know."

"I think you need help."

"Me, too."

"I can't believe it. That is *so fucked up*. After everything we've been through, last fall, the last five years, *everything*, and you would do that to me!?" he snapped.

"I had a very similar thought, when I walked in on you fucking her," she snapped back.

"I didn't do that on purpose!" he practically shouted. "I have never done *anything* to intentionally hurt you!"

"Oh really? Remember that time you accidently *anger-banged*

REPARATION

Rusty? Cause I haven't forgotten that – she still texts me about you, you know. Pretty '*intentional*'," Tate hissed at him. He turned a little red.

"Okay, well … so … Jameson is the goddamn devil, and you let him get away with murder!" he switched tactics. She laughed.

"Oh, no I don't. Not even a little. Not at all," she replied, her voice low.

"You're a crazy fucking bitch," Ang swore. She nodded.

"No shit."

"If my phone hadn't rang, we would've had sex. And you would've told Jameson, and you would've rubbed it in Ellie's face. Would that really have made you happy?" he demanded.

"At the time, I thought so. Now … not so much. I don't want to hurt you. I'm … tired of being a crazy fucking bitch," she finally laughed, and he chuckled as well. "I'm so tired, Ang. All the time. Tired, and lonely, and I feel like a crazy person. I hate it. I hate myself most of the time. Just … just tell me you didn't sleep with Ellie on purpose. Tell me it was an accident so I can save my soul."

"*I did not sleep with her on purpose.* Why do you think I hid it for so long? I was … ashamed. Mad at myself. I knew you would hate me for it, Tate. I felt like a piece of shit. I'm really, really sorry," he told her, reaching out and sliding his hand over hers.

"Any chance of you dumping her? Preferably in some horrific, public manner?" she asked. He smiled at her.

"Is that what you really want? I'll do it, if that's what you *really* want," he replied in a soft voice.

"Ang," she sighed.

"Hmmm?"

"Why didn't we fall in love?"

"Great mysery of life. I tried my hardest, but couldn't seal the deal. I was never mean enough for you," he teased. She laughed.

"No, I guess you weren't. Don't dump Ellie. Do whatever you

want, have weird, pregnant sex. Whatever. *God.* I just ... well ... don't fuck anyone else I hate," she snapped, pulling her hands away to wipe at her eyes.

"Deal. And next time you're this upset with me – upset enough to try to use me in some horrible plan to ruin both the relationships we're in – *just talk to me*, you silly cunt."

"Deal."

Tate walked across the driveway, feeling lighter than she had in a while. Since Paris. It felt good to get it all out with Ang, better than she would have thought possible. She didn't know why she always went against Sanders' advice; it was *always* right.

That's why when she got out of the car, she hightailed it to the guest house. The back of it faced the main house, so she had to practically beat her way through hedges and bushes. By the time she got to the front door, Sanders was standing on the porch.

"There is a path," he pointed out. Tate kicked her way through a rhododendron bush and took the hand he offered. He pulled her up the side of the stairs.

"Too easy. How are you?" she asked, brushing her hair out of her face as she walked through his door.

"I am well. How was dinner with Mr. Hollingsworth?" he asked, reaching to take her jacket. She slid it off and he hung it on a coat rack.

"Good. Great. I finally did what you said, I talked to somebody. I told Ang I didn't want him dating Ellie. I told him that I had basically been plotting their deaths this whole time," she said quickly. Sanders raised his eyebrows, but that was it.

"And how did he respond?" he asked, leading her into his living room.

"He was angry. Called me a crazy fucking bitch. We yelled at each other. Then we laughed, and we forgave each other, and I told him he could do whatever he wants with her," Tate replied.

"Good. Do you feel better?" Sanders asked.

She leaned into him then, wrapped her arms around his shoulders from behind. He stiffened up and hesitated for a second, but then she felt his hands clasp her wrists. Give her a squeeze. She pressed her cheek to his shoulders.

"Yes. Thank you," she whispered. He squeezed her again, then let her go.

"Good. I'm glad. I told you, communication is key," he reminded her. She nodded and walked around to stand in front of him.

"I know, I know. I shall always listen to you, from this day forth," she prattled on, then looked around the large room. "What's going on in here?"

Much like in the main house, the living room of the guest house had a bar built into it, though much smaller. More of a group of cupboards against a back wall. All of them were open, and the counter tops were filled with all different kinds of liquor and spirits and mixers. Sanders cleared his throat.

"The last person to stay in this house was a business associate of Jameson's. He had me fully stock the bar. I have been organizing what's left, alphabetically, and marking on the bottles were the liquid levels are," he explained. She laughed.

"Afraid someone's gonna sneak your booze?" she questioned, walking forward and looking through the alcohol.

"No. It just makes me feel better to know," he replied. She nodded.

"Understandable. This is impressive, Sandy, he doesn't have this much stuff in his bar. Angosturas? Lillet? You guys don't mess around when you stock up," she commented. She heard him fidget from behind her.

"I was actually thinking about that. I wondered if you would do something for me," he said. She turned around, surprised.

"Of course, anything. Shoot," she told him.

"I wondered if you would make me a drink."

Tate was shocked. Sanders didn't drink. As far as she knew, he had never drank. Along side Jameson, he had been to world famous night clubs and top-of-the-line bars and the best wineries in Europe, but he didn't drink.

"Why?" she asked. He shrugged, his eyes not meeting hers.

"I have never done it. I have been curious about it for a long time. There is no one else I would trust enough to do it with," he replied in a bored voice. She felt all warm inside. Her? Not Jameson?

Take that, Satan.

"Sandy, you're so sweet to me. Alright! What'll it be? You are dealing with South Boston's best bartender!" she said, clapping her hands together.

"I was hoping you could suggest something. I have never done this before," he reminded her. She laughed and turned to the cupboards, searching for shakers and glasses.

"Hmmm, let's see. Perfect drink ... well, you look like a sexy James Bond, so how about a martini. Shaken, not stirred," she did a crap Sean Connery impression.

"I do not look like James Bond."

"A *sexy* James Bond, I said."

It was his first time drinking, and she didn't want to get him wasted. Plus, she wasn't about to let him drink alone, and she didn't want to get drunk, either. So she made the drinks light. The martini didn't go over very well – she didn't understand the appeal, herself. So she tried a Manhattan. He informed her that it was tolerable. After that, she switched it up and made him a Mojito.

"Jameson likes Long Island Iced Teas," Sanders commented. She raised her eyebrows.

"I'm not making you that, you'd be on the floor. How about Sex on the Beach?" she teased, winking at him. He cleared his throat and looked away.

He said it was by far his favorite. Huh, Sanders liked girly drinks. Who would've thought? She made him a Tequila Sunrise after that, but then cut him off. She could see the effects. They had been at it for a while, she had spaced them out and made him take his time, fed him pretzels and made him a sandwich. But it was still clear that he was a little toasted.

"Is it normal for your lips to be numb?" he asked, staring at the wall behind her. His speech was still clipped, but his voice was soft, his eyelids heavy. His features relaxed. Small things to a normal person, huge things for Sanders. She laughed and sank into a chair across from him, putting her feet up on an ottoman.

"Yeah, sometimes that happens to me, too. How are your toes?" she asked. He glanced down at his shiny shoes.

"Toes?"

"Mine tingle sometimes, when I drink. Fingertips, toes, lips, all that good stuff. How's your vision?" she went on. He shrugged.

"Perfect."

"I meant," she laughed, "are you seeing double yet? Things a little blurry?"

"No. Should they be?"

"Not necessarily. So is it everything it's cracked up to be?" she asked. He shrugged again.

"I'm not sure I see the appeal. I feel like I am stuck in slow motion. How does anyone get anything done like this?" he said, his words coming out slow. She laughed again.

"You're not supposed to get anything done. You do it to relax, have fun, be brave, whatever," she told him.

"Brave?"

"*Liquid courage*. Makes you uninhibited, makes you do things you wouldn't normally do," she explained.

"Like take a whole bottle of xanax and swim in a pool?"

He could've hit her and she would've been less shocked. She licked her lips.

"Yes, things like that," she whispered. His eyes finally met hers, and he stared right into her.

"That's not very courageous, or brave," he commented.

"I know. Sometimes, alcohol can make you the stupidest fucking person on the block," she managed a laugh.

"I was very upset with you. You *worried* me," he told her, his voice full of bite. Another shock.

"I'm sorry, Sandy. I wasn't in my right mind. I won't ever do that again," she replied, staring back at him. He looked angry. She didn't think she'd ever seen him look angry.

"And Jameson … I was so upset with him. Angry. I was *angry* at him," Sanders stressed. Tate nodded.

"I know. Me, too."

"But *I* have forgiven him. Why can't you?" he demanded.

"See, this is that uninhibited thing I was talking about," she pointed out. He waved his hand in the air.

"I was counting on this," he replied. "Why can't you forgive him?"

"I'm trying, Sandy. I really am. You know, don't you, that I wanted to hurt him, too, like I wanted to hurt Ang," Tate said softly. He nodded.

"I had figured that much out. I just couldn't quite understand why. You *said* you forgave him, for Petrushka, for his cruelty," he explained, leaning forward and resting his elbows on his knees. She had never seen him in such a relaxed posture.

"I know. I lied. I didn't believe him. I don't know if I believe him, now. I just can't stop feeling this way. Like, why was Pet in Spain? Did he tell her he was there? Did he tell her what night club we would be at? When we were going to the apartment? And Ellie and Ang. I refuse to believe he didn't know about that – how could he not!? I mean, he booked them onto a plane he paid for! He keeps things from me, he messes with my head, and I —," she started to ramble, and could feel her blood pressure rise as the memories flooded into her brain. Sanders held up a hand.

"No. He doesn't. *I do*," he said quickly. She blinked at him.

"Huh?" she almost grunted, stunned.

"I knew Petrushka was in Spain, I saw it on the internet. The other things were merely a coincidence – Jameson frequents the restaurant that he took you to, he is friends with the owner. I'm sure she knew he would turn up there sooner or later. I never told him she was in the country," Sanders explained, rolling his glass between his hands, his eyes never leaving hers.

"Why wouldn't you tell him that?" she breathed. She felt like she had been tasered. She had been so angry, the whole time, at the wrong person. And the right person … she didn't think she could be angry at him.

Not him. Not fair.

"Because it would have upset him and I do not like to do that. It would have upset you, and I do not like to do that, either. I knew she was a problem between the two of you that needed to be dealt with it, so I left it to happen. Which it did. Rather nicely. I am not prone to violence, but I can honestly say, there was something enjoyable about watching you hit her," he said, and she thought she could detect a hint of a slur in his voice. She gave a half hearted laugh.

"Glad I could entertain you," she whispered.

"I found out about Mrs. Carmichael coming with Mr. Hollingsworth the day before they were to arrive, the airline sent me an updated itinerary and bill. Her name was on it, of course. That one confused me for a time. I knew if I told Jameson, he would tell you. That wouldn't have been right, it was Mr. Hollingsworth's confession to make. Obviously he was bringing Mrs. Carmichael along with him in order to do so. I did not agree with his actions or his decisions, but I was not in a place to advise him that he shouldn't do those things. So it had to happen," he explained, and then hiccuped into his fist.

"You weren't '*in a place*' to advise him," Tate almost laughed again.

"So I have been having my own battle with my conscience. Watching you be angry at people for deeds that were my own fault. Realizing that almost everything that has upset you, I could have prevented in some way," he said calmly, but he couldn't stop spinning his glass, his fingers deftly moving around the crystal. She shook her head.

"No, Sandy, you didn't make Jameson bring Pet home, you didn't —," she started to defend him – *from himself* – but he stopped her again.

"*But I knew*. And I never said anything. I am beginning to think I'm not a very good person," he told her.

Tate let out a moan, closing her eyes. She wanted to be mad. She had been mad at Jameson, when she thought it had all been him, so it was only fair. But she couldn't. Jameson did things on purpose and with intent, just to make them hurt. Ang did things without forethought and out of stupidity, which still hurt. Sanders … Sanders only ever tried to do what was right. Not what was fair, not what made her feel best, or sheltered her, or helped her. But what was right.

And what was right didn't always feel so good.

"Sanders," she sighed, climbing out of her chair. "You are *the best person* I know. If you ever think otherwise, *that* will upset me."

"I don't understand. When you thought it was Jameson keeping these things from you, you wanted to hurt him. You wanted to leave him, leave us. But when it's me doing these things, it's alright?" he asked, a wary look in his eye as he finally sat his glass down on the coffee table. She shook her head.

"It's not alright. I'm hurt. But I know your heart was in the right place. I can't be mad at that. Just do me a favor?" she asked, moving to sit next to him.

"Anything."

"Next time something weird happens, or some bullshit gets said, or I get attacked by Jameson's Amazonian love child," she babbled as she swung her legs across his lap, "*fucking say something.* You aren't protecting anyone by letting us all bumble around in the dark. Alright?" He actually laughed.

"I will try my best."

"That's all I can ask."

"Are you sure you're not —,"

"I love you, Sanders," she breathed, leaning in to kiss him on the cheek. "There is very little you could do to make me mad at you."

"You were mad at me in Spain," he reminded her as he leaned back into the couch. She snorted.

"You practically kidnapped me and handed me over to the devil, I get to be mad when you do things like that. But see, that was pretty fucking awful, and I still love you. So we're good," she assured him. He nodded, though he continued to fidget.

"Are you going to leave Jameson?" he blurted out. She blinked at him.

"Why do you ask?" she countered, propping her knees up over him.

"Because I think you are planning on it, and I really would like you not to do that," he answered, and there was definitely a slur to his voice. She sighed.

"Are you going to repeat this conversation to him?" she asked.

"If you ask me not to, than no, I won't."

"*Don't repeat this.*"

"I won't."

"Sandy, I … what he did, with Petrushka. That's a hard thing to let go. I say I'm fine, and I mean I'm fine, and then it's like … like I'm back in that pool," she whispered. "Like I'm eighteen again, and he's looking at me like I'm trash. I don't know if I want to live life this way, waiting for the next thing Jameson's gonna do to me, and I don't think he'll ever change, or ever admit anything is wrong. I'm not leaving today, or tomorrow, but … I can't make any promises."

"Then I guess that's all I can ask. But Tatum, he *does not* think you are trash. He has strange ways, and he doesn't know how to talk to you at all, but he cares very deeply for you. If you left him, he would be devastated, in his own way. *I know this,*" Sanders replied, resting a hand on her knee.

"'*In his own way*' loosely translates to '*so devastated, he fucks every woman in the tri-state area,*'" she joked. He made a face.

"I wouldn't have put it quite like that, but yes, pretty much like that," he said, but she knew he was joking.

"What about you? If I decide I'm not strong enough for Mr. Jameson Kane, are you going to disown me? Let me go? Or would you run away with me?" she asked. He thought for a long while.

"I would never disown you, because I don't own you, and if you have to go, then I have to let you go. Sometimes, running away sounds very appealing, but in my experience, it just makes things worse. I suppose we could be penpals," he offered, and she burst out laughing.

"Okay, I'll take that."

She pulled him close and hugged him, wrapping her arms tightly around his shoulders. For once, there was no tensing up, no hesitation, he just hugged her right back. Sighed into the side of her hair.

"I used to hate it when you touched me," he said softly. She laughed.

"I know, I think that's why I liked doing it so much," she replied, scratching his back.

REPARATION

"Now I almost think I like it. Sometimes. Thank you, Tatum."

"You're very welcome, Sanders."

She squeezed him tight, and he finally pushed her away when she tried to leave a hickey on his neck. He walked her to the door after that, though she hesitated to leave him. He waved her away, assuring her that he would be perfectly fine, that he would just go to bed. They said goodbye and she made her way back around to the main house, using the path he had pointed out. She shoved her hands in her jacket, guarding against the cold as she made her way home.

Home.

Her universe had, once again, shifted a little. So many things she had been holding against Jameson, poof. Gone. So angry at Jameson, all because Sanders was loyal to a fault and because she was a crazy bitch.

She was telling the truth, though; the incident with Petrushka would probably never sit right with her. Jameson had done that to *hurt*, had no regard for her feelings. He still had never officially declared how he felt, probably because he didn't feel any certain way towards her. Sure, he wanted her, wanted to own her, wanted to be the *only person* to own her. But that didn't equal feelings, or caring.

Or love.

As Tate stomped up the porch, she decided she needed just a little more time. She had learned a lot of new things – from Ang, from Sanders, from herself. She felt like one more blow, and she would be thrown irrevocably into crazy-fucking-bitch land. Then no one would want to be her friend.

As she pushed in the front door, she took a deep breath. Tomorrow. Or the day after. Then she would have a nice, long, *chat* with Mr. Kane and he would definitely —,

"Where the fuck have you been!?" his voice snapped from behind her. But before she could turn fully around, she was being grabbed around the waist. Thrown over his shoulder. Carried down the hall.

"Out to dinner! What the fuck are you doing!?" she demanded.

"It's almost midnight. Who the fuck has dinner from eleven o'clock in the morning until midnight?" Jameson demanded.

"Apparenly *I* fucking do! What is your problem!? Wait, *stop. What are you doing!?*" she all but shrieked as she heard a door get kicked open.

"It is most definitely time to rip off the band aid," he growled, and then he was walking through the door he had just opened.

I just needed a couple more days, then I would've done anything you wanted.

She threw her hands out and gripped onto the door frame, wiggling her hips against his head. He had one arm wrapped around her thighs, and he dug his fingers in painfully. His other hand went up and grabbed one of her arms, yanking it free. She shrieked and tried to pull away, but it was too late. A couple strides, and she was in the library.

"What the fuck, Jameson!? You can't just grab people and make them do —," she started to yell, but it ended in a shriek as she was tossed onto a couch. She bounced around and gripped onto the back of it.

"Apparently, I fucking can. I have been waiting all day for you. Do you not answer your phone anymore?" he asked, leaning over her. He looked *pissed*. She felt a shiver run over her skin.

"It's in my purse! I was *busy*," she told him.

"Too busy to answer your phone. I see. So what were you and *Angier* up to for so long?" he asked.

"Humping our way across Boston," she snapped back.

"Goddamn, took you long enough."

"Not everyone can be as quick as you."

His hand was at her throat in an instant.

REPARATION

This is not quite how I imagined this evening ending.

"Watch what you fucking say to me," Jameson growled. "I have babied you. I have been nice to you. I have bent over fucking backwards for you. I have done things for you that I have never done for anyone else. The least you can do in return is *answer your goddamn phone when I call.*"

"Someone missed me," she said softy.

"*Fuck you,* Tate," he spat out, his fingers digging in harder. He wasn't pressing down on her, though, so she slowly sat up.

"Is that what you've been sitting at home doing? Worrying all night? About what Ang and I have been up to?" she asked.

"Don't flatter yourself," he replied.

"*You* flatter me, by being this upset. If I didn't know any better, I'd think you actually cared," she laughed lightly, holding onto his wrist with one hand.

"You'd think *wrong.*"

She stared up at him for a second. Really looked at him. For the past month, she had been working very hard to blind herself to him. Always tried to glance at him, past him, *through him.* Never directly at him. He was too much. Looking at him, he would invade her. Possess her. It was too easy. It had happened last fall. It had happened in Spain. So she had avoided it.

But if it was true, if Sanders was telling the truth – which he must have been, because Sanders didn't lie – then everything Jameson had done for the past month, had been for her. Everything he had said in Spain, had been the truth. That moment in Paris, it had been real. Those pearls ...

She felt her eyes tear up, and Jameson looked shocked. He let go of her throat and lowered himself, so they were eye to eye. She looked away. Around the room. At all the furniture. Everywhere, but at him.

"You rearranged," she sniffled, realizing for the first time that she was in the middle of the room. He nodded.

"Yes."

"I like it," she said, her voice getting even more watery.

"*Tate.*"

"Oh my god, is that the Rothko from your office?" she asked, sitting up straighter. The couch had its back to the fireplace and Jameson's desk, and was facing the far wall. The bookshelves had all been rearranged, and the large painting was hanging in the middle of the wall.

"Yes."

"When did you bring it here?" she asked, wiping at her nose as her eyes wandered over the painting.

"Today."

"Why!?" she exclaimed. She felt his fingers curve around her jaw, and he slowly pulled her head around until she was facing him.

"Because one time, you said you liked it."

The tears couldn't be held back, after that. She didn't stop crying until he had laid her out in their bed. He left the room and she sniffled, took off her clothes, curled up under the sheets. It was a couple minutes before he came back in the room and she sat up, hugging the sheets tight around her body.

"Tea?" she asked with a laugh, taking a steaming mug that he was holding out.

"Yes. Here," he said, producing a handkerchief from his pocket and holding it in front of her face. She simply leaned into it and blew her nose. He made a face like he wanted to vomit, but he didn't say anything, just stepped away and threw it into a hamper.

"Thank you," she sighed, sipping at the hot tea. He crawled onto the bed and sat across from her.

"Care to explain?" he asked, cocking up an eyebrow at her. She looked into her tea. It was hard to bare her soul when he was always looking at her like she was annoying.

REPARATION

"It was just a lot to take in. It was an intense dinner with Ang, an intense talk with Sanders, and then *that*. Believe it or not, I have my breaking points," she joked. He didn't laugh.

"What did you talk about with Sanders?" he asked. She chewed on her bottom lip.

"Stuff. Europe. You," she answered sort of truthfully.

"Sounds dangerous."

"God, you have no idea. That man has a wild side none of us know about."

"Cut the shit, Tate. What's going on?" Jameson demanded.

"It's not easy, being with you," she blurted out.

"No one is keeping you here. Like I said, I have been trying my hardest. Maybe that's not good enough for you, and that's fine, but if it's true, then there's the fucking door. Because this is all you're gonna get," he told her, gesturing to himself.

That's it? Feels like too much and not enough, all at once.

"I didn't necessarily mean it like that, I meant … I'll like you one minute, and hate you the next. I'll be having fun, and then remember how awful you are. You *made me* bipolar. I didn't even know that was possible," she laughed into her tea.

"I can only apologize so many times, Tate. Maybe you just can't accept it," he pointed out.

It was a fair and honest statement. She should just let him go, if she couldn't accept his apology. But stupid man, it wasn't that easy. She had tried. A million times in her mind. Three months ago, she had convinced herself that she would never see him again. Two month ago, she swore to herself that she wouldn't let him win his little game. A month ago, she was promising herself that she would rip his heart out.

Now, she was realizing that none of those things had happened, or would happen. She would never be rid of him. He had branded himself onto her soul. Like it or not, he was a part of her, and she was a part of him.

"I don't want to go," she whispered, staring into her tea.

"You need to decide if that's how you really feel. No more of this back and forth, hot and cold, bullshit. You say you want to be with me, but two weeks ago, you were plotting to fuck *Angier* in my bed, just to push me away," he reminded her. She nodded.

"I know. You make it a lot easier to hate you than to like you," she pointed out.

"Deal with it."

"I'm trying."

"Try *harder*."

"I think you need a nap," she laughed. He rolled his eyes and took the mug out of her hand, set it on a night stand.

"What am I going to do with you, baby girl," he grumbled, grabbing at her legs through the sheets and dragging her closer to him.

"Sometimes, I ask myself the same question," she sighed.

"No more games?" he asked. She shook her head.

"No. I had this whole game plan, you know. I was gonna eat you alive," she warned him. He nodded, pulling her legs out and settling them on either side of himself.

"I know. You weren't exactly subtle. You have a lot to learn from me," he informed her.

"*Pfffft*. You're about as unobvious as a sledgehammer to the skull," she replied.

"When you're a sledgehammer, you don't need to be unobvious. You just need one good hit."

"Stop being a smart-ass."

"No more plotting my imminent demise," he continued. Tate sighed.

"God, I suck at being a bad girl."

"Excuse me?"

"That was my whole goal. I mean, I'm fucking Satan. How come none of your badness rubs off on me?" she asked.

"Because," Jameson said, wrapping his arms around her waist and pulling her closer. "I hate to tell you this, Tatum, but you wouldn't know bad if it smacked you in the face. You're practically an angel."

"For the last seven years, I thought I was nothing *but* bad," she told him, leaning in to hug him. He sighed, kissed the top of her head.

"Just because you have sex with anything that moves, that does not make you bad. A slut, yes. Bad? No. There is nothing wrong with liking sex, and whoever taught you that is very, very bad," he informed her.

"At least I'm very, very good at it," she murmured, settling her head on his shoulder. She let her eyes drift shut. She felt so drained. So tired. So warm.

"Yes, baby girl, that you are."

"Oh!" she exclaimed, lifting her head. He groaned.

"What now?"

"You might want to check on Sanders," she told him.

"Why?"

"Because when I left him, he was pretty drunk."

Jameson completely froze.

"You got Sanders – *my Sanders* – drunk!?" he exclaimed.

"It was his idea. When I left, he seemed to be doing okay, but I think he's actually kinda partial to cheap vodka. You might want —," she started, but Jameson was already rushing out the door before she could finish.

5

TATUM WOKE UP THE NEXT morning alone. She thought she remembered him climbing into bed next to her at some point, but Jameson wasn't there. She glanced around the room before realizing there was a note on the pillow next to hers. She picked it up.

Be good.

She smiled and slithered down the bed, stretching her arms up over her head. It sounded corny, but she really felt like it was a brand new day. She felt like she had woken up without a heavy weight on her shoulders. Sure, thinking about what he did to her last fall still made her want to claw his eyes out, made her want to hold him underwater in a cold, dark swimming pool. But he also made her happy. He made her feel alive. He made every nerve ending, every synapse, come alive with want for him. He was right – she either needed to get the fuck over what he had done, or get over him.

She made her way downstairs. At first she was surprised not to see Sanders. He was almost always up and puttering around before anyone else was home. Then she remembered the night before and she laughed. She threw one of Jameson's coats on over her tank top and underwear, then tripped over to Sanders' house. She didn't even bother with shoes, just hurried along in her knee high socks.

He was up, and he was dressed, and he looked immaculate, as always. But he had a set of bags under his eyes that made her laugh and laugh. He didn't look her in the eye, just pressed his lips together so hard that they turned white. She linked her arm through his and walked him back to the main house, promising to cook him breakfast.

"The very idea of food makes me want to pull my own tongue out of my head. No thank you," he replied curtly.

He said he remembered everything they'd talked about, and he wasn't embarrassed at all about being "*over emotional*". He did, however, apologize for bringing up her stint in the pool. She pointed out that if that's what he considered to be "*over emotional*", she was dying to see hysterical.

"Have any plans for today?" she asked as he followed her into Jameson's bedroom.

"Not really. I was hoping for it to be peaceful. Quiet," he replied. She laughed, heading into the closet.

"I was going to go downtown. Wanna go with me?" she asked, shrugging out of Jameson's jacket. Sanders came to stand in the closet doorway and stared at a wall while she hopped up and down, trying to squeeze into a pair of leggings.

"Of course. What are we going to do?" he asked.

"I never got Jameson a birthday present, I wanna take him one," she replied, yanking off her tank top before rifling through a bunch of shirts. She settled on a loose, grungy, black tank top with a band logo on it. She pulled it on and looked in the full length mirror. It was a shirt from her life before Jameson, a thrift shop special she had cut the sides low on, so it showed off her lime green bra. She nodded at her reflection and traipsed out of the closet, moving over into the bathroom.

"Oh really. How were things when you got home last night? I know before I left, he was not happy about your absence," Sanders told her, not moving from the closet doorway.

"He's never happy about much, is he," she laughed, digging through her makeup bag.

"He is. Sometimes."

"We talked a little bit. He told me some things. Things I need to understand, if we're gonna do this," she explained, leaning over the counter as she carefully drew eyeliner around her eyes.

"And may I ask what it is you're going to do?" Sanders' voice floated to her. She was quiet while she finished her eye makeup, making it all smudgy and dark. *Dirty*. She looked over her handiwork, then moved onto powder and lip gloss.

"*This*. What you want. I'm going to try – *try* – to get the fuck over my hang ups, his hang ups, *everybody's* hang ups, and just … see. See what happens, see where this goes. Pick up where we left off last fall," she said, examining her face in the mirror. Done. She finger combed her hair, swung her head up and down a couple times to give it volume, then called it good.

"You're sure this is what you want?" he asked as she walked back into the bedroom.

"I think so. Isn't this what *you* want?" she asked in return.

"Of course. I am just making sure. I don't want to see either of you hurt because of rash decisions," he replied. She rolled her eyes.

"Stop confusing me. How do I look?" she asked, holding her arms out wide and smiling broadly at him. He took his time, his eyes sweeping over her whole form. When he got back to her face, he cleared his throat.

"You look exactly like the woman I first met back in August," he replied. She sighed happily.

"Good. We haven't seen her in a long time."

The drive to Boston took roughly half an hour, depending on

traffic. She offered to drive, because of Sanders' condition, but he refused. If he was going to be in a car, then he was going to be the one driving it.

She had him stop at a store first, told him to wait outside. Then they stopped at a little shop right downtown, and Sanders insisted on coming into that place. Then they stopped at a party shop and she got a *"Who's The Birthday Boy!?"* balloon. Satisfied with her purchases, she had him take her to Jameson's offices.

"Should I call him to tell him we're headed up?" Sanders asked as they walked towards the front doors. She shook her head.

"It's a surprise party," she laughed.

Jameson hadn't been lying, the secretary in the main lobby was a knockout. A chesty brunette with a blunt bob and bangs, she looked like Bettie Paige. She smiled sweetly at them as they headed into the elevators. The secretary in front of Jameson's office wasn't as polite, however, and made a racket when Tate burst into the anteroom that connected to his office. She didn't shut up till Sanders strode into the room, staring at her. She closed her mouth pretty quick and Tate walked through Jameson's door, sticking her tongue out at the lady.

"Excuse me, what do —," Jameson started to bark out, and then he saw who it was. "Oh. What are you doing?" He looked suspicious.

"Sandy and I wanted to surprise you," she laughed, taking off her coat and throwing it in a chair.

"To clarify, I did not want to surprise you. I simply drove," Sanders interjected.

"Surprise me with what? What's with the balloon?" Jameson demanded, still looking between both of them like they were there to assassinate him. Tate took the small brown bag from Sanders. The ribbon for the balloon was tied around the top of it.

"Happy birthday!" Tate shouted, waving her free hand around. Jameson still stared.

"My birthday was January ninth," he replied. She dropped her hands.

"I know. I kind of ruined it, I didn't even get you a present. So I got you something now," she explained, holding the bag out towards him. If anything, he looked more suspicious.

"What's gotten into you today?" he asked. She groaned and stomped forward, plonking the present down on his desk.

"I had the very bad idea of doing something nice for you," she told him, folding her arms across her chest.

He narrowed his eyes, but he leaned forward and untied the balloon. It floated up to the ceiling while he opened the brown paper bag. He cocked up an eyebrow, glanced at her, and then back at the bag before pulling out a bottle.

"Very original, Tate. No one's ever gotten me one of these before," he said in a snippy voice, holding a bottle of Jameson Irish Whiskey.

"Not like that, they haven't," she replied, slipping into her seat. He flicked his eyes up, then back to the bottle. He turned it over in his hands, and finally realized she had scrawled across the label in black marker. He lifted his eyebrows.

"Sanders?" he called out, not looking up.

"Yes, sir?"

"Thank you, for the surprise."

"It was nothing, sir."

"Good. Now you can leave," Jameson ordered. Sanders nodded and walked out of the room, closing the door behind him.

"You like it?" Tate asked, smiling as she slunk lower in the chair, her arms resting over the sides.

"It's interesting. You're right, I have never gotten a bottle quite like this," he chuckled, looking over the label again.

"Do people buy you a lot of bottles of Jameson?" she asked. He nodded and pointed across the room. Behind her was a large bookshelf. On the top of it were all different kinds of bottles, with labels in different languages, colors, styles.

"Everyone thinks they're clever," he replied.

"What's the most expensive one?"

"Jameson Rarest Vintage Reserve, only about $250."

"*Only.*"

"Tatum. What brought this on?" he asked. She turned back towards him.

"I've been thinking, about what you said. About needing to get over it. About you bending over backwards for me. While I don't agree entirely with that last part, I still want to call a truce," she offered.

"Oh really?" his voice was soft, and he finally set the bottle down.

"Yes. You need to not be such a dick to me. If you have a problem with me, or you think I'm lying or bullshitting or fucking around, then you need to say it – not hide in a different country and get mad about things you don't know anything about," she told him bluntly.

"Bold words, baby girl," his voice held a warning in it.

"And I need to deal with the fact that this is you. You *are* a dick. If I can promise not to freak out every ten seconds about it, then you have to promise to at least check with me before you decide to rip me in half again," she laid out her deal.

"I don't have to check with you for shit. But maybe, if I'm feeling *generous*, I'll give you a heads up," he replied, but he was smiling.

"I *never* want to deal with Petrushka again," Tate warned him, and she hoped her voice conveyed just how much she meant that.

"Me, neither. I won't use her against you, ever again."

"I have never dated Nick. We are not boyfriend and girlfriend, and we never were. I haven't slept with him, since that very first time," she said.

"I knew he couldn't handle you," Jameson chuckled.

"*You* can't even handle having me as a girlfriend," she snorted.

"So if everything between us is all good, does that mean I get to fuck the secretary downstairs?" he asked.

"I don't think things between us ever were, or ever will be, '*all good*', and *no*, you cannot fuck that secretary," she replied.

"What if I fire her? Could I fuck her then?"

Tate snorted again.

"Would you like to see what you got me for your birthday?" she changed the subject. His eyebrows shot up.

"What *I* got *you?*" he clarified. She nodded.

"Yes."

"Christ, I'm scared to ask," he groaned, leaning his elbows against his desk. She scooted even lower in her chair and stuck her leg up, jutting it over his desk so her shoe was in his face. It took him a second, and then he saw it. He curled his fingers around her ankle and pulled it closer.

"Like it?" she asked. He shrugged.

"It's okay. At least they're real this time. Why did I buy you the tiniest pearl bracelet you could find?" he asked, still examining the pearls she had strapped around her ankle.

"I'm not comfortable spending money the way you do, I needed it to be cheap," she explained.

"Why did you do this?" he asked, letting go of her ankle. She sat upright and put her foot back on the floor.

"I bought it so … you would know that I can remember things, too. Good things. You said I deserved them. I listened. I did it so you'd know that I hear you. I'm not very good at it, I'm still trying to figure out how to speak your language, but I'm trying. It isn't necessary to spend $50,000 on a necklace for me. Don't get me wrong, it's nice to know you would have, that you think I '*deserve*' them. But real pearls or fake pearls – I wouldn't know the difference anyway. One is just as good as the other to me," she explained, laughing a little at the end.

"Depending on the intent with which the gift is given," he re-

REPARATION

peated what she had told him so many months ago. She nodded.

"Yes. You don't have to spend $50,000, Jameson. Sometimes it's okay to get me the crappy, junior high prom style, pearl necklace. It's okay to just say you like me. You don't have to buy me," she told him.

"Tatum, come over here."

She got up and walked around his desk. He swiveled his chair towards her and she moved next to him, swung her leg over his knees, then sat on his lap. He grabbed her by the hips and helped her to adjust, so she was sitting as close as she could get, her face inches from his own.

"Hi," she laughed, as the chair rocked back and forth.

"Tatum O'Shea, sometimes, I almost think I like you," he told her.

"See? Such a dick."

"Shut up. When do I get my real present?" he asked, using one hand to pick up the bottle from off his desk. He turned the front of the whiskey towards her. She had used the label to address him, then wrote her own little note.

When this bottle is empty, you may return it for one night of anything-you-can-think-of-sex, and the giver **must** *comply. ANYTHING. Happy Birthday, Satan.*

"It says it right there, when the bottle is empty," Tate replied. Jameson let go of her entirely and unscrewed the lid.

"You do realize, I have a very vivid imagination. You wrote 'anything', and I'm going to hold you to it," he warned her, before lifting the bottle to his lips and taking a healthy swig. She nodded.

"I know what I wrote. I'm just very glad you don't own any double ended vibrators," she joked.

"*Yet.*"

"I said *anything*, meaning anything *you want*. I'm a woman of my word," she assured him. He narrowed his eyes and took another drink.

"Sometimes," he amended her statement.

"But I'm begging you, please, no threesome with the busty secretary," she pleaded. He laughed and his hand cupped her jaw, tilting her head up.

"You said anything I want, baby girl," he reminded her, then poured the Jameson down her throat.

Doesn't taste as good as him.

―

Since she was on a roll with the apologizing and forgiving, she decided it was time to face her sister. She wasn't sure if Ang had already told Ellie about their dinner, but Tate figured she had to talk to her anyway. Just get it all out there. So she invited her sister out to the house that night.

She made Jameson promise to stay hidden in the library. He wasn't very happy about it – he'd had plans to finish the bottle of whiskey then possibly fuck her with it. She told him it was quite a waste of such an extravagant gift, was that the best he could think of? She was literally thrown out of the library after that comment, and told not to come back unless she was on her knees.

As she watched her sister waddle across the driveway, she couldn't help but wonder what Ellie was thinking as she stared up at the grand house. In another life, Ellie had thought everything would be hers. The house that Tate felt was more like home than the one she had grown up in, was meant to be Ellie's. The man Tate slept with, had been picked out for Ellie. The apartment in Spain, the penthouse in New York, everything, all meant for Ellie.

It must be hard. I should be nice to her.

REPARATION

"Did you find the house okay?" Tate asked. Ellie leaned down to air-kiss her cheeks.

"Yes. It's very beautiful," she commented, and the wistful look was plain-as-day on her face. Tate shut the door and led her into the kitchen.

"There's a formal dining room, but I figured we could just snack in here," Tate explained, gesturing to some stools at the end of the large island which sat in the middle of his kitchen.

"I can't believe I'm here. I always wondered what this place was like," Ellie breathed, her eyes roaming over everything.

"You knew about this house?"

"Yeah, his father talked about it, a lot. His dad was originally from this area," Ellie explained. Of course, Tate already knew that – but she didn't say anything.

"Oh. Well, he's done a lot of remodeling. The conservatory on the back is new, and he had all new hardwood floors put in, wiring, new modern bathrooms, the works," Tate explained, waving her hand around. Ellie frowned.

"Pity. I would never have let him do that, I would've kept it as close to the original building as possible," she commented. Tate frowned. She didn't care for Ellie's tone. It was one she recognized well; Ellie's *"I would've been soooooo much better than you, at everything you've ever done"* voice. Like Tate wasn't keeping Jameson in line enough, or something.

"I love it. You should see the master bedroom, he completely gutted it, doubled its size. The bed is *huge*," Tate couldn't resist adding. Ellie frowned.

"I'll take your word for it."

They sat in silence for a while, nibbling on snacks Tate had sat out. She and Ellie had never really reached a place where they were comfortable just chatting. They were a lot better than they were a year ago, but still not besties. Sometimes they could laugh and have fun together. Other times … other times were more like old times, and Tate felt like she was in a competition. This felt like one of those times.

"So when is the baby due?" Tate asked, glancing at Ellie's huge stomach.

"About six weeks. God, I'm over this. I'm just ready to meet him," she laughed, patting her baby bump. Tate smiled.

"Still gonna name him Mathias?" she asked. Ellie scrunched up her face.

"I've been having second thoughts. Daddy still won't speak to me," she replied.

"Join the club. I think we're better off," Tate assured her. "What about Robert, is he coming down for the birth?"

Ellie's abusive ex-husband, Robert Carmichael, lived in upstate New York. Or rather, he hid. Jameson had once threatened to rip his jaw off, after he had slapped Tatum. When Ellie had first left him, Robert tried to get back together with her, but after he found out she had run away to Tate's apartment, he had left her alone. Granted her anything she wanted in the divorce.

Sometimes, Jameson being the devil was a very good thing.

"I hope not. I'll call him after it happens. He's not getting any custodial rights, so I don't know why he would," Ellie snarled. Tate nodded.

"Good plan. So does Ang, like, go to lamaze classes with you?" Tate couldn't help but snicker. Ellie shook her head.

"Oh, no. We're not into all that, we're more like you and Jameson," she said quickly. Tate's ears perked up.

"Excuse me? What do you mean?" she asked.

"Just sex. You know, like —," Ellie started to explain again. Tate shook her head.

"Wait, wait, wait. What are you saying? You guys just have sex, and that's it? You're not boyfriend-girlfriend?" she clarified. Ellie nodded.

"Well, yeah. We don't go on dates, or stuff like that," she said.

"But … but I thought you guys were dating. The word dating implies *going on dates*. He calls you his *girlfriend*," Tate stressed. Ellie rolled her eyes.

"I know, it's horrible. I can't figure out how to tell him we're not like that," she replied. Tate nearly choked on a pretzel.

"Apparently you *are* like that! Ellie, Ang hasn't had a girlfriend the entire time I've known him. He's a sex-machine, only uses women for one thing. If he calls you his girlfriend, then you're his goddamn girlfriend!" Tate snapped. Ellie frowned.

"I thought you were the liberal thinker, here. I'm just trying to be like you, you know, sow my wild oats. I never meant for him to get so attached," Ellie whined.

"*Be like me!?* Ellie, I never pretended to be a guy's girlfriend so he would fuck me. I would *never* do something like that – I'm always honest. And don't say you guys are like Jameson and I, you don't know the first thing about us," she argued. Tate. Was. *Pissed*. Ang had defended Ellie. Tate had felt guilty over Ellie. Ellie had only cared about Ellie. Big fuckin' surprise.

"I know that you guys use each other for sex. How come it's okay for the two of you to do it, but no one else!? Not me, not Angier?" Ellie snapped back.

"*Don't call him that!*" Tate yelled, jumping out of her chair and slamming her hands on the counter top. "His name is *Ang!* And you better fucking call *Ang* and tell him exactly what you just told me, *or I will!*"

"Stop being so dramatic, Tatum. I'll tell him in my own good time. It's not like I hate him. I like spending time with him, we have fun. I'm just never going to *be with* someone like him, we both know that," Ellie stressed.

"I don't think *he* knows that. I can't believe you. Daddy won't even speak to you because he's such a fucking snob, and you're still the exact same way! You need to talk to him, Ellie. Seriously," Tate insisted. Ellie sighed and lumbered to her feet.

"If I had known you were only going to bring me here to yell at me, I wouldn't have bothered," she grumbled, pulling on her purse.

"I wasn't planning on yelling at you – but you're using my best friend. You came between us, made us fight. *Serious shit*, Ellie. You can't just tell me it was all over nothing, over *sex*," Tate said, following Ellie out into the hallway.

"I'm so surprised at your reaction – I honestly thought you'd be proud of me. The way Jameson talked at home, the only thing you two care about —,"

"*Shut the fuck up*, right now. You don't know shit about what goes on between me and him. Is that what this is about? I fucked your boyfriend, so you fucked Ang!?" Tate demanded.

"No. I mean, it's still messed up that you slept with Jameson, when he was my boyfriend. Even you have to know that wasn't right. Angier was never your boyfriend, so I still haven't done anything wrong," Ellie replied, standing in front of the door. Tate let her jaw drop open.

"Jameson and I never planned that night, it wasn't like we were carrying on some illicit affair behind your back for months and months. It just *happened*. Get the fuck *over it*. You are *using* Ang – I *never* did that to you," Tate pointed out, her voice loud. Heated.

"No, what you did was worse. You always bitch that I ruined your life. Well, you kinda ruined mine, too, you know," Ellie reminded her. Tate threw her hands up.

"Seriously!? HE WAS NEVER GOING TO MARRY YOU! It is time to let him go!" Tate insisted.

"I have, I *am* over it, I just don't think it's fair. I don't think it's right, that you're sitting in this house, pretending to be some fairy tale princess with him, when I was the one —," Ellie started.

REPARATION

She had expected it to happen sooner, so Tate wasn't shocked when she heard the library door open. Jameson casually strode down the hall and stood behind Tate. Ellie looked stunned; no one had told her that Satan was in residence.

"Ladies. I am trying to get some work done. What seems to be the problem?" he asked.

Tate knew he was being facetious, but both she and Ellie burst out yelling at the same time. Curses were thrown, fingers pointed, Ang's name yelled *a lot*. Sanders eventually appeared from somewhere, and soon the two men were between them. Sanders was urging Tate backwards towards the library. She hopped around on her toes, watching as Jameson blocked Ellie from her.

"You're a snob, Eloise! A fucking snob! You're not fit to lick the ground *Angier* walks on!" Tate shouted.

"He knows what he got into with me! And at least we're consenting adults! You were practically a child when you stole my boyfriend!" Ellie yelled back.

"And it only took me one time, to get him to break up with you! So *GET FUCKED*, Eloise!"

Tate was completely shocked into silence when Sanders' arms went around her waist and he picked her up. She always underestimated his size, his strength. He carried her into the library like she weighed nothing. She didn't say anything, just let him deposit her in the middle of the room. She stood there while he shut the door behind them.

"I apologize, but you need to calm down," he informed her. She nodded.

"I know, I know," she breathed, almost panting from all the adrenaline rushing through her body.

"I don't know why you always let her goad you. You are better than her. It is beneath you to act this way with her," Sanders pointed out. Tate groaned.

"I know," she agreed, dropping her head. The library door swung open and Jameson strode inside.

"Outstanding, Tatum. You've really topped yourself, fighting with a pregnant woman. Why did I have to explain to her, *again*, that she and I would never have stayed together?" he asked.

"Because she's a stupid bitch who doesn't think I belong somewhere like here, with someone like you. And she's using Ang," Tate replied. Jameson nodded.

"Yup, that'll do it," he whistled through his teeth. Tate licked her lips.

"Did she leave?"

"Yes, I personally escorted her to her car and politely informed her that if she ever insulted you again, she wouldn't be welcome in my house," he replied.

"She drove off?"

"Yes."

Tate took off down the hallway, grabbing her coat as she went out the door. Jameson caught up with her on the porch steps, following her down onto the driveway. She had been the last person to use the Jaguar, and the keys were still in her pocket.

"I have to talk to him," she breathed, when Jameson asked what she was doing.

"Jesus, Tate, you can call him, you know," he pointed out.

"I know. But I have to talk to him about this in person. After everything that's happened, I don't think he'd appreciate a phone call," Tate explained, unlocking the Jag and opening the driver's side door. Jameson shut it again.

"This is fucking stupid. All this because —," he started. She stood on her tip toes and kissed him, as forcefully as possible. He looked a little surprised when she pulled away.

"Just stay here and finish the damn whiskey," she told him, then she hopped into the car.

REPARATION

She didn't know if Ellie had already called him, or even if she'd be at his place, but Tate had a hunch she wouldn't. Ellie wasn't a "feelings" kind of person, it was probably what had drawn her and Jameson together – something in common. When Tate pulled up in front of Ang's apartment building, she didn't see Ellie's car anywhere. She figured it was a good sign. She shivered on his stoop, pressing the buzzer for his apartment until he picked up.

"What the fuck!?" his voice crackled over the intercom.

"It's freezing out here, let me in!" she shouted back. There was a buzz, and she yanked the front door open.

His apartment was on the fourth floor, and the elevator was broken. By the time she got to his door, he was holding it open for her. He was yawning, standing in only a pair of pajama pants, his hair completely standing on end. She glanced at her watch as she walked in the door. Eight o'clock at night.

"Yeah, yeah, I know. I was filming all last night, some crazy kinky fetish take on Pride and Prejudice, and then I had to waiter some wedding this morning. I was so fucking asleep," he grumbled as she went straight to his room.

"Kinky Pride and Prejudice?"

"*Pride and Pre-Ejaculate*."

"I don't want to watch that film."

"What's up, sweetie pea? You usually don't come slum it anymore," he yawned again, stretching out on his bed. She patted his stomach.

"No sleepy-time Ang. Up, up, up," she instructed. He pulled himself up so he was resting back against his headboard.

"Is someone on fire somewhere? Oh god, you're not gonna tell me there's some other incident you've been festering over for like the last year," he groaned. She actually laughed.

"Shut up! No. Has Ellie called you?" Tate asked. He frowned and glanced at his phone.

"No. I haven't heard from her since the day before yesterday, actually. I tried to call her last night, to tell her all about your little melt down, but she never called me back," he explained. Tate licked her lips nervously.

"Why didn't you tell me? I mean, if your relationship with her is just based on sex, why did you let me feel so guilty for trying to break you up?" she blurted out. His eyebrows shot up.

"What the fuck are you talking about? Based on sex? Tate, two weeks ago, we talked about me *moving in* with her," he said. Tate winced.

"You and her? Or just *you?*" she stressed.

"If you came here just to be a bitch, you can go right back home to Satan, I'm sure —," Ang started, moving to get off the bed.

"She was just at my house. She said she's only using you for sex, and that she would never really '*be with someone*' like you," she rushed out all in one breath. He paused for a long second.

"You're lying. You just thought that your little show last night would —," he was angry, obviously. Tate held up her hands.

"I'm really not! I promise! We got into a huge fight, I almost beat up a pregnant lady for you. Ask Jameson. Ask *Sanders*, he had to carry me out of the room. I told her she had to tell you, or that I would," Tate explained.

She watched as Ang warred with his emotions. He had known Tate longer, but she knew she had been weird lately; trust was shaky between them. He was sleeping with Ellie and calling her his girlfriend, but he knew that she was capable of being almost as shitty as Jameson. It was a tough call to make.

"If I call her, and she denies all of this, I am going to be very pissed," he said slowly, picking up his phone.

"Not fair! What if she denies it just to prolong it!? Call Sanders!" Tate demanded. Ang held up his hand and pressed his phone to his ear.

REPARATION

"El? Hey, Ang. Uuugggg, don't call me that, I hate my full name. I know, but he's the devil. Yeah. Yeah. So, something really weird happened … uh huh. Uh huh. She … called," his eyes moved to stare at Tate. "Uh huh. I see. I see. Really. Really? Ooohhh. I didn't realize. No. No, not at all. Just glad to know how it is – I totally feel the same, I just thought you would freak out. No, we're totally cool. You're sure about this? Yes, I'm fine. Yes, she told me. No. No. I told her it was cool, she's coming over so I can chill her out. Yeah, I will. Don't talk about her that way, you know I don't like that. Sure. See you then. Okay. *Okay.* Bye."

Tate was a little shocked. He had seemed so angry a moment ago – he was really okay with it? Why hadn't he said that from the beginning? She felt very confused. Up until a couple days ago, she had been plotting the destruction of their relationship. If she had just chilled the fuck out, it would have dissolved on its own, anyway.

"Wow, Ang, I had no idea you felt the same way, I'm sorry I —," she started.

"No! Fuck that! I was fucking lying through my teeth! That fucking bitch! Used *me!*? Came between you and I? Shit, Tate, what if that's what this has been about this whole time, her just pissing on you!?" Ang snapped.

"I don't think it was. Really. I think something happened between you two, she liked it, she kept it going, then it got out of hand and she didn't have the balls to back off. She could never be like us," Tate said quickly. He shook his head.

"I'm so pissed. Do you know how many women I could have been having sex with? This whole time?"

"I'm sorry, Ang," Tate said softly, rubbing her hand against his leg. He sighed.

"I was stupid. You O'Shea girls, I swear," he grumbled. She nodded.

"I know. Who ever raised us, *that* was Satan," she joked.

"Totally. *God*. I could *really* use that revenge fuck now," he groaned. She laughed.

"You had your chance. Should've taken it."

"I mean … just … what the fuck!? I haven't had a legit girlfriend in like six years, since I was nineteen. I haven't had sex with one single other woman since I got with her!" he snapped.

"Such a waste. The world is missing out."

"I know! Fuck. Fucking bitch," he growled.

"I know."

"I thought … I thought she liked me," he mumbled, running his hand through his hair. Tate frowned.

"If it makes you feel better, I don't think she knows how to like people. Not for real. She was still talking shit about me stealing Jameson. It's insane. She's sleeping with you and pregnant with another guy's baby, and she's *still* obsessed with him. Half the time, I feel like I can't get rid of him, and here she is, wanting him," Tate laughed.

"Kitty cat?"

"Hmmm?"

"Could we, just this once, *not* talk about the goddamn devil?"

"Of course."

Ang suddenly scrambled to get off the bed, almost knocking her over in the process. She ducked under his legs and stared as he hurried to pull clothing out of a hamper. He changed into a pair of expensive looking jeans, dug a little more, then pulled out a really nice, slim fitting, button up shirt. He rolled the sleeves up to his elbows then bent to look in a mirror, raking his fingers through his hair.

"How do I look?" he asked, hopping into a pair of shoes. Tate blinked up at him.

"Uh, really good, actually," she replied. He held out his arms.

"Like how good? Fuckable good?" he asked.

She let her eyes wander over him. She had always thought Ang was sexy, since the first time she'd ever met him. In a completely different way from Jameson, Ang wasn't predatory at all. He was more subtle. Like the guy who would've snuck in her bedroom window and stolen her virginity, right before her prom date was supposed to pick her up. He had a naughty-fun smile and his hair always looked like some woman had just clawed her hands through it, not to mention that his lean body just looked built for fast times. Tate nodded.

"*Very* fuckable. Why?" she asked. He grabbed her hand and pulled her up, practically dragging her out of his bedroom.

"I just can't believe her," Ang grumbled, letting go of Tate's hand and stalking around the apartment. She watched as he undid the bolt lock and chain lock from the door. Then he ducked down to stare out the peephole.

"Ang. What the fuck are you doing?" she asked. He waved an arm at her.

"Shut up. She's gonna be here any second," he mumbled, leaning to the side, obviously trying to look down the hall.

"What?" Tate was a little shocked. "Ang, maybe I should go. It's, like, between you two, and I don't want to get arrested for beating up a pregnant woman."

"You won't beat her up, I just want to —, *shit! She's here! She's here!*" he hissed, and hightailed it back to her side. Tate could hear the sound of a key in the lock.

"Good god, Ang, you gave her a key!? I didn't even —,"

She couldn't finish her sentence, however, because his tongue was suddenly in her mouth. She gasped as his mouth completely enveloped her own. She was vaguely aware that the door was swinging open and then Ang was dipping her slightly, raking his fingers down her back before grabbing onto her butt. She squealed against his mouth and pushed at his shoulders.

"What the hell is going on!?" Ellie's voice squeaked from the doorway.

I have no fucking clue.

Tate finally managed to shove Ang off, breaking the kiss. But he kept his arms around her, swinging her around so his back was to Ellie, Tate almost bending in half backwards. She glared at him, shoving at his hand as it worked its way over her breasts.

"What are you doing!? Jameson is gonna kill you!" Tate hissed, all while Ellie shouted behind them.

"Just go with it!" Ang growled, then kissed her again.

"*Angier!*" Ellie shrieked.

Tate shoved him hard, finally gaining arm distance between them. She glared at him, wiping at her mouth. He smirked back. Ellie fumed in front of him. How come when Tate wanted to break them up by having dirty, nasty, fun time with Ang, it wasn't okay – but suddenly he wants to suck her face off to make Ellie mad, and it's fine!?

"What's up?" he asked casually, turning to face Ellie.

"Are you kidding me!?" she demanded before turning towards Tate. "And you! I thought this was, like, against the rules or something! You're such a slut!"

"Hey!" Tate snapped. "Technically, what I do is none of your business. And second of all, pretending to like some guy just to fuck him is pretty goddamn slutty!"

"It becomes my business when you make out with my …" Ellie's voice trailed off, her face turning red.

"*Your what*, Ellie? You just explained to me how I'm nothing more than sex to you," Ang pointed out.

"No! *We* just said that's all we are, *to each other*," she stressed, waving her purse between them.

"Yeah. So, I think that means I can make out with whoever I want," he replied, coiling his arm around Tate's waist. She began smacking him in the chest.

"This is sick. You two are sick. I'm getting out of here. I hope

REPARATION

you're happy together, you … sluts," Ellie cursed, then stomped out of the apartment, slamming the door behind her.

"That was pretty awesome," Ang laughed, still holding onto Tate. She shoved at him.

"No it wasn't! A little warning, maybe, next time you feel like shoving your tongue clear down to my stomach!" she snapped at him.

"Oh c'mon, you always loved lots of tongue," he reminded her. She snorted, trying to pull free from him.

"Shut up. This is so fucked, you know that, right? I try to sex you up to piss Ellie off and I'm a bad person, but you get to do it and it's no big deal!?" she pointed out.

"It's completely different. You and I are a team – you can't make plays against me."

"You're retarded."

"Shut up."

"*You* shut up!"

He grabbed her then, pulled her into a hug. Tate was a little shocked at first, then she wrapped her arms tightly around his waist. Ang sighed into her hair. He had really liked Ellie. Shocking. No one seemed to like Ellie, and Tate's best friend had gone and fallen in total-like with her. She was a little miffed at being used, but her heart hurt a little for him.

"Oh, Angy wangy," she sighed.

"Tater tot," he mumbled back.

"That was very bad. You shouldn't have done that. We're bad people," she whispered to him. He shook his head.

"No we're not. We're not very good, but we're not bad. She's a bitch and we're spiteful. Everyone wins," he replied.

"I don't know if I agree with you. But it was fun," she chuckled, combing her hand through his hair.

"Yes, it was. God, we used to have so much fun. Do you ever

think about it?" Ang asked. Tate nodded, pressing her cheek against his chest.

"All the time. Every time I saw you with her," she replied.

"Jealous?"

"Of course. Part of you belongs to me. I never wanted to share that with her."

"I gotta say, Tate, it feels fucking awesome to hear that," he groaned. She wiggled against him, trying to pull free. His arms stayed locked around her.

"Good. Cause I think now we are finally, officially, completely, even. For everything. No more being mad at each other? Or weird?" she asked. He nodded.

"No more."

"Ang?"

"Yeah?"

"Let go of me. Your hard on is digging into my stomach."

He burst out laughing.

"Now there's something I never thought I'd hear you complain about."

"Shut up. Makes having a heart to heart kinda awkward."

"You love it."

Ang let go of her and groaned, stretching and lifting his arms over his head. Tate dug her cell phone out of her pocket and winced. A missed phone call. She could guess who it was from; he was already mad at her for missing his calls the day before, he would not be happy about her missing them for Ang. She still had only ever called him once, just one time ever. When he had been in Berlin. He hadn't answered. She had resisted doing it again, ever since then. She debated whether or not to take the leap.

"I should head home," she mumbled, staring at Jameson's contact info.

"No, stay here tonight," Ang said quickly. She looked at him with her eyebrows raised.

"I'm not fucking you, Angier," she stated. He laughed.

"Thank you for that. *No*, you cow, just hang out. I feel like shit. Cheer me up. You owe me," he told her.

"We just got finished saying we're even, and you're already —," Tate started to complain when he clamped his hand over her mouth.

"Just shut up and hang out with me. Satan can miss you for one night. Please, honey-pot? I could really use some cuddles tonight," Ang begged, pouting out his lower lip.

Tate groaned. She was a sucker where he was concerned. Geez, sleep with someone a couple dozen – or maybe hundred? – times, and suddenly she's over a barrel, emotionally. She glared at him, then an idea struck her. She held out her cell phone.

"You get to call Satan and tell him I'm staying here," she told Ang. He glanced at the phone and grumbled.

"God, he's gonna be such a dick. Does he own a gun?" Ang asked, taking the phone.

"Several. Be nice. Sometimes it works with him."

"Does it really?"

"No. Good luck."

"*Fuuuuck.*"

She dragged him to sit on the couch, then yanked him down to her height so she could listen to the phone call. It rang three times before the line connected.

"You better not be calling to ask for bail money," Jameson's voice barked. "I don't care if you're in prison – if you ever ignore one of my phone calls again, I swear to fucking god, I'll —,"

"This isn't Tate, so please keep your weird style of flirting to yourself," Ang snapped. Tate reached up and yanked on a lock of his hair. There was a pause for a long moment.

"*Angier.* Why are you calling me? What did she do?" Jameson demanded. Ang glared down at Tate.

"Do you always assume she's done something wrong when she calls?" Ang demanded in return. Jameson laughed.

"*She never calls.*"

Ang raised his eyebrows at Tate, and she just waved him away.

"So you're saying *your* girlfriend calls *me* more than she calls *you*?" Ang asked, his smile audible. Tate pulled away enough to slap at his arms.

"As lovely as it is to hear from you, what the fuck do you want?" Jameson asked. He sounded bored.

"Look. We don't like each other. But I needed some help with something, so I need you to be understanding. You know, *not* an asshole. Just this once," Ang stressed.

"I make no promises."

"I needed to borrow your girlfriend, for like two minutes, to piss Ellie off," Ang said it quickly. It was the second time he had referred to Tate as Jameson's "*girlfriend*"; she was waiting for Jameson to correct him.

"Oh jesus. I don't want to know."

"Mostly tongue, not a big deal, I promise. She absolutely refused to fuck me," Ang said assuredly. Tate slapped him across the back of the head.

"She kissed you?"

"More like I kissed her. Totally rape-y. She was very respectful of you, I promise."

"You're both insane. I don't know why I bother. Tell her she needs to come home, *now*," Jameson growled.

"I need her for a little longer," Ang said. Jameson laughed, but it was evil sounding. Satan was on the phone.

"I don't give a fuck, *Angier*."

"Hey, she was my friend long before she was ever with you," Ang reminded him. "Just let me borrow her for the night. It's been a shitty day. I promise, nothing bad will happen. I won't touch your girl-

REPARATION

friend '*inappropriately*'."

"You won't be touching her *at all*. I want her home."

Tate didn't hear the next part of the conversation. She was shell shocked. Jameson hadn't corrected him. Had actually fed the assumption that she was his proper-girlfriend. It was almost as if he had said the words out loud. She shook her head. Didn't mean anything. Jameson didn't believe in titles.

"… fine. Fine, anything, as long as you never fucking call me again, understood? Tell her to be at my office tomorrow, noon. *Sharp*," Jameson's voice was hissing when Tate dove back into the conversation. Punishment sounded imminent. She shivered at the thought.

"Of course, of course, whatever," Ang was grumbling.

"*Angier*, if I find out you so much as looked at her while she was sleeping, I will cut your nuts off. Understood?" Jameson said in a cool voice. Ang laughed.

"You do realize I have seen her naked. Like a million times. I can shut my eyes, and see her naked right now," Ang pointed out.

"Stop."

"Too late. Doing it right now. Naked Tatum, all up in my brain," Ang rubbed it in.

"The idea of strangling you and dumping you in the harbor is suddenly becoming very appealing to me."

Ang stopped laughed.

"I'm not gonna try anything. She only has eyes for you anyway, she's mental for you. Believe me, once upon a time, I tried to talk her out of it. I've given up. So don't worry," Ang told him.

"I never do."

Then the line went dead.

"What the fuck is your problem!?" Tate shrieked, slapping at Ang. He finally sat upright, almost out of reach.

"What!? What!?" he exclaimed, batting her hands away.

"Why do you have to piss him off like that!?" she demanded.

"Uh … because it's, like, my purpose in life?" he offered.

"You're such a dick. He wouldn't be half as bad, if you weren't always provoking him," Tate pointed out. Ang rolled his eyes and handed her cell phone over.

"Just because you're butt-crazy in love with him, doesn't mean the rest of us are – I'll probably still be making fun of him when you're both old and gray," he laughed. She gasped.

"I am not butt-crazy in love with him!" she yelled, then pushed away from him, getting up off the couch.

"It's okay, Tate," Ang said, getting up as well.

"I know it is, but I'm not."

"Stop. It's okay. Like I said to Satan, I'm over it. If there's anything this whole fucked up situation has taught me, it's you can't choose who you like, who you love. It's okay that you love him. I'm not mad," Ang assured her. She stomped into the bathroom.

"But *I don't*. Till a couple days ago, I was planning on ripping his heart out and eating it for breakfast," she pointed out, grabbing a rubberband out of his medicine cabinet and using it to put her hair up. She finally turned to face him and he was smirking at her.

"Yeah. Seems to me you'd only be that angry at him if you were in love with him. Why else would you go through all this shit together?" he asked.

The breath flew out of her body and Tate slumped against the sink. Ang asked if she was okay, dipping his knees so he could look her in the face. If she had been shell shocked earlier, she was blasted now. *Obliterated.*

She didn't love Jameson. *Couldn't* love him. Sometimes, she was pretty sure he didn't even like her. How could she be in love with someone like that? Sure, she was growing more accustomed to the idea of just being with him, in whatever capacity she could, just like old times. But love!? No. No, she refused to believe it.

REPARATION

"I can't love him, Ang," she said softly.

"Huh?" he asked, his hands gripping her shoulders.

"He'll never love me back. I can't ... that would be it. Game over. He would own me," she whispered. Ang smiled.

"I think he already does," he pointed out. She closed her eyes.

"I didn't want to like him. When this all started, remember? I just wanted to play. You told me not to lose my heart. What happened?" she asked.

"He's a lot better at whatever game it was you were playing."

"Too good. I thought we were only playing for sex," Tate laughed, looking up at Ang. "I didn't realize we were playing for hearts."

"Pity he doesn't have one."

She cried then. She hated crying.

Goddamn Jameson Kane, you make me cry even when you're not around.

6

THEY STAYED UP AND ATE pizza and ice cream. Talked about boys and girls. A good old fashioned slumber party. Ang admitted that part of what had drawn him to Ellie had been her good girl-richie varnish. But he had liked her. He was so chaotic and crazy and over-sexed. She was so structured and crazy in her own way and repressed. It had worked. Or at least, *he* thought it had worked.

Tate admitted she felt guilty for wanting to be with Jameson. He had treated her like garbage, had hurt her so badly. What if he did it again? It was her constant fear. What was wrong with her, wanting to be with a person like that? Ang pointed out that all of that just came with the territory of being in love. She tried to make him eat a pillow.

She was *not* in love with Jameson Kane. She refused to believe it.

"I always thought I was just a freak in bed. Why is it so much easier for me to listen to one guy talk filth, than to listen to one say something nice?" Tate asked, looking at pictures of Nick on her phone. She hadn't talked to him in about a week. Why couldn't she love him? He was such a better option.

"Guilt," Ang replied so matter-o-factly, she almost missed it.

REPARATION

"Huh?" she asked, lifting her head off his bed. He was sitting on his floor, playing some race car game on a playstation.

"You feel guilty, about what you did to your sister," he said. She frowned.

"But I like it, so it's not much of a self-inflicted-penance. I mean, I love the way Jameson talks to me. I *beg* for it."

"But then you freak out when he says nice stuff. Because you think you don't deserve it."

"That's not true."

"Okay."

"Shut up."

"*You* shut up."

She laid her head back down. God, was that true? Tate had never really thought about it. She hated when Jameson said nice things, because she didn't believe him. She always figured he was just talking, patronizing. Saying what he thought she wanted to hear, not how he felt – *that* hurt. She couldn't stand that feeling. Why couldn't she believe him? Did she really think she didn't deserve his affection?

He's so much smarter than you. Classier than you. Worldlier than you. He would never love someone like you, **trash** *like you.* **You're just a waste of time.** *He'll leave you.*

It was like Ellie's voice, her father's voice, *everyone in her family's voice,* had been living in her brain, her whole life, and Tate was just now realizing it. A little whisper, always running up and down her spine. Warning her away. Telling her she was only good for one thing, so just ignore everything else. And Tate had – she just ignored everything, and became *very good* at that one thing.

"Who needs therapy, when they have a pornstar bestie?" Tate laughed at the ceiling. Ang snorted.

"I should start charging you."

She slept in his bed, with him spooning up behind her. Ang had always been an affectionate person, right from the get go with her.

It was natural. She woke up to him snoring, halfway laying on top of her. His phone was ringing, and she groped around to find it. She kept her eyes closed against the sunlight that was pouring in his window.

"Angy wangy's phone," she croaked out.

"*Oh my god you slept together you are such a slut does Jameson know oh my god you're such a whore.*" Ellie's voice, talking so fast, all her words ran together. Tate snorted.

"It's too early for this, call back later," she groaned, rolling onto her back.

"It's after noon!" Ellie snapped back. Tate opened her eyes.

"Holy shit, we really stayed up late," she commented.

"I can't believe you! I can't believe you'd do that, *again*, after —,"

"Ellie, shut up. Just shut the fuck up. I didn't sleep with Ang, but if I had, it wouldn't be a bad thing. Me being a slut, isn't a bad thing. Me fucking Jameson, isn't a bad thing. Stop trying to make me feel bad about everything. God, I fear for your child. The insecurities you're going to give it. Just calm the fuck down and get the fuck over yourself. You wanna live a wild life? Have sex with no strings attached? You're not very good at it so far," Tate pointed out.

Ellie was silent for so long, Tate had to check to see if she was even still on the phone.

"No, I guess I'm not," she finally breathed. Tate laughed.

"I'm sorry we made out in front of you, I didn't know he was going to do that. He was really upset," Tate explained.

"It was pretty awful," Ellie managed a laugh.

"He liked you. Still does. You hurt his feelings. You can't do that, Ellie. *I* don't do that," Tate said in a soft voice.

"He really liked me?" her sister's voice was quiet.

"Yeah. For the life of me, I can't figure out why, but he did. Something about pregnant nipples. You think *I'm* weird, geesh. Look, I gotta go, but call him in like an hour when he's had coffee and a chance to masturbate, he'll be in a much better mood then," Tate told her.

"I heard that," Ang grumbled, his face in a pillow.

"You are so gross," Ellie's voice shuddered.

"*Byeeee*," Tate sang, and hung up the phone. She let it drop to the bed as Ang snuggled even closer.

"What did she want?" he asked, his voice hoarse and scratchy with sleep.

"To talk to you," Tate yawned. "I think she kinda wanted to yell at you, but really, she feels bad."

"*Good.*"

"It's after noon," Tate warned him. He made a clucking sound with his tongue.

"Uh oh. Satan said be at his office, noon sharp. Someone's getting a spanking," he chuckled.

"If I'm lucky, that'll be it," she replied, pulling away from him. He held onto her.

"C'mon, it's early still. We could cuddle some more, maybe have just a tiny bit of sex, then go for breakfast," he suggested in a sleepy voice. Tate laughed.

"Just a tiny bit, hmmm?" she joked, pulling at his arm. He pressed his hips to her side, leaving her in no doubt of how serious he actually was; he had never been shy about his body around her. Ang slept in the nude.

"Just the tip," he offered.

"Jameson would cut off '*just the tip*' if he found out. He might still, as it is. Gotta go," she told him, then finally broke away. She sat up and scooted off his bed.

"Can't upset the devil, now can we? You're no fun now. You know that, right? I liked you much better when you would fuck anything that had a penis," he said through a yawn, rolling onto his back.

"I had slightly higher standards than that."

"Barely."

"Why are you so okay with Jameson and I, all of a sudden?" Tate asked, wiggling back into her skinny jeans. She had worn one of his t-shirts over her underwear to bed, and she pulled it over her head. "Before Paris, he was still the worst thing ever. Now you're almost cool with him, telling me to be all head-over-heels for him. Very hot and cold, Ang."

"I have two choices – hate him and lose you, or get over him and keep you. He's not going away, no matter how hard I pray about it. Besides, seems to me, he worked pretty hard in Spain to get back into your good graces," he replied, watching as she pulled her tight black tank top back on.

"He did some pretty shitty things, too," she grumbled, putting on her jacket as she remembered getting tossed into the ocean.

"Yeah, but you like the shitty things best of all," Ang laughed.

Tate rolled her eyes and bent to look in a mirror. Her hair was psychotic looking. She finger combed it all into a ball on top of her head. Her eye makeup was smudged everywhere, giving her that slutty-startled-Panda look, but sometimes Jameson was into that, so she just ran her fingers around the edges, cleaning it up a little. She turned back to Ang and crawled over him on the bed.

"You are a very good friend, dear. Thank you," she said quickly, kissing him fast.

"*Pleeeease,* just the tip?" he whined when she crawled back off of him. She laughed again.

"*No.* Tell me how things go with Ellie," she called out as she dashed out of his bedroom.

Tate hopped on the subway and the red line took her all the way downtown, just a couple blocks from the financial district and where Jameson's offices were, on State Street. It took her a little over half an hour, but she was finally standing outside his building at one o'clock. Only an hour late. He was going to be *pissed.* She was excited *and* nervous. She still wasn't sure how she felt, after her all night heart-to-heart with Ang. She felt giddy, and nervous. Excited and confused. A lot like she was going to either throw up, or shit herself.

Not fun.

She took a deep breath and was about to pull the door open, when her cell phone started ringing. She scrambled to yank it out of her pocket, positive it was him. If she missed another phone call, he would probably lose it and go find Ang. Put him in a pair of cement booties and drop him in Boston Harbor. Tate snickered at the thought, but then stopped when she saw her screen. It wasn't Jameson. It was Nick.

"Hey, how are you?" she asked, taking a couple steps down the sidewalk.

"Good! I have something exciting to tell you," he said, sounding a little breathless. Wherever he was, it was noisy.

"Oookay, what's up?" she asked, moving around the corner of the building.

"Guess where I am?" he asked back. She leaned back against a wall.

"Hmmm, I don't know. Some pre-game exhibition?" she replied.

"Nope."

"Bangkok?"

"Nope."

"An airport?" she guessed for real.

"Yes," he answered. She perked up.

"An airport, huh. New York?"

"Nope."

"*Boston!?*"

"Yup."

"What are you doing here!?" she exclaimed. He hadn't mentioned visiting. It was the beginning of February, spring training was going to start in like two weeks.

"They flew the whole team up for some charity dinner thing at the Hilton. I need a date," his voice was teasing sounding. She almost swallowed her tongue.

"How long are you here for?" she asked, glancing around the corner. She halfway expected Jameson's psychic abilities to call him down to her hiding spot.

"Just a couple days. I was hoping we could catch up. Feels like I haven't seen you in forever," he groaned. She nodded.

"Yeah, since December. A date, huh," she mumbled, a plan formulating in her head.

"Yeah. Should be kind of stuffy, but I figured we could go out for drinks later and you could be my wing-man, help me pick up chicks," he joked. She cocked up an eyebrow. Nick did fine picking up chicks all on his own – he had gotten her pretty easily. She wondered if he had a specific chick in mind. Wondered if it was herself.

"Look, I was just about to go to a … meeting, thing. Place. Can I call you back when I'm done? Maybe we can do lunch, or dinner," she said.

"Yeah, yeah, sure. So long as I get to see you. Are you still with …" he let his voice trail off.

"Don't worry about him, that's my job," she laughed.

"Yeah, and worrying about you has somehow become my job," he laughed back.

"I promise, I will chew through my restraints and come see you tonight. I'll call you," she assured him.

"You had better," he stated, but there was a smile in his voice, and she hung up the phone.

She breezed into Jameson's building and smiled saucily at the sexy secretary. The woman gave a broad smile back and Tate figured if Jameson chose to use his birthday gift to have a threesome, that woman wasn't such a bad choice. At least she wasn't Petrushka. Or Sanders. *That* would be awkward.

REPARATION

She listened to his personal secretary squawk long enough to learn that he was alone in his office, then Tate waltzed into the room. Jameson was on his phone, but his stare practically screamed at her. He didn't take his eyes off of her until she was seated in her chair, across from him. She leaned back, sitting casually while he talked about numbers and stocks and bonds and things she knew nothing about. He was wearing another suit with a fitted vest, and he'd gotten his hair trimmed, though he'd been leaving it long on top. He looked very much like a wolf in sheep's expensive designer hand tailored clothing. She squirmed around in her chair.

"You're very sexy when you're working," she said in a soft breathy voice.

He held up his middle finger.

He talked for a while. It was obvious there were several people on the other end, as he switched tones of voice and languages. Fluidly between German and English, a little more haltingly between French and English, and the Mandarin was choppy at best. Though he still managed to sound like he knew exactly what he was talking about, at all times. Finally, after about fifteen minutes, Jameson got off the phone.

"Where *the fuck* have you been?" he demanded, steepling his fingers in front of his chest. Tate gestured to her crazy hair.

"Sleeping. I literally jumped out of bed and onto the red line," she assured him.

"I don't give a fuck. I said noon, not noon-ish," he reminded her. She shrugged.

"Too late now. We stayed up late," she told him.

"Doing *what*, exactly?" he asked.

"Just some light bondage, nipple clamps, car batteries, things like that," she said with a smile.

"Nothing in comparison to what I plan on doing to you."

A shiver ran over her whole body and she had trouble not drooling.

"Sounds fun."

"What did you to two do last night? Why am I giving *Angier* persmission to spend the night with you?" Jameson pressed. Tate sighed.

"He got upset about the Ellie thing, had a silly plan to make her jealous by making out with me. We stayed up late and ate pizza and ice cream. Very tame and non-sexual, I assure you," she promised.

"I won't be allowing that again," he informed her.

"Jameson, you can't me tell who I can and can't spend time with," she pointed out.

"*Wrong.*"

She licked her lips and leaned forward.

"I actually have something to ask you. A favor," she started, twiddling her fingers. He groaned and let his eyes fall shut.

"Just some sex. That's all I want out of life, money and sex. Why is sex the difficult one?" he breathed, dropping his head onto the back of his chair.

See? Just sex. That's all you are to him. Just sex, and eventually, he'll get bored and —

No. He's upset that you were with Ang. He's upset that you weren't with him. He cares.

FUCK, now I'm arguing with MYSELF. I need medication.

"I promise, I will give you sex any time you want, all the sex you can handle, if you'll give me a couple days," Tate told him. Jameson lifted his head.

"What's your game, baby girl?" he asked softly. She shook her head.

"No game. I just want to borrow your condo," she said. His eyes got wide.

"You want to borrow my condo? Well, gee, as long as you promise to bring it back," he replied snidely. She rolled her eyes.

"I will. Just a few days."

"*Why?*"

"Because Nick is in town."

Jameson stood out of his chair and moved towards her quickly. Tate leapt up as well, moving away from him, putting the desk in between them. She had expected this part. Jameson always got mad at first, but then he usually capitulated. She could handle this, she just had to stay out of his grip long enough. If he caught her, sex was imminent, and when they had sex, he could get her to say and do anything he wanted. If she withheld sex, sometimes – rarely, but sometimes – she could get what she wanted. And then have sex. Win-win, really.

"You want to spend the night with *Angier*. You want to spend a couple days with Nick, in *my* condo. Anyone else you plan on fucking before I get my turn?" he asked, casually circling the desk. She kept skittering away.

"No, I think that's it."

"*Tatum.*"

"I didn't sleep with Ang. I'm not going to sleep with Nick – he's going to stay in his own place. He's just visiting, and I know you won't want him at the house, so —," she started.

"*No shit.*"

"So, I thought maybe I could take a vacation," she suggested. Jameson's eyebrows went up and he stopped moving.

"A vacation?" he asked. She nodded, standing in between his chair and his desk.

"Yes. Things are ... confusing for me, right now. I thought maybe some space would help," she said in a small voice.

"Ah. This is about the other night. Your talk with Sanders," he filled in. She shrugged.

"A lot of things. Sometimes it feels like you take me over, and when I remember the bad stuff, it's like I'm drowning. I just want some time. You told me I needed to figure shit out. That's what I want to do," she stressed.

"And how does darling Nick figure into this?" Jameson asked.

"He doesn't, really, just gave me the idea to get away," she replied. "I won't sleep with him. I won't even touch him. We're just friends, hanging out."

"He's not coming into my fucking condo," Jameson snapped, and Tate smiled. She had won.

"Of course not."

"How come all your friends are men, huh? What happened to the tiny red head?" he demanded.

"Rusty? She's in school," she replied.

"Well, introduce *her* to your baseball player – tell him he needs a new fucking friend. I am *not* okay with this, Tatum," he growled, prowling towards her. She held her ground.

"I know, that's why it means a lot that you let me do it," she replied.

"Just keep that in mind – *I'm* letting you do this," he reinforced the notion. She nodded.

"It's just a few days, Jameson," she pointed out.

"I have worked very hard for every day I've spent with you. I am not accustomed to giving some up," he replied. She felt warm inside.

"That's very sweet."

"Shut the fuck up. You better have shit figured out after this, because you will be coming back home, regardless of your boy-toy's feelings or yours," he snapped. She nodded.

"I'm okay with that."

"I *do not* like this, Tatum. I don't want to do this."

"But you will, for me."

"For you."

He was standing in front of her, so close they were almost touching. He stared down the length of his nose at her, and the look of disdain he usually wore was front-and-center. She smiled at him. Reached out and straightened his tie.

"You're such shit at this," she mumbled, adjusting his tie-pin. He grabbed her hand.

"Sanders is coming with you," he informed her.

"Really? You wouldn't mind?" she asked, surprised. Sometimes she wondered if Jameson would be able to survive without Sanders.

"You can't be left alone in the world without a babysitter. *No getting him drunk*," Jameson growled. She laughed.

"That was all him. I just made the drinks," she pointed out.

"You are a bad influence," he said.

"What, on Sandy?"

"On *all* of us."

"Duh."

He yanked her close and kissed her, and she moaned. They hadn't had sex since before the night Sanders got drunk, over two days ago. A long time, in their terms. He shoved her backwards against his desk and she fell onto it. She didn't even have time to find her balance before he was leaning onto her, his tongue invading her mouth. She moaned again, clawing her nails down his back.

"You sure you just slept next to *Angier?*" he growled, shrugging off his jacket and tossing it to the floor.

"Next to him, on top of him, po-TATE-o, po-TOT-o," she laughed, wrapping her legs around his waist.

"I can *smell him* on you. God, I wanna hold you under a hot shower till your skin turns red," he hissed. She shuddered, combing her fingers through his hair.

"Sounds exciting," she whispered. He grabbed her throat then, pinned her to the desk.

"*Stop fucking talking.*"

"You're the one getting turned on by smelling Ang," she pointed out. His fingers squeezed harder.

"I always did love fucking a whore."

She couldn't stand it. She began clawing at the buttons on his vest, trying to undo them while his hands ran under her shirt, pushed it up over her breasts. She let out a gasp when he sucked on a nipple, through her bra. She moaned, her head hitting the desk. She felt like she was going to explode. He hadn't even hardly touched her, and she was ready to pop.

She knew it was a bad idea, to have sex. Not with her emotions all over the place. She would probably wind up screaming that she loved him, then cry like a girl afterwards. He would love it, fuck her again, and then leave her a broken mess. He would've gotten what he wanted, won the game. She wasn't ready, not yet. But she couldn't stop. She pressed her hips up against his, felt the bulge in his pants, and wanted to feel more. Her fingers wouldn't stop moving. She left his vest and trailed her hands down to his belt, began yanking at it.

"*Mr. Kane*, your one-thirty is …"

Saved by the bell.

Tate opened her eyes. The squawking secretary was a couple feet into the room, and turning bright red. Tate smiled and flicked her eyes to Jameson. His chin was resting on her chest, and one of his hands was halfway down her pants. He looked casual, but his secretary looked ready to burst into flames. Tate wondered how many women he'd fucked in his office. Maybe she was the first. She wiggled her hips underneath him.

"Yes, Mrs. Janette?" he asked, scratching his fingers up Tate's stomach as he pulled his hand free of her pants.

"I'm so sorry," the other woman breathed.

"It's quite alright. Do you mind, Tate?" he asked, not looking down at her.

"Nope."

"What did you need?" Jameson asked the secretary as he slowly backed off of Tatum.

REPARATION

"Your ... your one-thirty appointment. Mr. Yamamoto. He's —, he's here," the secretary stuttered, looking everywhere around the room but at them.

"Of course. Tell him ten minutes," Jameson replied, and the secretary fled from the room. Tate pulled herself up so she was sitting.

"Ten minutes isn't very long," she told him. He shook his head, buttoning his vest back up.

"No, not nearly long enough for all the things I want to do to you. As sexy as your whore-y ways are, I don't think I can be inside of you, knowing that Ang might have just been there," he explained. She snorted.

"*I didn't have sex with him,*" she snapped. Jameson smiled.

"I know. Still. The mental image. You have five days, baby girl. You better make sure that *no one else has been here*, when I get you back," he said softly, stepping forward to run a finger up and down the seam between her legs. She rubbed her lips together.

"You think you can go a couple days without fucking me?" she asked, widening her legs.

"I've gone a lot longer than that before, I think I can manage it again. Besides, I'm submitting the termination papers to the secretary downstairs. I may not be so bored while you're gone," he whispered, his finger pressing harder. She curled her fingers into his shoulders.

"I swear, if you fuck her, I'm definitely gonna fuck Nick."

"Threaten me again, and I'll beat your ass so hard you won't even be able to walk during your little sabbatical with Nick."

God, I missed this.

"Maybe," she breathed, his fingers starting to make her pant, "maybe we could be really fast. We still have, like, six minutes left." Before she could say more, he stopped touching her and pressed the finger to her lips.

"*Shhhh.* Good things come to those who wait. You want to spend the next few days with your boyfriend? *Fine.* Then you have to wait for me to give you what you need," he replied.

It was only fair. She continued to squirm around on top of his desk, wanting his finger back. Wanting him to finish what he'd started. She wanted to finish *him*. Her eyes flicked down to the desk, then to his crotch. Down again, then up again.

"How much time is left?" she breathed, shoving him back and hopping off the desk.

"Maybe five minutes. Why? What are you thinking?" he asked, eyeing her suspiciously.

"I'm thinking I might be able to fit under this desk almost as well as the desk at home."

"Such a whore, baby girl. *I love it.*"

Of course Jameson didn't like the idea of her spending time downtown, *alone*, hanging out with Nick Castille. He fucking hated the idea. When she first brought it up, he had wanted to slap the idea right out of her fucking head. Who did she think she was!? Who did she think she was dealing with!? She wasn't allowed to galavanting off, just fucking whomever she pleased, and using *Jameson's* condo to do it. *Fuck that.*

But then she had asked for the time to think. And thinking was good. She was so close to just letting go. He could feel it. Whatever she and Sanders had talked about had changed something. Brought her around in a way Jameson hadn't been able to. She looked at him different, treated him different. There was a wall that was gone. The detachment was gone from her eyes. She was finally really looking at him again. After so long.

It was nice.

So if he needed to let her go, *again*, so she could figure shit out,

REPARATION

then he would do it. For her. Only for her.

But good god, was she going to pay when she got home.

7

TATE MET UP WITH NICK later that evening, at a sushi place on a busy street. She got there before him and was able to watch as he approached. He was an exceedingly good looking guy. He smiled at everyone, a sort of sideways smile, his bottom lip pulling to the right. Chocolate brown eyes, soft brown hair. Built body. Kind soul. She smacked herself every day, for not being able to just like him back. But apparently she preferred ice cold blue eyes and fangs for smiles. She liked her toys to have a little bite, and Nick was all cuddle.

"How are you!?" he exclaimed, bustling up to their table. She had barely stood up when he wrapped her in a hug.

"Good! God, it feels like forever!" she laughed, hugging him back. He finally pulled away and held her at arms length.

"You looking amazing," he breathed, letting his eyes travel down her form.

"I guess you haven't seen me in a while," she commented, looking down at herself. The shirt she was wearing showed more bra than shirt at the top, and her leggings had a geometric pattern sweeping all across them.

REPARATION

"You look more like you, like the girl I met in the bar," he replied. She burst out laughing.

"*Oh god.*"

"No, it's nice. You look like you feel comfortable in your own skin again," he explained, sliding into a chair. She sat down as well.

"Well, I'm still not that girl, just so you know. There will be no free-fucks in the back of bars this week," she warned him.

"Jesus, your mouth is amazing."

Huh, Jameson always says the same thing.

"So what's up? How've you been? How is Arizona?" Tate asked, pulling out a menu.

"Hot. I'm not a big fan. You ever gonna come visit me?" he asked, looking over a menu as well. She winced.

"I don't know. Things are complicated right now, I don't think flying across the country to stay with another man is gonna help anything," she pointed out. He smiled at her.

"You really like him, don't you?" he asked. She frowned.

"Does that make me a horrible person? I really worry about that, that I shouldn't be allowed to like him, after everything he did," she said quickly. Nick shrugged.

"No. You can't help it. What makes you a horrible person is not liking me," he teased. She groaned.

"Don't remind me – I tell myself that *every day*," she assured him.

"Maybe if you slept with me again, I could help you forget him?" he suggested, in a halfway joking tone.

Yeah, right. There aren't enough men in the world to fuck Jameson Kane out of my memory.

"You know what, if he fucks me over again, I will definitely take you up on that offer," she joked.

"So that's it, huh. You're going to stay with him? Try to be with him?" he asked. She sighed.

"I don't think I have much of a choice. I can't … get away. My brain. He owns it," she replied.

"But what about your heart?"

"My heart …." she paused for a while, staring off into space. "I think he's had that since I was eighteen."

"Well, shit. I don't stand a chance," Nick tried to joke, to lighten the mood. She reached out and grabbed his hand.

"If I could choose anyone else, trust me, it would be you," she said softly. He nodded.

"Sure, sure. Whatever. C'mon, help me drown my sorrows in sake."

Nick drank sake, Tate drank water. It was one thing to get tipsy with Sanders and cry in front of Jameson. She wasn't about to do any of that with Nick, and after his second bottle was done, she distracted him from ordering another.

They walked around for a while after that, catching up. She had always had an easiness with him that kind of surprised her. She had used him for sex. Good sex, but that had been it, a one night stand. Something to piss off Jameson. She had never expected to get a friend out of the deal. She looped her arm through his, leaned against him while they walked.

"You're happy?" he sighed as they made their way towards his building. His condo actually wasn't too far from Jameson's. Scary.

"Sometimes," she joked.

"I think I could make you happy all the time," he replied in a soft voice. She let go of his arm.

"Nick, someday, you are going to make some woman *so happy*, she won't know what to do with herself," she warned him.

"I hope she knows what to do with me."

"She will."

"I wanted her to be you."

She smiled sadly at him, standing outside the front doors.

REPARATION

"I wish I was her," she replied, straightening out his jacket.

"You still could be," he whispered. She glanced up at him.

"I don't think I ever could," she laughed, trying to lighten the mood. His arm snaked around the waist.

"Sometimes, I think you were meant to be," he challenged. She put her hands against his chest, pushing away.

"Nick. I appreciate everything you've done for me. You were there for me in a way no one else was, after the hospital. I don't think I can ever repay that, but I can't be ... I just can't," she breathed.

She didn't want to break his heart. She never wanted to hurt anyone, that's why she was always so upfront and honest. The night they had slept together, she had bluntly told him she didn't plan on ever seeing him again. After the hospital, she had told him she wouldn't sleep with him again. She didn't know how else she could put it.

He stared at her for a while, then smiled. Kissed her on the cheek. Told her he would call her tomorrow, then went inside. She stared after him for a while, chewing on her bottom lip. She had needed closure with the whole Petrushka/Jameson incident. Now, she could get some closure with Nick.

Sanders was waiting at the condo when she got there. She was kind of surprised – she had forgotten that Jameson said he was going to send the other man. She smiled, sitting across from him in the living room. When they'd left, Jameson had everything packed up and prepped for shortage. She and Sanders sat on couches covered in sheets, surrounded by boxes.

"How are you?" he asked. The only light in the room was coming from the kitchen, backlighting him.

"I'm okay. And you?" she asked. He was looking over her shoulder.

"Is this some kind of game?" he asked. She widened her eyes.

"No. Why would you ask me that?" she was surprised. He sounded angry. Well, angry for Sanders.

"Because you surprised me, this all came out of nowhere. I don't particularly like surprises. I don't like staying downtown," he told her. She snorted.

"No one is making you stay here, Sandy. You're free to go home," she pointed out. He finally glanced at her.

"I wouldn't feel comfortable with that, I worry about you," he replied.

"I'm a big girl, sometimes capable of making halfway adult decisions. I'll be fine," she assured him.

"Are you going to leave Jameson for Mr. Castille?" he asked bluntly.

Ah, Sanders. So scared of losing your happy home. So sweet.

"No," she stated.

"Then, may I ask, what is all this about?" he pressed.

"Nick is only in town for the week. I wanted to spend time with him, he's my friend. And I wanted to take some time off, to think. Think about things *you* told me," she said. Sanders frowned.

"Alcohol is not as much fun as everyone makes it out to be."

Tate burst out laughing and got up, walked over to him.

"No, no it's not. But at least you didn't cry," she snickered, pulling him up and into a hug.

"I don't want to see him get hurt," Sanders said in a soft voice. She sighed.

"And what about me, Sandy? What if I get hurt again? I almost didn't survive the first time," she pointed out.

"He won't do that again. He promised me. He promised you. *I promise you,*" Sanders promised.

"Okay, then. Just give me some time. I'm not going anywhere, *I promise you,*" she mimicked him. He pulled away from her.

"Sometimes, Tatum, I very much wonder how he puts up with you."

She started laughing again. Sanders could be very, very funny, when he put his mind to it.

The next two days were relatively peaceful. Nick picked them up, and all three of them went out to lunch. Sanders always seemed uncomfortable around Nick, probably because he felt like his loyalties were being pushed to the limit, but Nick never seemed to care. Nick could probably dine with Hitler, and do it with a polite smile. He was just that nice of a guy, he always wanted everyone to feel comfortable around him.

They got all dressed up for the charity event that he had come to town for, and it was actually a lot of fun. Sanders refused to come along, and though she loved him dearly, Tate was a little glad. Sometimes, Sanders made her feel guilty about having a good time. Which was silly – she was allowed to have fun, with or without Jameson. The only thing she didn't like was the photographers. There were a lot of them about, snapping photos with large flashes. She chewed on her lips.

"I don't want my picture taken," she told Nick for the hundredth time. He put a hand on the small of her back.

"So you've said. I'm trying, but it's probably going to happen. What's the big deal?" he asked.

"Pictures of people on the internet is what started my whole problem," she grumbled, letting him lead her to their seats.

"They're just pictures, who cares. He'll get over it. It's not like I've got my tongue down your throat in any of them," Nick laughed.

"Oh jesus."

He was right, though. Photographers from every newspaper were there, so it was going to happen. Tate just made sure it happened with a lot of different people, and not just Nick. No use pissing off Jameson more than was necessary. She had photos taken with almost every ballplayer on the team, and one with her hugging the team manager.

It was fun to be around the team again. It felt nice to be wanted, nice to be liked, for something other than her skills in bed. She could make the pitcher laugh, talked the alcoholic outfielder out of having a drink, and helped the mother of the umpire to the restroom. She felt pretty good about herself.

That you ever thought you could be a 'bad girl', is hilarious. You're Mother fuckin' Teresa.

There was an auction at the end of the night, put on by Sotheby's. All the proceeds were going to a charity for a specific type of lung cancer. The amount of money being thrown around blew her away a little, which really said something, considering the kind of money Jameson had, and spent, on a day to day basis. Nick bid on, and won, a perfect condition 1958 Karmann Ghia. Only $60,000, that's all. The highest bid made was on a Ferrari, which went to some older gentleman in the crowd. There were also several anonymous buyers, bidding via phone calls. A delicate China tea set went to one, a vintage Cartier necklace to another, and a bronze dog sculpture to the last one – she didn't understand that piece, but apparently it was worth $8,000 to someone.

"You people are insane with your money," Tate laughed while Nick helped her into her jacket.

"What, you're telling me Mr. Kane doesn't buy lavish things?" he chuckled, walking her out the doors.

"Oh, he does, just not quite so publicly. He'd be more likely to buy everything in one go, then sort out the shit he doesn't want, just to save time," she joked.

"Jesus, wish I had that kind of money."

"Don't we all?"

"You don't get to talk, he spends it on *you*."

REPARATION

They climbed into a cab after that, and she was quiet for a while. She wasn't sure what to make of his statement. Jameson didn't really spend that much money on her, comparatively speaking. But that he spent any at all on her, was amazing in it's own way. She had worried people saw her as a slut for the baseball team. She also worried that people saw her as a whore for Jameson. Not okay.

When they got to her building, Nick surprised her by walking her inside. She had told him at the beginning of the week that Jameson *"wasn't comfortable"* with Nick being in the condo. She had put it politely. He had respected that, didn't even question it, so she was fine with him coming into the lobby. She was a little surprised, however, when he got into the elevator with her.

"I had a really good time," she assured him, a little nervous.

"Good. I'm glad. Tate, I go home the day after tomorrow, and I just wanted to tell you —," he started. She winced.

"God, please don't say something that'll make this awkward," she begged, and he laughed.

"*I wanted to tell you*, that my offer still stands," he said. She raised her eyebrows.

"Huh?"

"What I told you, when you were in Paris. You like him, or you think you like him, or he might like you, or whatever. *I'm still here*," he stressed.

"Nick, I don't get what you —,"

He practically dove into her, kissing her hard. She gasped, completely stunned into immobility, and he wrapped one arm around her waist. Cupped the back of her head with his other hand. He was trying to tell her something, something she obviously didn't want to hear. But she was getting it, loud and clear now. Every part of him screamed with want for her, from his fingertips in her hair, to his lips against her own, to his chest against hers, to the rock solid erection pressed against her. The elevator doors dinged open, and she finally broke away. Of course, Sanders was standing in the open doorway.

Of fucking course he is. Cause nothing ever happens easily with me.

"I'll be there for you, if anything happens. *I'll wait,*" Nick stressed. She struggled to get out of his arms, glancing at Sanders.

"Don't do that, not for me," she urged him through clenched teeth.

"*You're worth it.*"

She finally shoved him, hard enough to push him off of her. She pulled at the material on her dress as she huffed off of the elevator. She turned back, praying that he wasn't following her. He hadn't. He was staring at her with sad, puppy dog eyes, ripping her heart in half.

"I'm not, Nick. I'm really not. Don't wait for me, I won't be coming," she warned him. He managed a smile.

"All the same, if you ever need me," he replied, and then the doors slid shut.

"I think it would be in your best interest to call —," Sanders started in a immediately. She let out a small shriek, stomping through the front door.

"He's not God, Sandy! He doesn't need to know about everything, the minute it happens!" she yelled at him. He blinked at her, clearly surprised, then followed her inside, closing the door.

"I don't think he's God, but I do think he will be upset when he learns that —," he began again.

"Sandy, right now, right this moment, he is fucking that playboy-secretary, which means a lot more than kissing her. *I know he'll be pissed*, but I didn't do that. I didn't know Nick was gonna do that, I have been very honest with him. You heard me, you heard what I said," she pointed out, kicking off her heels as she walked back to the bedroom. Sanders picked them up behind her.

"I know. I appreciated it. Does that mean you have thought about the situation with Jameson?" he asked, standing near her as

REPARATION

she let her jacket fall to the floor.

"No. Yes. *God,* why is everything so difficult?" she whined, lifting her hair off of her neck and turning her back to him. He immediately stepped forward and pulled the zipper down on her dress.

"Because you both over-complicate things," he replied simply. She threw a glare over her shoulder at him, then walked into the closet.

"My life was very un-complicated before Mr. Kane, you know. I probably wouldn't have ever met Nick, ever slept with him, if it hadn't been for Jameson," she pointed out, peeling herself out of the dress and changing into a t-shirt of Jameson's. She padded back into the bedroom.

"Mr. Castille would have come to your bar that night, regardless of whether or not you were sleeping with Jameson, so the result would still be the same," Sanders returned her logic.

"Maybe I wouldn't have just slept with him, maybe I'd be Mrs. Castille by now," she bit out, yanking her hair up into a ponytail while she glared at him.

"Is that what you'd like? To be Mrs. Tatum Castille?" Sanders questioned.

"No," she replied quickly, crawling onto the bed.

"And why not?"

"Because."

"Because *why?*"

"Because, it'd be boring," she answered softly. He nodded.

"And that answer, right there, is why your life is so '*difficult*,'" he told her. She groaned while he walked into the closet. She heard hangers clanking around, knew he was hanging her dress up.

"Your attitude doesn't help, Sandy! Holier than thou, know better than all of us mere mortals, blah blah blah!" she snapped. He came back into the bedroom.

"I apologize. Would you like me to stop offering advice?" he asked. She frowned, wouldn't look at him.

"No."

"Alright then. What *would* you like me to do?"

"Will you sleep with me again?"

"Of course."

Their first night in the condo, Tate had woken up from a violent nightmare. Screaming, hands pulling at her own hair. She had been under water, fighting with someone, though she wasn't sure who. Sanders had been standing over her, looking scared out of his mind. But after she started sobbing, he climbed into bed next to her, let her hold onto him till she calmed down. Till she fell asleep. When she woke up the next morning, he had been laying in the exact same spot. After that, they slept together every night.

"Sandy," she said softly, long after he'd changed into his pajamas and she'd turned out the light.

"Hmmm?" he responded, clasping his hands together on top of his chest.

"The first time I saw Jameson again, that first time we talked together, *I'm* the one who turned it all into a game. I'm the one … who felt like she couldn't lose. I'm terrified of losing to him. Why do I still feel this way?" she asked, rolling towards him.

"Because he is a lot to take in, to absorb. Because he never loses. And because you've already lost, you just won't admit it," he said plainly. She winced at his words.

"Ang said that I'm in love with Jameson," she whispered.

"I have never thought Mr. Hollingsworth to be a stupid man."

"What if he never loves me back?" her voice kept getting quieter and quieter.

"Is that really what frightens you?" Sanders questioned.

"I'm scared … I'm scared that I'm unlovable. That I'm just this dirty human being, a waste of time," she told him. He sighed and unclasped his hands. She immediately grabbed onto one of them, held it between her own.

"You are none of those things. Mr. Hollingsworth loves you. Mr. Castille loves you. I love you. It seems to me that everyone you know, loves you. So that is a very ignorant statement," he pointed out.

"But not Jameson," she clarified. He cleared his throat.

"I said *everyone*."

"I don't think he loves me."

"Tatum, I am not entirely sure that you know what love is."

"Sandy?"

"Hmmm?"

"*Shut up.*"

"Of course."

The next day, Tate avoided seeing Nick until dinner time. It was his last night in town, and she had already agreed to go to dinner with him. She and Sanders had stayed up very late the night before, talking. She had woken up curled around him, almost hugging him from behind. He woke up, and then they talked some more. As blunt as he was, he never once said outright that Jameson was in love with her, and he never once told her exactly what she should do. Just that it was obvious she was happiest with Jameson, to anyone with eyeballs, so why was she fighting against it?

Obviously, Sanders had never had convulsions and been admitted to a psych ward. Obviously, Sanders hadn't spent every day for the past couple months, worrying and waiting for the other shoe to drop. The other hand to strike. Nothing was ever smooth sailing with Jameson. Something was going to happen. She still couldn't say if she honestly wanted to see what it was.

Dinner with Nick was awkward. He laughed and tried to make

her feel comfortable, but the kiss laid heavy between them. Words were almost easier to forget than a kiss. He assured her that he was fine, his heart wasn't broken. But before they parted ways, he hugged her tightly and made her promise that if she ever needed anything, *anything*, that he would be the first person she called.

Tate could've gone home, back to Weston. She had originally planned on going home the next day, because she had wanted to see Nick off at the airport, but that wasn't going to happen anymore. Still. She wasn't ready.

So she invited Ang over to the condo. Sanders protested vehemently, insisting that Ang coming over was *almost* as bad as Nick coming over. Tate just shushed him and told him to go back to Weston.

"You don't want me here?" he sounded shocked. She laughed and hugged him.

"I always want your around, Sandy. But I know you don't like it here. And Nick is gone, I don't need a babysitter. I'll be home, I'm not going to run away," she promised him. He frowned.

"I think this is a bad idea," he insisted.

"Stay, if you want. We're going to do a marathon of Ang's first ten porns. They start getting almost good after the first three. Anal was new to him, he didn't —,"

She had never seen Sanders move quite that fast.

Ang really did come over, though they opted not to watch the porn. She hadn't had sex in almost a week. After being celibate for so long over the winter, her sex drive was back with a vengeance. She didn't want to tempt fate.

Ang and Ellie had made a truce of sorts. She admitted to knowingly leading him on, and had apologized. He apologized for making out with Tatum, just to hurt her. She asked if they could still have sex once and while. He told her that she couldn't afford him.

Laughter all around.

REPARATION

"You know who was good?" Ang breathed, passing a joint to her. She didn't really drink anymore, and hadn't smoked any cigarettes since Jameson had tossed her in the ocean. But Tate saw no problems with marijuana. A fine, smoky haze drifted around the condo.

"Who?" she asked, taking a hit and holding the smoke in her lungs.

"Rusty," he replied, referring to her old roommate, the one he had slept with to piss Tate off. She started coughing.

"Seriously!?" she exclaimed, patting her chest. He nodded.

"Yeah, surprisingly. That shy, virginal thing kinda does it for me," he replied. She swatted him in the arm.

"Shut up, you loved it with me."

"Tater tot, no one will ever be as good as you," he told her, and she smiled. "But Rus was pretty hot. I think I was like only the fourth dude she'd ever had sex with."

"One time, I had to listen to her and some dude, all night. Jameson was over. I thought we were gonna die, we were laughing so hard. It sounded boring," Tate said. He shook his head.

"She's one of those chicks that just needs the right kind of man to turn her out," he explained. She made a face.

"Such a pig. What about Ellie? Closet freak?" she asked. He picked the joint off the ashtray, put it between his lips.

"Nah. I mean, it was kind of obvious she was exploring her '*wild side*' with me – she loved getting it on in public. Cracked me up. You should see peoples faces when you get caught going down on a pregnant chick in the public library," he commented before inhaling deeply.

"Oh god, I feel sick."

"What about you and that little sidekick? Sanders seems to have googly eyes for you," Ang pointed out, blowing a stream of smoke away from her head. She made a face.

"Sandy? No, not like that. I think I'm like a cross between a springer spaniel and an incompetent child, to him. He doesn't look at me like that," she replied.

"Does he look at *anyone* that way? Guys?" Ang asked. She smiled. "Interested?"

"*No.*"

"No, he's not gay. I've caught him peeking at me when I'm changing, I've seen the way he looks at other women. It's not obvious, you have to know him really well, but you can tell. He's probably banged more women than you or Jameson put together," she told him and he laughed.

"Very true. It's always the quiet types. So what about you and Satan. Did you tell him that you *loooooooooove* him? Do you *make love* now?" Ang teased her. She snorted.

"I don't *loooooooooove* him, and the last time we had sex, he bent me in half over a lawn chair and fucked me so hard, I'm pretty sure the neighbors heard me screaming – the closest house is two miles away. A postal worker came to check on us, and Jameson just waved. I don't think that's '*making love*'," she told him.

"Fuck, that's hot. Can I watch you two sometime?" Ang asked. She laughed.

"No. But yeah, it's pretty hot."

"Can you record it for me?"

"I'll think about it."

Ang passed out not long after that; weed put him to sleep like a baby, half the time. Tate left him on the couch and crawled into her bed. Thought some more about Jameson. After they had come back from Paris, she had used sex as a weapon. As a distraction. As a way to keep him from her heart. Not that she hadn't enjoyed it – of course she had – but she detached herself a little. Separated herself from the act. Sex with Jameson had always been too much, she couldn't let him get to her that way. So she had cut herself off.

Now, as she was remembering some of their more adventurous

REPARATION

times together, it was like opening her eyes. She stretched out on the bed, bent her legs at the knees. Remembered the first time he had told her he'd slept with another woman; other *women*. Two. At once. Pretty hot. She walked her fingertips across her stomach, pushing her t-shirt out of the way. Let the cool air in the apartment wash over her skin.

Remembered the time at her parents' house, when she had him screw her against the wall, making sure Ellie and Robert heard everything. Remembered the time in the bathroom on his boat. God, that time. It had been quick for them, but hot. Hotter than anything had been in a long time. Her finger tips crept down to the waist of her leggings.

After Jameson had come back from vacation and found out that Ang had been in the house. Worn his clothing. Had almost slept with Tate. Jameson had been onto her, her little plan. After going down on her like it was his job, he had flipped her onto her stomach and practically pounded her through the mattress. She'd thought she'd had whiplash for the next few days. She closed her eyes as she worked her fingers under her leggings. Under her panties. She could hear his voice, like he was in the room.

"*Starting without me, baby girl? Very naughty.*"

Only for you, Mr. Kane. Anymore, it's only for you.

8

IT FELT LIKE A LOT longer than three days. She'd spent most of the last day with Ang. For the first time since … since Jameson had reentered her life, she felt like she was back to the same old friendship she'd always had with Ang, just minus the sex. It was nice. It was amazing. She actually cried a little when he left to go home. He called her a stupid cow and kissed her goodbye.

Sanders pick her up, but instead of driving her straight home, Tate convinced him to stop and have dinner with her. She apologized for making him feel like he had to leave, and explained that she had just wanted some time. Some time to pretend to be the "*old her*", so she could figure out exactly who the "*new her*" was and what that person wanted.

"Did you figure it out?" Sanders asked. She smiled at him.

"I think I did."

By the time they pulled up in front of the house in Weston, it was after seven o'clock at night. She had guessed that Jameson would be in a foul mood, and Sanders warned that he would be in a foul mood, but she didn't care. She was actually excited to see him. Be in his presence. The couple days apart had rejuvenated her. Made her really like him again. Sometimes, loving a person was easy, the heart went and did that all on its own. Liking a person, however, was a little more difficult. That involved the brain. And the brain was a fickle bitch.

He wasn't waiting for her at the door, as he had a tendency to do whenever she was tardy. In fact, the whole house was mostly dark. She made a face at Sanders, laughing at him as he carried her bag upstairs. Then she crept down the hallway, to the only light source in the house.

A fire was raging.

"Hello," Tate called out softly, edging into his library. It was her first time entering the room, since he had dumped her in there, that her skin didn't crawl.

"You came back. *Shocker,*" Jameson commented. He was sitting in one of the wing back chairs, facing the flames. So close, she worried he'd burn his feet.

So, the same spot as always.

"Ooohhh, there's a tone. Someone is feisty already," she teased, walking over to the couch and plopping down on it, folding her legs under herself. He didn't move.

"Just surprised. It had occured to me that this was all an elaborate ruse, a way to sneak out of my clutches," he told her. She laughed.

"You give me too much credit. Wasn't Sandy talking to you? I was a good girl, all week," she assured him.

"I highly doubt that, and sometimes I think Sanders is working *for* you, and *against* me. Though he did inform me of a kiss," Jameson said.

"Such a tattle tale. *Yes,* there was a kiss. I hope he also told you that I put a stop to the kiss, and told Nick that I wouldn't be running away with him to his castle in Arizona," she stressed.

"There was some mention of that. Mostly babbling. I try to ignore him when he gets to the facts."

"Obviously."

"*Shut up.*"

"Nothing happened, Jameson. I'm *here*," she pointed out.

"Yes. And you could've been here last night, but you chose to spend it with *Angier*," he practically spit out Ang's name. Tate laughed and began taking off her scarf and jacket.

"You know, for such an amazing man who is always going on and on about not worrying or caring or any of that bullshit, you're awfully insecure," she told him. He finally turned his head towards her, his jaw visible below the wing of the chair. She leaned over the back of the couch, folding her arms.

"*Fuck you*, Tatum. It's post-traumatic stress, from dealing with *you*," he snarled. She snickered.

"Such a *bitch*."

She was provoking him on purpose, so she didn't move when he got out of his chair and stalked towards her. She had missed him all week. She wanted him, *now*. She was ready to let go, to give in to him. He had won, after all. She was finally ready to admit that.

"Care to say that again?" he growled, coming around the couch to face her. She turned around, settling back onto her heels.

"Bitch. I called you one. As in, *you're acting like a little bitch*. You won, Mr. Kane. I'm here. *He's* in Arizona. *Ang* is at home. But *I'm here*, with you. So stop being a *bitch*."

His fingers were around her throat instantly, forcing her back into the couch at first. She sighed, her hand gripping his wrist, fingernails digging into his skin. The harder she dug, the harder he squeezed. She gripped as hard as she could.

"Someday, you will learn to *watch your fucking mouth* around me," he hissed.

"Probably not, Kane," she wheezed out. "You should probably just get used to it."

"I don't have to get used to shit. So was he any good? Still bor-

REPARATION

ing? How about *Angier*? I know he was always a fave," Jameson said. She managed a laugh, though it sounded more like snorting, and she trailed her free hand across his chest, gripped onto his shirt.

"If I didn't know any better, I'd say you missed me," she whispered. He glared at her, but the pressure on her neck loosened a little. She was able to sit up.

"No shit."

"Aw, poor baby. Sexy secretary not hot in bed?" Tate cooed at him.

"I wouldn't know."

"Please. I don't believe for an instant that you spent all week alone, especially after firing her," Tate snorted. He rolled his eyes.

"I fired her because she couldn't file for shit, Tatum," he snapped. "I'm not entirely sure she even knew how to read. And while usually stupid women tend to be good fucks, *no one* is as good as you."

She yanked on his shirt and pulled him close, kissing him. Electro-shock therapy, all over her body. Something she hadn't allowed herself to feel, in a long time. She gasped into his mouth, struggling to climb to her knees on the couch. She wanted to be closer; much, much, *much* closer to him. As close as she could possibly get.

He let go of her throat and quickly pulled his shirt off. He had barely tugged it free of his head before her hands were on his chest, scoring his skin hard enough to leave red dashes on their way down. He grabbed her wrists and yanked her forward, his tongue invading her mouth as he pressed his body against hers, forcing her back into the couch.

"Please," she realized she was whispering as she fought to kick off her shoes. "Please, Jameson. Please."

"Apparently little Nick wasn't very good, if you're already begging for it from me," he chuckled, yanking her shirt over her head.

"Why do you always want to talk about other men when we're fucking? If you want to fuck men, Jameson, it's okay. Can I watch?"

she asked while he tried to pull her pants and underwear down. When she lifted her hips, he smacked her on the ass.

"I wouldn't even let you watch me fuck myself, you stupid bitch. You don't deserve a treat like that. Where the fuck were you all day?" he demanded, yanking her clothing free and throwing it over the couch.

"Downtown, with Ang. Then dinner, with Sanders," she told him, chucking her bra across the room while he slipped out of his own pants.

"I don't like waiting."

"See? Such a whiny bitch."

"*Watch your fucking mouth,*" he hissed, slapping his hand down between her legs. She gasped, and then his fingers were soothing the sting. Slicing through her, like butter. She moaned, letting her legs fall open to him. "Jesus, Tate. I was expecting a battle when you came in here, not an easy fuck."

"Kind of one and the same with us," she panted. He slapped her again between the legs and she shrieked, almost coming right then.

"Something's got you all riled up. Did your day with *Angier* get you all excited?" he asked, burying his middle finger in her. She squirmed around.

"No."

"You're awfully wet."

"I usually am."

"Not without reason. What set you off, hmmm?"

"You. Just you."

"*Good answer.*"

His hand was on her breast bone then, pressing her down into the couch. Forcing her down. He propped one of her legs along the back of the couch, and then he was slamming into her. No hesitation, just hips meeting hips in an instant. She shrieked, her hands flying to her breasts, squeezing.

REPARATION

"Oh my ... *fuck*," she groaned as he immediately began pounding into her.

"*Fucking slut*. Spent all day with him. Tried to fuck him in *our* bed. Probably tried to fuck him in *my* condo. Who the fuck do you think you are!?" Jameson demanded. She had her other foot touching the floor and he grabbed that leg, held it out away from her body by the knee, forcing himself so deep inside of her, it felt like he was interfering with the rhythm of her heart.

Like that's anything new. Remember the first time you saw him? Heart attack.

"Originally, I wanted to fuck him in *here*," she taunted, and the hand on her chest moved to her throat. He wasn't playing around, no butterfly kisses with this hand – he practically squeezed her neck in half.

"*You wouldn't fucking dare*," he hissed.

"Didn't have enough time."

"*Stupid whore*, didn't have enough balls. Fuck. *Fuck you*, Tate. Fucking always making me do things I don't want to do," Jameson growled, his grip on her neck loosening.

"I think you *always* want to do these things," she cried out.

"*Always*," he moaned.

"I couldn't do it, though," she whispered.

Why is it that sex always makes an honest girl out of you? Why can't you just fake it, like everyone else?

"Of course you fucking couldn't. I *own* this pussy, *you stupid cunt*. You thought you could use it without my permission? *Wrong*," he informed her.

"I know, I know," she breathed. The hand on her throat finally released her, and she gasped in air, only to moan again when his fingers moved to her nipple, pinching it hard.

"I *made* this pussy. It has belonged to me for the last seven years," he whispered, letting go of her leg and leaning down on top of her.

"Yes, yes," she whimpered, squeezing her eyes shut tight. She felt him press his forehead against her temple, his teeth bared against her cheek.

"*Mine*," he growled.

"*Yours*," she agreed.

"*Stupid fucking whore*, doesn't even know who she belongs to. *Slut. Cunt.* You said you wished I didn't exist. *Fuck you*," he swore, and she gasped as his hand let go of her breast and slithered between their bodies.

He was talking about when she had screamed at him in the hospital. She was shocked he even remembered the things she'd said. That he ever remembered *anything* she said. It must have hurt, to have stuck with him for so long.

"I didn't mean it," she told him, then gasped again as she felt one of his fingers sliding inside of her, right on top of his dick. He was not a small man.

So. Fucking. Full.

"Of course you didn't fucking mean it. I *created you*, you *came from me*. If I didn't exist, *you wouldn't fucking exist*," he snapped. Realization suddenly dawned behind her eyelids.

Not Satan. Not Lillith. Eve was created from Adam's rib. We're part of each other. That's why I can't get away. That's why he can't get away. I'm not his subject, he's not my lord and master. **We're the same**.

Getting philosophical during sex usually wasn't her thing, but apparently it worked for her, because Tate came so hard that when she bit down on his earlobe, she drew blood. He roared and pulled back, his fingernails biting into her throat as he grabbed it, forcing her down onto the couch. He held her there while she shook and cried, her whole body ripping apart around him. He finally stilled, but she didn't stop coming for another solid twenty seconds.

"No," she breathed when she finally felt like she could again. "No, I wouldn't."

REPARATION

Without a word, he picked her up from the couch. She squealed, clinging to his shoulders as he walked them across the room. She wasn't sure what his intentions were, until she saw that he was walking around the desk. Back to where it all began. He practically dropped her onto it, forced her back down hard against the wood, and began thrusting into her again.

"Why do I always have to fuck you, to get you to agree with me?" he demanded, raking his claws down her chest. She managed a laugh.

"The question is, why do you like it so much?" she replied as he gripped onto her hips.

"Are you kidding?"

"*Harder,*" she moaned, and he complied. The desk began to rattle and shake, edge forward.

Just like old times.

"*The question is,* why do you make me do it?" he sighed, his head leaning back. She rubbed her hands across his chest.

"Because no man has ever made me come the way you do," she purred.

"*No shit.* You don't deserve it. I should make you work harder for it," he groaned, his hands moving to her knees. Forcing them wider apart.

"You make me work *too hard* for it," she countered.

"*Fuck you,* I should make you pray to my dick. That fucking mouth. *Fuck.* Are you this mouthy with *Angier?*" he growled.

"It's always about Ang," she sighed.

"You're the one always talking about *fucking him,* and every time I see him, he's bragging about *fucking you. Fucker. Fucking bragging.* Couldn't have been that fucking good. He should have at least taught you how to shut the fuck up," he snarled, his thrusts getting brutal. She felt another orgasm approaching like a freight train.

"He was a good enough teacher," she moaned.

"Excuse me!?" Jameson's head snapped down to look at her.

"You should know – *you benefit from him every day.*"

It hadn't happened since last fall. Not since that very last time they slept together, before the shit hit the fan and hurricane Jameson ripped her heart in two. And hadn't even happened once when he had been busy putting the same heart back together in Spain.

He slapped her across the face and she screamed, coming so hard, her vision went black around the edges.

"*You goddamn cunt, don't you ever fucking say shit like that to me again,*" he snapped at her.

"Yes! Yes! Oh my *god, please,*" she moaned, not even aware of what planet she was on, let alone what she was saying. He grabbed her by the neck and roughly yanked her forward so she was sitting up. She tried to gasp, still caught in multiple orgasms. His other hand grabbed onto her ass, forcing her closer to him, as close as another human being could get, and he jackhammered his hips against hers, his forehead resting against her own.

"*You fucking bitch.* Fuck you. *Fuck you. I goddamn hate you,*" he growled, and then he was coming.

It seemed to go on forever. He would shudder, pump, release, and it would trigger another wave of pleasure through her own body. She was practically sobbing by the end, her arms wrapped around his waist. When he finally let go of her throat, she fell back onto the desk, and he fell with her. Pressed his head to her breasts while he tried to catch his breath.

It felt like they had run a marathon. She and Jameson had wild, roadrunner sex all the time, but this time … she felt like she would never be able to walk again. Talk again. Do *anything*, ever again.

Except maybe have sex. She would *definitely* do that again.

"Oh my god. Holy shit. *Holy fuck,*" she panted, pressing her wrist to her forehead.

"Yes," Jameson breathed in agreement, not moving.

REPARATION

She was very aware that they were in an almost identical position to the first time they'd had sex in his library. Spread out on his desk, him on top of her, both of them gasping for air. Except this time, there was slightly less clothing. A lot bigger orgasms. *Definitely* a lot scarier feelings. Tate cleared her throat. Tried to talk. Had to clear her throat again. Felt her eyes well up with tears.

"That was …" her voice was barely above a breath. He chuckled.

"A week is too long, baby girl. See what happens when you make me wait?" he told her, still out of breath, as well. She cleared her throat again.

"So," she managed to choke out loudly enough to hear, her voice raspy.

"Hmmm?" Jameson mumbled, his hands gliding up and down the backs of her thighs. Her legs were still wrapped around his waist.

"You hate me, huh?" she asked, managing to laugh. A tear slid down the side of her head. He chuckled.

"Tatum, what have I told you about listening to the shit that comes out of my mouth during sex? It's all rubbish," he replied, the gliding turning to scratching.

"You've said you hate me before, one time. Before you went to Berlin," she pointed out. He paused for a second, then his hands continued their path.

"That was different. Sometimes … sometimes I feel like I do hate you. I didn't want this, I wasn't looking for this, this isn't what I asked for. I wanted someone to play with, not someone for keeps. You changed the game on me," he said quietly.

"I did?" she replied, another tear escaping. He nodded his head against her.

"Yes, and I don't know this game. I'm not good at this game. I'm learning as I go, and you don't make it easy, when you fight me at every turn. When you change the rules. You change your mind. You make me slip up. I hate that. Sometimes it all makes me wish for the old days. Sometimes, it all makes me hate you a little," he confessed. She laughed. The tears were free falling now. No turning back.

Not that there ever was.

"Pity," she whispered.

"Why?"

"Because it all makes me love you a little."

9

"WHAT ARE THE RULES?"
"No rules."
"Shut up."
"*Fiiiiiine.*"
"What are the rules?"
"No Angiers in the house."
"Yes. And?"
"No plotting your imminent demise."
"*And?*"
"No corrupting Sanders."
"Good girl. I'll be back in four days."

Jameson leaned down and kissed her. Went to leave, made it a couple steps, then came back.

"What!? I haven't corrupted him yet," Tate held up her hands defensively. Sanders shifted from foot to foot, tried to blend in with the door frame.

"Any rules for me, baby girl?" he asked, glancing in a large mirror and fiddling with his tie. She batted his hands away and worked at the knot.

"You are shit at doing this," she grumbled, pulling the whole thing free and starting over.

"*Watch it.* Why are you so good at it?" he asked, watching in the mirror as she deftly tied a knot.

"Fucked a lot of professors," she replied. He shoved her hands away.

"You're not fit to touch me," he informed her.

"That's not what you said last night."

"Last night was a completely different story. Any last words?" he asked. She thought for a second.

"Don't do anything I wouldn't do," she replied with a smile.

"What a horrible thought. *Be good,*" Jameson kissed her again, then sailed out the door, Sanders carrying his luggage behind him.

It was Monday. He would be back Friday. She had told him she loved him Saturday night. Things hadn't exploded. The earth hadn't swallowed her whole, Satan hadn't carried her off to his temple of doom. Though he did carry her off to his bedroom.

"I know you do, baby girl."
"When did you know?"
"Paris."
"How? I didn't even know."
"You're not very subtle."
"I'm sorry."
"Never be sorry, Tate. I never am."
"Does this change things?"
"No. Not a thing."
"Please, don't hurt me."
"I'll do my best."
"That's all I can ask."

He had kissed every inch of her skin, practically worshiped her

REPARATION

with his mouth. She had felt like dying on top of his desk, but fifteen minutes later, and he had her so super charged, she felt like her fingertips could jump start a jet engine. Just when she was ready to beg for it, he had slipped inside of her, and eased the tension.

And things really hadn't changed. They fucked all weekend, making up for lost time. Sanders was scarred on more than one occasion, by walking into the wrong room at the wrong time. Jameson still called her filthy names, and she still loved it. Still treated her to heavy hands, and she loved that even more. But best of all, when he did say something nice, it didn't hurt. It didn't scar. It just folded in with the rest.

Finally.

"I bought something," he said Sunday afternoon, striding into his library.

She was back to laying on the floor, stretched on her stomach. There had been an *"incident"* with the couch. It had gotten flipped over and a leg broke off. It was being repaired. Jameson told her she had to be more careful in the future – his shit wasn't cheap. She told him that maybe he shouldn't go around fucking people so hard. He told her to shut her mouth. It just went uphill from there, and then they broke his desk chair.

She had laughed a lot.

"What is it?" she asked warily, sitting up and taking a box he held out towards her.

She recognized it instantly. A vintage Cartier necklace, mostly pearls and diamonds. Purchased by an anonymous buyer over a phone.

"Got it at some stupid auction," he commented, sitting in his wing back chair. "Don't know why. Waste of money. For some charity function."

She wanted to cry, but she was trying to make it a habit not to do that anymore. So she game him a blowjob instead. Was practically of equal value, she was sure.

But Sunday evening, he got a phone call. They were still in the library, so she was there when he got it. Something about his offices in Germany. She heard everything, he tried to get out of going. Had even offered to send Sanders in his place. But he was needed. He had to go – it was easy to forget, but he did have obligations. He *had* to go to Berlin.

Of course, a panic attack was the first thing on her mind. But then she calmed down. Saying *"hey, I'm kinda sorta in love with you, you sadistic bastard"* was kind of like making a deal. She had to trust him, to a certain extent. So she just smiled and told him to come home soon. He tried to talk her into going with him, but she told him she wouldn't go for all the tea in China. Fuck that. Letting him go was baby steps. He would have to wait for the giant leaps.

She requested that Sanders stay behind, though, which made everyone happier. Sanders didn't like going to Germany. Jameson didn't like leaving Tate alone. Tate didn't particularly like being alone. So it all worked out.

It really wasn't so bad. That's what she kept telling herself. She tried to ignore the fact that the last time she had confessed her feelings to him, he had run away to Berlin. Awfully big coincidence. But it was just that, it had to be – she would have to trust that it was, *trust him*. So she did her best.

"What should we do without him?" she asked when Sanders finally came home.

"Same thing we usually do when he is not at home," he replied, walking into the kitchen.

"I'm not making brownies. You called me fat a couple weeks ago," she reminded him.

"You made me angry. I was provoked into saying that."

"I didn't provoke shit. You were being *a brat*."

"Though technically, you are a couple pounds overweight for

your height."

"Shut up! I am not!"

"Well, a couple *more* pounds, and you will be."

"*I WILL NOT!*"

She laughed and threw flour all over him. A small baking fight ensued. Something about Sanders being messy just did her in. Perfect, pristine Sanders, coated in baking soda and canola oil, made her laugh endlessly. Even when she slipped in the oil and fell onto her back. Even when he dumped an entire ten pound bag of sugar on her. She couldn't stop. He finally pulled her up and dragged her to the bathroom, where he pushed her – fully clothed – into the shower. She shrieked when the cold water hit her.

"*I am not amused,*" was all he said before he stomped out of the room.

But he came back, clean and showered. He changed into pajamas and they enjoyed brownies while they watched a movie in the sitting room. She lamented about cleaning the kitchen, but he told her he would have a cleaning service come take care of it in the morning.

"Sandy, does Jameson know you have spooned with me? Multiple times?" she asked, shoving almost a whole brownie into her mouth.

"Yes. I tell him everything."

"He doesn't mind?"

"No. Why should he?" Sanders asked, not taking his eyes off the television screen.

"He hates it when I so much as smile at Ang," she pointed out.

"Mr. Hollingsworth is a threat. I am not," Sanders pointed out. She nodded.

"Fair enough."

They woke up the next morning, still on the couch. She was stretched across his chest, drooling. Attractive. He hid his disgust well when they got up, but she still laughed. Then he cooked them breakfast and they ate it outside, shivering in their pajamas. She found herself thinking that some of her happiest moments in life had been spent doing absolutely nothing with Sanders.

"Should I call him?" Tate asked, jumping up and down in the middle of Jameson's bed. Sanders stood in the doorway.

"If you want to," he replied.

"Of course I want to. But I've never really called him before," she told him.

"I know."

"So, I kinda wanted it to be special, the first time I call him," she tried to explain, jumping high and doing a toe touch.

"You are going to hurt yourself," Sanders warned.

"*Pffffft*, no I won't."

"Why would a phone call be special? Are you going to wait for his birthday?" Sanders asked.

"Don't be silly, it's because —, *ACK!*" she hit the mattress wrong and took off at an angle, almost bouncing clear into the closet. She hit the floor with a thud.

"I told you," Sanders' voice called out to her.

She didn't have to worry about whether or not to call Jameson, though, because he called her.

"Have you been good, baby girl?" he asked. She was in the library and she looked across the hall, watching as people swept and cleaned in the kitchen.

"Uh … sure. You could say that."

"Oh god."

"Sanders is still in one piece," she assured him.

"I don't want to talk about Sanders," Jameson replied.

"What would you like to talk about?" she asked.

"How wet you are."

"Oh my."

"I'm waiting for an answer."

REPARATION

By the time they got off the phone, she was laying on the floor behind the desk, her pants around her ankles. Breathing hard. The phone resting on her chest. She probably should've shut the library door, but she didn't really care.

Not when she was sitting on cloud nine.

The next day she and Sanders hit the town. She didn't want to go shopping, but she did want look into job options. She didn't tell Sanders until they were sitting on a bench, her perusing the want ads in a newspaper. He frowned when he realized what section she was reading.

"I don't think Jameson would like this idea," he warned her. She shrugged.

"I have to do something, Sandy. I can't just sit in that house all the time, hanging on Jameson's every word. I need *something*," she stressed, shivering and scooting closer to him.

"Jameson once mentioned that you were accepted to Harvard. That must mean you are smart," he said. She snorted.

"Thanks, Sandy."

"Why don't you go back to school? Surely, there is something you are interested in," he suggested.

"Harvard costs an awful lot of money, Sandy. You gonna float me fifty grand?" she asked.

"If you were serious about going, yes, I would."

She was shocked.

"I'm not gonna let you pay for me to go to school," she grumbled, concentrating on the paper.

She hadn't really ever thought of going back to school. Before Jameson, she had been too busy hustling. Too busy having a good time. During Jameson, she couldn't think of anything but him, and after Jameson … well, really more of the same. School had never been something on her radar.

But Sanders had a good point. She was smart, or at least she used to be – it couldn't be that hard to get back into the swing of things. She had originally gone to school for political science. Daddy's requirement. She hadn't ever taken the time to think of what she would go back for, if she ever went back.

"Would you let Jameson?" Sanders asked in a soft voice.

"Hmmm. And what should I go to school for?" she asked, letting the paper fold down.

"You are very good with people. You could be a social worker," he suggested.

"Or a stripper."

"Sometimes, I'm not sure why I talk to you."

They walked around after that, and Tate stopped in at a couple bars which were hiring, grabbed applications. But she didn't stop thinking about what he had said. Going to school. Pretty amazing. Something to think about, for the future. She was just taking baby steps towards Jameson. She wasn't about to run and leap into his arms, asking for a hand out that would bind her to him for years.

Later that night, Sanders had to take part in a video conference with Jameson and some suits, around two in the morning. Eight in the morning, Berlin time. Tate laid upstairs in bed, staring at the ceiling. Sanders' voice was a distant murmur in the otherwise empty house.

She couldn't sleep, so she got up and wandered into the sun room. She hadn't spent much time in there, not after she and Ang had been in there. She scooted in behind the computer and stared at the big screen. It was dark. She shook the mouse, and everything turned on, lit up. She chewed on her bottom lip and glanced around.

Tate hadn't looked up anything about Jameson since that night. *The* night. At first, she hadn't wanted to, and now … she was scared to, she realized. Scared of what she might learn, might see. She should trust him. She should give him his privacy. She should not care. He didn't waste his time investigating her. Why should she waste her

REPARATION

time on him?

She had already typed his name into the Google search bar before she even realized what she was doing. She figured she was halfway there already, so might as well jump all the way into it. She hit enter, and watched the pages come up.

There was a lot of news about his trip to Los Angeles, him selling his part in a film company. A *big* film company. Tate wondered why he had gotten out of it, but then another article talked about him turning around and investing a god-awful amount of money in an oil company, so she figured it was a trade of sorts. She never asked him about his money, or what he did with it. She didn't really care, and it wasn't her business.

She hesitated with the mouse over the tab for a while, but then she clicked it. Images. Pictures immediately filled the screen, and she sighed. He still had the ability to turn her into a giggly, stupid girl, no matter how many times she saw him. No matter how much time they spent together naked. He was just so handsome. She sighed, scrolling through the photos.

Tate was relieved to see none of him and Pet, not since the old ones. There were pictures of him in Marbella, from a Spanish tabloid. One of him and Tate, standing on the bow of his yacht, talking to each other. Or arguing, she couldn't tell. Neither of them looked happy.

She moved on, found more pictures of them. One of them at a cafe in Marbella, another of them leaving a shop. Tate would never get used to seeing pictures of herself online. There was even one of them leaving the restaurant, after her run in with Pet. It was at night, and it was grainy, but it still made her smile. Him mid-stride, walking confidently ahead of her. Her laughing, holding onto the hem of his jacket, bent over a little as she struggled to keep up with him. He almost looked happy as well, a small smile playing at the edges of his lips.

She printed the picture out, and while she looked at it, she realized she had no pictures of them together. She subjected Sanders to selfies all the time, and of course she had tons of pictures with Ang. Even Nick, with the amount of team events she went to with him. But no real pictures of her and Jameson together. At least, none that were taken on purpose with their express permission.

She frowned and moved back to the search bar, typed in their names together. She was astounded at the amount of photos that popped up. Them everywhere together, all over Boston. Pictures of them in the Bentley, in restaurants, coming out of his building, going into his building. In front of his building. Lots and lots around his office building.

Her favorite was an old one, one from before their brief split, where they were caught in the rain. She was soaking wet, because she had been standing outside waiting for him. When he had come out to meet her, he had taken one look at her and gone back inside. He came back with an umbrella and held it over her. She laughed, and he had kissed her. The photographer caught that moment. She was still smiling through the kiss, and Jameson had one hand against the side of her neck. They looked … they looked almost *normal*.

She printed that picture out as well.

"What are you doing?"

Tate screamed so loud, she was pretty sure the police would be showing up. Sanders jumped a little, took a step back from her. She bent over the keyboard, trying to catch her breath. He had just shaved about ten years off her life.

"*DON'T EVER FUCKING DO THAT!*" she yelled.

"I'm sorry. I assumed you heard me come in, my apologies. What are you doing?" he asked, glancing between her and the screen.

"Looking up pictures," she replied, leaning back in the chair, still trying to breathe.

"Last time you did that, things did not end so well. He hasn't seen her, since he's been there," Sanders assured her. She nodded.

"I believe you. I was looking up pictures of us, together. I don't have any. Look! Here's one of me and you!" she pointed out, making the picture larger. Sanders squinted at it.

Jameson was in the foreground of the photo, talking on his phone. They were in the background, Sanders standing very straight, with Tate leaning on him, her arms around his shoulders, smiling up at him as she held her face close to his own. Probably teasing him about something. Tate looked at the title of the article and burst out laughing.

"What?" Sanders asked. She pulled up the webpage, pointed out the headline.

<u>Trouble In Paradise:</u> *Is Jameson Kane's Current Play-Thing Cheating With His Guy-Friday?*

"We're an item, Sandy," she told him. He snorted.

"This is why I don't look these things up. They are full of lies and a waste of time."

"At least you got a sorta-title. I'm just a *'play thing'*," she pointed out.

"Please, turn it off," he asked. She obliged, closing the windows. She held up the two photos she had printed out.

"I just wanted these, I wasn't trying to dig up dirt," she promised him. Sanders took the photos and examined them under the desk lamp.

"They're nice. May I take them?" he asked. She raised her eyebrows.

"Uh, yeah. I mean, sure, I guess," she replied, a little caught off guard.

"I will find them frames," he explained.

"Good. I thought maybe they were for your secret shrine," she teased.

"No. I only use solo pictures of you for that."

She laughed until he cleared his throat.

"I'm sorry, yes?" she gasped for air.

"Jameson would like to speak to you, that's why I'm up here," he told her. She jumped out of the chair.

"God, has he been on hold this whole time?" she asked, hurrying down the hall. Sanders nodded.

"Yes."

When Tate picked up the phone in the library, she could hear the sound of Jameson drumming his fingers against whatever kind of desk it was he was sitting behind.

"Sorry," she breathed. "I didn't know you were on the phone."

"Sanders failed to mention it?" he asked.

"He was ... distracted," she explained.

"How are you?" Jameson asked.

"Good. We've been having fun," she told him.

"Mmm hmmm. And how much do you miss me?" he pressed.

"On a scale of one to ten? Maybe a two," she mocked him.

"Liar."

"How is your trip?" she asked.

"Tiring. Frustrating. I could very much use some of your relaxation methods," he told her. She laughed and glanced at Sanders, who was sitting in Jameson's wing back chair.

"Might be kind of awkward, Sandy is sitting in front of me. Or kinda hot. I think I may be an exhibitionist," Tate wondered out loud.

"I *know* you're one. But no, it's probably not a good idea. I was just checking to make sure you weren't doing anything you shouldn't be doing," he told her.

"Oh? Like what?" she asked.

"Running away."

"I'm not going to do that," she replied in a soft voice.

"*Yet.*"

Ooohhh, he's in a mood.

REPARATION

"Tell you what," she started, leaning back in his chair and putting her feet on his desk. "I promise not to run away *until* you fuck things up again."

"*Fucking bitch.*"

"Feel better?" she asked, smiling. He chuckled.

"Yes, yes I do. I'll be home soon."

"I know."

"Be ready."

"I will."

Then the line went dead.

Falling in love with him had been easy, much easier than she would've thought. That first time, when she had been a silly, stupid, eighteen year old girl, she had fallen a little in love with him. And then last fall, he had walked away with most of her heart.

Jameson Kane wasn't scared of much, but apparently feelings terrified him. Saying she loved him, saying it out loud, had been so much scarier because of that; but knowing that it scared him, and now knowing that he wasn't running away, made it all that much better.

"Sanders," she said softly, staring off into space.

"Yes?" he asked, turning towards her.

"I need you to get something out of the safe for me."

―※―

When Jameson got home Friday night, he felt like shit. A shitty trip, shitty plane ride, and shitty traffic. *Shit.* He was cranky. He wanted to walk in the door, have a drink, and then sleep for the next three days. Possibly four. He walked into his home and dropped his suitcase on the floor, the thud echoing through the dark house. Not a single light was on in any of the rooms.

"Hello?" he barked out. No answer. Sanders had walked back to the guest house, after parking the car. But he had said Tatum was at home.

Jameson went upstairs, but she wasn't in the bedroom. He left his suitcase at the foot of the bed, then went back downstairs. She wasn't in the bathroom, or the kitchen. On his way back through the hall, he finally heard something. A crackling noise. There was a fire going in the library. He pushed open the door, walked into the stifling hot room.

He loved the heat.

"What the fuck are you doing? I've been looking for you," he snapped, his eyes searching the room for her.

"Yeah, and I've been waiting for you," she replied. His eyes snapped towards his desk chair. She had her back to him, and he could see her bare feet propped up on a bookshelf.

"I am not in the mood for bullshit, Tate. It was a long flight, and I —,"

"Hey, I finally found them!" she interrupted him.

"Huh?" he asked, too tired to even be annoyed.

"Your glasses! I haven't seen you wear them since that day in Spain. I found them, by the computer," she said.

"I honestly couldn't give two fucks. I'm going to bed," Jameson growled, but before he could make a move, Tate swiveled around in his chair.

"I think they look better on me," she told him, smiling at him, his glasses sitting on the bridge of her nose. His eyes wandered over her form and he groaned.

"Baby girl, why do you do this to me? I'm tired," he moaned, slipping his tie over his head.

"I'm not doing anything," she replied, leaning back in his chair and stretching her legs over his desk.

"I'm sore, and I'm mad at the world, and I just want to be pissed off at everything, and you do this," he grumbled, unbuttoning his shirt as he walked towards her. She smiled up at him.

"Well, you can be pissed off at me. Sometimes, I think it's more fun."

She was wearing his glasses, the Cartier necklace he had bought her from her ballplayer's auction, and nothing else. Not a stitch of clothing. Her hair was piled up on her head in a messy bun, and she wore heavy eye makeup behind the glasses, but that was it. He grabbed her by the ankles and swung her legs around, spinning her in the chair so she was facing him.

"You're going to have to do most of the work, baby girl. Mr. Kane is very, very tired," he warned her, pulling her legs apart and walking up between them.

"Don't I always?" she replied as he leaned down close to her.

"Shut the fuck up. I'm too tired for your lip," he growled, gripping her hips and scooting her forward.

"Maybe you're too tired for *anything* fun," she said, then squeaked as his fingers dug into her flesh. He yanked her forward, his hands going under her ass as he picked her up.

"Probably. Wake me up if I fall asleep," he told her, carrying her out of the library. She hooked her ankles together behind his back.

"Never do."

"I am going to fuck you so hard, just for this attitude."

"Promises, promises."

He made good on his word, not stopping till she was panting and listless underneath him. And even then, he dug deep into his reserves, and managed to get another orgasm out of her with his tongue. Then he made her go down on him; made a mess coming all over her and the bed.

While she went to take a shower, he kicked the comforter to the floor and slipped between the sheets. He didn't care about taking a shower. He wanted to slip into a coma for a couple hours. Or days.

But just as he was about to, something caught his eye. A light from the closet was glinting off something silver on the nightstand. He rolled closer and turned on a light. A picture frame, one that hadn't been there before he'd left. He picked it up and looked it over.

He didn't know where she had gotten it, but it was a picture of the two of them, kissing in the rain. He couldn't remember the time, but it looked like last fall. He ran his fingers down the glass, across her face.

She's stunning.

She had said she was in love with him. He had said it was okay. He hadn't said it back. She said that was okay. He was still a little blown away by it. By his reaction as much as by hers. From the very beginning, he hadn't wanted a relationship with her. He had told her that, from the very start.

The first time around, when Tate had admitted to having feelings for him, he had freaked the fuck out. Jameson could admit that now. She couldn't just like him – she would want something, in return. Something he might not ever be able to give. Too much. He would give her anything else; sex, money, diamonds, gold, whatever else. But he couldn't make a promise if he didn't know whether or not he could keep it.

This time around was different. He had worked to get her back, fought for her. That in itself was its own kind of promise. In Paris, when she'd had her breakdown over the pearls, that's when he had realized. Any kind of game they had been playing, he had long since won. She wasn't over him. She had never been over him. In fact, she was so much farther down the rabbit hole than either of them had guessed, she probably couldn't make it back out. Somewhere along the line, she had fallen in love with the devil. And being the devil, of course, Jameson had known.

He rolled onto his back, holding the picture above him. It was a good photo, it kind of encapsulated their relationship. Tatum doing something stupid, like standing in the rain, getting soaking wet, when she could've gone inside. Jameson holding an umbrella over her, trying to shield her from the damage she had experienced while waiting for him, but a moment too late. Them meeting in the middle. Kissing. Touching. Not asking for anything, not demanding anything. Just being themselves.

"I thought you'd be unconscious by now, the way you were complaining," Tate laughed, rubbing a towel over her hair as she walked out of the bathroom. He glanced at her.

"Where did you get this?" he asked, holding up the frame. She sat down on her side of the bed and looked at it.

"Oh, Sandy did that. I printed it out, and he saw it, asked to put it in something. I didn't realize he'd left it in here," she said.

"Where is it from?" Jameson asked, looking at it again.

"Like last September, I think. Maybe the end of August. We're outside of your work," Tate told him.

"Who took the picture?"

"I don't know. It was online."

"Seriously?"

"Yeah. You're an *'international playboy'*, paparazzi *loooove* you," she teased him. He grunted.

"Fuck off."

"It's true," she pressed. He frowned.

"I don't like people taking pictures of us," he grumbled. She stretched out on her stomach next to him, a large towel still wrapped around her middle.

"Why? Embarrassed to have me as your *'play thing'*?" she asked with a laugh. He didn't quite know what she meant by that, or really care.

"Don't be fucking stupid. You're part of my life, I like to keep that private. Other people aren't fit to witness us," he snapped. She smiled big at him, and his satanic heart skipped a beat.

"You are so sweet sometimes," she said softly.

"Shut the fuck up."

"Alright, fine then. Don't look at it," she snapped, reaching for the frame. He held it out of her reach.

"No, I like it," he said. She stretched across his chest, clawing at his arm.

"Apparently not, all you've done is bitch about it," she grumbled, her towel falling loose.

"You have gotten way too lippy lately. Don't think I haven't noticed. Refer to me, or anything I do, as '*bitch*' again, and I'll teach you who the *bitch* around here really is," he warned her, but he smiled as he switched the frame to his other hand. She laughed as well, swinging her body the other way, till she was almost completely on top of him, still reaching for the picture.

"I'm not scared of a little *bitch* like you, *bitch*, so quit *bitching* and just —,"

"Dammit, Tate," he started, rolling over on top of her. "Always making me do things I don't want to do."

"*Dammit, Jameson*, always *bitching* about things I don't want to hear about," she teased back.

"*Shut the fuck up*. If you want pictures, I would be happy to take some of you," he groaned, pulling her towel away from her body.

"Really?"

"Sure. Just let me grab a camera," he started to get up, but she clung to his arms.

"*Clothed*, Jameson," she told him. He pushed her hands away, rolled her onto her stomach.

"I don't want pictures like that," he said, his voice low as he ran his hands down her back. Dug his fingers into her skin. She groaned and stretched underneath him.

"What kind of pictures would you like?" she whispered. He pulled her hips into the air, ran his hand up between her legs.

REPARATION

"This is a particularly nice angle for you," he commented. She wiggled against his touch.

"God, you're like a machine," she groaned as his fingers worked their way inside of her.

"A robot," he chuckled.

"I won't argue with that."

He slapped her on the ass.

"You argue with me even when I agree with you," he snapped, taking his fingers away. He held onto her hip with one hand and stroked his cock with the other.

"What are you waiting for?" she breathed, stretching her arms out on the mattress.

"For you to beg," he replied.

"*Please*," she whispered.

"Please what?"

"Please, fuck me again."

"Why?"

"Because I need it."

"You don't deserve it."

"No, but I *need it*. I *want it. Please.*"

"Hmmm, let me think about it."

She chuckled, and one of her hands slid down the mattress. Disappeared beneath her body.

"Not like I really need you, for what I want," she whispered, and he could see the tips of her fingers between her legs.

"*Fuck you*," he growled, and then shoved her fingers away. He pressed himself to her entrance, pushed his dick inside. She gave a full body shudder.

"*Yes*," she hissed.

"Shut up," he snapped, slapping her on the ass again. She squealed.

"God, so much for being tired. You should go out of town more often, if this is how you're going to be when you get back," she told him. He held onto her with both hands, closed his eyes.

"I *am* tired. You wouldn't be so fucking chatty if I was myself," he warned her.

"Big talk."

"*Shut the fuck up, whore*. Why do you want me gone so bad, Tate? What did you get up to while I was gone?" he demanded.

"What *didn't I* get up to would narrow it down," she laughed.

He smacked her ass until she begged him to stop. Until she was coming.

"You're too easy, baby girl," he groaned, rolling her onto her back, then nailing her to the mattress.

"I know. Why did I bother taking a shower?" she panted, her fingers working their way into her own hair. He wrapped a hand around her throat, cut his fingernails into her skin. She moaned.

"Tatum," he breathed, his hips picking up speed. He was very close.

"What?" she gasped, pulling her hair. He squeezed her throat tighter.

"This time, when I come on your tits, you're going to sleep in it."

"God, you're filthy."

"*You love it.*"

"*I know.*"

10

"SPRING TRAINING OFFICIALLY STARTS IN a couple days."

"I know, Nick," Tate replied. "You tell me that every time we talk."

From across the room, Jameson made a sound in the back of his throat. It had been a little over a week since his trip to Berlin. She was back to living in paradise. Living in orgasm-city, as Ang liked to call it. Things almost felt the way they had last fall. Almost … perfect, she hesitated to say.

Everything was awesome. She and Ang were great, saw each other every couple days. Sanders seemed happier than ever, though a person couldn't really tell with him. Jameson even seemed lighter, easier. So when she sat down in the library to check in with Nick, it was with a feeling that all was right in the world.

Which is usually when things go wrong.

"Do you have to talk to your boyfriend in here? *I'm working,*" Jameson snapped in a loud tone. She laughed and grabbed a remote, turning on his TV.

"I'm sorry, what was that?" she asked, turning it to a random channel and turning up the volume.

"What's going on?" Nick's voice could barely be heard over the television. There was the sound of drawers being opened, and then the TV was put on mute. She glanced over the couch. Jameson was sitting behind his desk, and he waved a remote at her. She crossed her eyes at him.

"Jameson's being a *bitch*," she said loudly. Jameson glared at her for a second, then looked back at his work.

"Oh my, those are fighting words," Nick laughed. She laughed along with him.

"I'm counting on it."

"Anyway," he steered her back to their earlier conversation. "I'm just saying, I assume you're not coming out here. It'll be hard after training starts."

"I just don't think so. Things here are ... don't count on it. I don't wanna say sure, and then something happens, and we don't come," Tate tried to explained, sitting back against the armrest and stretching her legs out.

"I notice you say '*we*' more often now," Nick pointed out, his voice soft. She curled her toes.

"Jameson would have to pay for my ticket, I couldn't *not* invite him," she chuckled. There was another snort from behind her.

"I'm never fucking going to Arizona," his voice warned.

She laughed and glanced at the TV screen. Some under-dressed, bleached blonde woman was sitting behind a sort of news desk, the large E! Entertainment logo next to her. When Jameson had put the TV on mute, the closed captioning for the program had immediately started working. The blonde bobblehead was talking about Leonardo DiCaprio vacationing in Brazil.

"What if *I* bought your ticket?" Nick suggested. Tate snickered, her eyes following the lettering. She swore she had ADD, sometimes.

"Good lord. A year ago, if anyone had asked me if I thought

REPARATION

several devastatingly handsome men would ever be trying to pay for everything for me, I would tell them they were cut off and I'd kick them out of the bar," she joked.

"You're spoiled, that's your problem."

"I know."

Nick rambled a little after that, talking about his adventures with his teammates. She laughed at his funny quips, but she was halfway distracted by the TV. Madonna said something else inappropriate on Twitter. Naomi Campbell threw her cell phone at another assistant. Kanye West had offended somebody. Petrushka Ivanovic was pregnant.

Tate sat up so fast, she almost got dizzy. Her eyeballs ate up the words. Paparazzis had caught the Ukrainian-Danish model while she had been walking out of a clinic. She was wearing skin tight leggings and a tank top, so it was easy to see her tiny baby bump. E! Entertainment had gotten the official release from Petrushka's publicist. The supermodel was almost three months pregnant. The phone dropped from Tate's hand, clattered to the floor.

Almost three months. November. She got pregnant at the end of November.

She was vaguely aware of Jameson asking her what was wrong. Of Nick's voice squeaking up from the floor. She couldn't say anything, she just kept staring at the screen. Ms. Ivanovic had gotten pregnant in Spain. Yes, she knew who the father was; of course she did. It was her on-again-off-again boyfriend, financial tycoon Jameson Kane.

"Holy shit," Jameson's voice said from behind her, and the television's sound came on, loudly.

"... Ms. Ivanovic is said to be thrilled, excited to have her first child. It's too early to know the sex, but it has been reported that she is hoping for a boy. We can only hope the little tyke will have his father's striking blue eyes and his mother's stunning good looks ..."

And of course a picture of Jameson was splashed across the screen.

The picture of him beside my bed is better. Our bed. Fuck. I am so fucking stupid.

"Stop fucking listening to it, right now!" Jameson demanded, hurrying across the room and opening the door. He hollered for Sanders.

"How can I not?" Tate whispered.

"*... Ivanovic and Kane were vacationing in the South of Spain in late November. Reports were flying about an American visiting him on his yacht, the same American he has been spotted with around Boston – Tatum O'Shea, the daughter of Mathias O'Shea, former CEO for Koch Industries. When asked about Ms. O'Shea, Ms. Ivanovic said she was aware of the American, but didn't 'waste much thought' on her ...*"

"Tatum, listen to me," Jameson came around the couch, squatting down in front of her. She couldn't tear her eyes away from the television screen. "She is *lying*. If she's pregnant – *if* – it's not mine."

Aaaaaand cue the ugly truth ...

"*... it would be the first child for both twenty-seven year old Ivanovic and thirty-one year old Kane. There were reports of their break up last year, but they have been spotted together several times since then, in New York, and they spent most of October together, in Berlin. Several people report seeing them together in Spain ...*"

And there it was, a picture of him and Pet together. In Spain. It was taken from a distance, probably with some huge telescopic lens. They were standing in a parking space, in front of the marina where his boat was docked. They were facing each, obviously in some sort of conversation.

So much for not having contact with her. You got one wrong, Sandy.

"Stop thinking whatever it is you're fucking thinking!" Jameson shouted. Sanders walked in the room and Jameson leapt to his feet.

REPARATION

*If he would have just said it in the beginning, that he wanted to sleep with her, couldn't **not** sleep with her, we could've been cool. One conversation. One sentence. There would have been no us. No hurt. No burning. No scars. God, why does this hurt so much? You knew it was coming.*

"What's going on?" Sanders demanded.

"I don't know," Tate managed to say. "He's freaking out."

They both stared at her like she was insane.

"Tate, stop it. I have never —," Jameson started, when she barked out a laugh.

"I'm not mad. Why would I be mad? It's not a big deal," she assured him.

"Shut up, Tate. You're freaking out about something that I —,"

"I'm not freaking out!" she insisted, holding up her hands. "Do I look like I'm freaking out? Why would I freak out? I mean, it's fine. We're allowed to —,"

"Shut her up. Just shut her the fuck up, I have to call my lawyers!" Jameson barked, striding back towards his desk. Sanders knelt in front of her. She was still babbling.

"Honestly, I don't care. I mean, it's not like we were together right? We're not together *now*. We weren't together then. I have no right to …" she continued, talking at light speed. Sanders put his hand on her knee.

"Tatum. It's not true," he insisted. She shook her head.

"… he can sleep with whoever he wants, I'm not the boss of him. I'm not even his girlfriend. It's just fun right, Sandy? Fun, fun, fun. Though it can't call me Auntie. The baby. That would just be weird …"

"*Shut up!*" Jameson roared from behind her.

"Tatum, please," Sanders whispered.

"… but I hope it does have his eyes. God, he has amazing eyes. And her bone structure. It would rule the world with those kind of looks. But it can't call me Auntie. Probably best if I'm not here when it comes over for visitation rights. That would be double weird. I'm not mad, Sandy. Do I sound mad? I'm fine. *I'm fine.*"

Sanders actually picked her up. Scooped her up off the couch, like she was a baby. Jameson was yelling into his phone while she was carried away. He had his back to the room, slicing an arm angrily through the air.

"No! No! I want this stopped, *now!* Any kind of lawsuit you can think of, just shut this bullshit up! I want a paternity test. I don't care, she can't claim it's mine without pro —," he was ranting, but then Sanders whisked Tate through the door.

"You're awfully strong, Sandy. Do you work out?" she asked, resting her head against his chest, trying to catch her breath.

"Pilates. I also run every morning. Weight training in the evenings."

"Pilates, huh. I wish I would've known. I love pilates."

"I would be very glad to work out with you sometime."

"Can we stop talking now?"

"Of course."

Tate closed her eyes while he carried her up the stairs. Clung tighter to his shoulders. When they got to the bedroom, he tried to sit her down, but she wouldn't let go. He wound up sitting on the side of the bed, resting her against his chest.

"He has never lied to you," Sanders whispered.

"Except one very important time."

"Technically, he —,"

"A lie by omission is still a lie, Sanders," she snapped. He took a deep breath, and his arms around her got tight.

"*He is not lying,*" he insisted. She took a deep breath.

"I know. I know, I'm just … upset. I'll be fine," she whispered.

"Please. Please, just talk to him," Sanders urged. She nodded, not lifting her head from his chest.

REPARATION

"Of course. Of course I will," she replied.

"You need to trust him. You said you loved him," he reminded her.

"I know what I said."

That's what makes it so much worse. Why did I have to say it out loud?

By the time Jameson stormed up the stairs, she had gotten off Sanders' lap. Though she was holding his hand. Jameson burst into the room, glanced at them, and continued on into his closet. Sanders and Tate glanced at each other.

"We're going to New York!" he shouted.

"Excuse me?" Tate asked.

"You fucking heard me. Pack a goddamn bag," he growled. She let go of Sanders and stood up. Took a deep breath. Walked into the closet.

"What's in New York?" she asked.

"My lawyers."

"I don't need to be there for that, I can just —," she started in a calm voice. He whirled around and he was so angry, she was actually startled. As he stalked towards her, she quickly backed away, bumping into shelving.

"*Pack. A fucking. Bag,*" he hissed. "I don't have time for this, for any of your crazy shit. I will deal with *us* later, but for right now, this moment, I have to stop this fucking publicity train. Got it!?"

He was leaning over her. Looming. She stared right up at him. Licked her lips, then pressed her hand against his chest. Jameson had always been a little psychic, so she knew she really had to sell it. She let her eyes wander over his features, cementing them in her memory. She always loved him best when he looked angry.

Always loved him, always.

"Jameson, I'm fine. I'll just slow you down. *I'll be here when you get back,*" she insisted in a soft voice, gently rubbing her hand over his chest. He narrowed his eyes.

"No, you won't. You *always* run away," he said. She shook her head.

"I will be here, I promise. I'm fine. Go, do what you need to do. Like you said, we'll deal with us later," she assured him, pressing herself against him.

"I don't believe you."

"I don't really care. You're wasting time right now, arguing with me. *Go,*" she urged.

He suddenly leaned down and kissed her, and it was all she could do not to cry. She had always loved his kisses. This one was soft, his lips pressing against hers, his tongue gentle against her own. His hands came up to cup her jaw, molding her to him. She sighed into his mouth, wrapping her arms around his waist.

"Promise me you'll be here when I come back," he breathed against her, resting his forehead to hers.

"*I promise.*"

Note he never said anything about later ...

Jameson was only gone for two days. Long enough to slap Petrushka with so many lawsuits, her management team was spinning in circles. A cease and desist was first and foremost. She could not talk about him in connection with her pregnancy, or she would be sued. But that didn't really matter, because there was nothing he could do about the media. He was requesting a paternity test, to see if she was telling the truth. She was fighting it. That one would take a bit longer.

Requesting a paternity test to see **IF** *it's true. Requesting proof to prove that it* **IS** *true. Doesn't sounds like he's as positive as he likes to pretend ...*

REPARATION

Jameson was wary of her. Eying Tate as if she was going to explode at any minute. Fair assumption to make. She teased him and laughed at him about the whole thing. Even Sanders looked at her like she was a little crazy.

"Do you *want* me to freak out? I mean, it can be arranged," she laughed one day. Jameson put his forearms on his desk.

"I want you to be truthful," he insisted. She swallowed thickly.

"I don't think either of us is ready for that right now. Later," she replied. And he nodded.

Petrushka even called one day. That was some awesome icing on the cake. Tate answered his phone. Syrupy sweet German words dripped down the line, laced in venom. Tate just shrugged and handed the phone over to Jameson. He looked astounded at her for a minute, then like he was going to strangle the phone in the next. He called Petrushka so many impressive names, Tate almost thought it was foreplay.

Maybe it is.

The final straw came a couple days after he had gotten back. Everyone had settled into the library for a nice, awkward evening of not speaking to each other, when Tate's cell phone started ringing. It was Ang. She hadn't told him about everything that had gone down. She answered the phone, worried that he would hear it in her voice.

"Hey, how are —," she started.

"*It's time.*"

"Huh?" she asked.

"Ellie. Having the baby. Driving to the hospital," he spat out. Tate leapt out of her seat.

"But she's got like another month, or something!" she yelled.

"I know. Apparently no one told the baby. Get down here."

She was halfway out the door when Jameson stopped her.

"What the fuck is going on?" he demanded. She laughed, hopping into a shoe.

"Apparently the whole fucking world is having a baby, not just your *girlfriend*. Ellie's in labor."

She really didn't want him there, but he had become like her shadow. Afraid to let her out of his sight. He insisted on going with her, so Sanders drove them both to the hospital. When Tate got to the waiting area, Ang was sitting in a chair with his head in his hands.

"She called you?" Tate asked, hurrying up to his side. He looked up at her.

"She was actually at my place. She had left some stuff, from before, and had come to get it all. We were just kinda chatting, whatever, you know, *stuff*, and she went into labor. Fucking scared the shit out of me," he breathed. Tate laughed.

"'*Stuff*'!? Ang, were you two getting it on?" she asked. He groaned.

"I'm scarred for life."

Normally, a first time birth took hours. Not Ellie Carmichael. That baby wanted out, and it wanted out *now*. Ellie didn't want anyone in the room while it happened, her modesty was firmly in place. Tate wasn't exactly surprised. What did surprise her, though, was seeing her mother and father strolling down the hallway.

"*Fuck*," she whispered under her breath. Jameson went to hold her hand, and without thinking, she yanked away from his touch. He cut his eyes to hers, but before he could saying anything, her father was upon them.

"Kane. Surprised to see you here," Mathias O'Shea barked out. Her father *did not* look happy to see them – the last time they had parted ways, Jameson had said some very choice words. But money talked, and Jameson had more of it than her father. Mr. O'Shea knew when to eat shit.

"Yes. Tatum got the phone call, we came straight here," Jameson stood up, shaking hands with the other man. Her father didn't even look at her. Tate glanced at her mother, who appeared to be swaying. Classy.

REPARATION

"Ah, yes. Tatum. You two are still …" her father grumbled. Tate was tempted to shout '*fucking*', but Jameson beat her to it.

"Yes. We just got back from an extended vacation in Spain, last month," Jameson filled in.

Not dating. Not together. Just got back. So perfect.

"Been a long time now. I never thought you'd put up with —," her father started.

"Yes, it has been a long time. And time *well spent*."

The innuendo was not lost on anyone. Tatum dropped her head into her hands.

She wondered how her life had gotten to that point. Jameson Kane on one side of her. Her father on the other. Neither of them speaking to her. Her feeling small. Insignificant. *A mistake*. That's what she felt like; like one big mistake. It was horrible.

"Tate," Jameson suddenly said. She glanced over to find him staring at her. "I want you to know, I meant —,"

"Is there a Tatum here?" an important looking nurse shouted out. Tate leapt to her feet.

"That's me! *Thank god*," she groaned, trailing after the woman.

"The baby is fine. Ten fingers, ten toes, a beautiful little boy. Your sister said you could see her now, but only you," the nurse informed her.

"Oh. Okay."

Ellie looked tired. A kind of bone weary tired that Tate couldn't even begin to imagine. But she also kinda looked relaxed, and happy. She smiled at Tatum and gestured for her to sit down on the side of the bed.

"I'm glad you're here," Ellie said through a yawn. Tate smiled.

"Of course I'm here. Everyone's here. Sanders is passing out water like we're at a cocktail party," she joked.

"Good, I'm glad. Ang? Is he okay? He looked kinda green," Ellie told her.

"Yeah, he was a little upset. Tell me, did your water break when you were on top of him?" Tate teased.

"God, you two are disgusting. No," Ellie grumbled. But then she smiled. "But a minute or two later, and it would have."

"Good for you."

"Do you want to see him?" Ellie asked softly. Tate nodded, and Ellie gestured to a sterile looking crib that sat against the wall.

"Is he okay? Isn't he early?" Tate asked, walking towards it.

"Only a little bit, the doctors said I was farther along than they nthought," Ellie replied.

He was beautiful. So beautiful. Tate picked him up and cuddled him to her chest. She normally wasn't a baby kind of person, not much into kids. But when he stared up at her with his dusky blue eyes, she felt her soul melt a little. A tear splashed onto his baby blanket, followed by another.

"Did you name him?" she managed to ask through her sniffles.

"I was thinking Shamus, after Daddy's brother. I always liked him. Shamus O'Shea Carmichael," Ellie said, yawning again.

"Christ, he's never gonna be able to pronounce it," Tate snorted, stroking her finger down one of Shamus' fingers.

"Don't use that kind of language in front of my son," Ellie corrected her.

"God, he's perfect, El. Good job, good for you," Tate breathed.

"At least I did something right," Ellie laughed.

The baby had big eyes. Beautiful eyes. Both Tate and Ellie had brown eyes, so he must have gotten his eyes from his daddy. A misty blue, almost like Sanders', but huge. He was very quiet, too, and he stared right into Tate's eyes. She felt like he was staring straight through her, straight into her soul.

I want this.

The thought came out of nowhere, and some more tears fell. She had never thought about having kids before, it was always more of a

REPARATION

"*someday*" kind of thing. But she was twenty-six. "*Someday*" really wasn't that far away. And here she was, caught on repeat with Jameson. He would never want to have kids. He wouldn't even call her his girlfriend, how could he have kids with her? He would never marry her, he had said so himself. It would never be anything more than what it was, right then.

What if I want more?

She'd had the thought before, and now she knew it would keep coming back. Keep coming, until it ripped them apart. Just as bad as Petrushka, if not worse. Yes, Jameson liked her. Yes, he cared about her, to a certain extent. But not as much as she wanted. As much as she needed. She laid the baby back down in the crib. Wiped at her eyes.

"Yes, Ellie, you did something very right with this little guy."

When she wandered back down the hall, everyone was standing. Her father was demanding to know how the baby was doing. Ang was demanding to know how Ellie was doing. Her mother was demanding to know where the bathroom was, and Jameson was demanding that everyone calm the fuck down. Standing apart from everyone was Sanders, calm and quiet.

She burst out crying and fell into his arms. Pandemonium broke out around her. Was the baby sick? Was Ellie hurt? What the fuck was wrong with Tatum? What was going on? Say something, say something!

"She's fine," Tate managed to choke out. "The baby is beautiful."

Then Sanders led her off down the hall, hugging her to his side. She cried harder, so hard she could barely walk right.

"I know, Tatum. I know," he said softly.

"You … always … do," she managed to get out.

He chuckled, then led her further away from everyone else.

11

TATE WENT TO VISIT HER sister the next day, all by herself. She was able to sneak out of the house and steal the Jag without anyone catching her, though she did get several angry text messages from Jameson. When she got to the hospital, she was glad to see that no one else was there, either. She carried a small bouquet of flowers and tiny stuffed bear.

"You awake?" she whispered, peeking into her sister's room. Ellie nodded, but held a finger to her lips.

"Yeah, but he just fell asleep," she explained softly, gesturing to the crib. Tate nodded and crept across the room.

"How are you doing?" she asked, sitting on the edge of the bed.

"Good. I actually feel pretty good. They're releasing me later today," Ellie replied.

"That's great. Do you have a ride?"

"Yeah, my friend is gonna come get me. Believe it or not, Mother is going to stay at the apartment with me, till I get settled," Ellie laughed. Tate laughed as well.

"Oh god. Well, I guess that's a good thing. I was gonna offer to stay with you, but I probably wouldn't be much help," Tate put out

REPARATION

there. Ellie nodded.

"Thanks."

They made idle chit chat after that; Ellie shared some of the more disgusting, lesser known facts about childbirth. Tate tried to hold down her lunch. They turned on the TV and watched some crap reality show, made fun of the contestants. But after about an hour, Tate grew restless.

"Ellie, I have a favor to ask," she started.

"Sure, what is it?" her sister responded.

"I hate asking when you're like this, in the hospital, but I really need your help," Tate continued.

"You're kind of freaking me out. What's up?" Ellie asked. Tate took a deep breath.

She asked Ellie if she could borrow some money. She hated doing it, especially after the little show she and Ang had put on, but she didn't have anyone else she could ask. She couldn't ask Sanders, he would tell Jameson, and she certainly couldn't ask Jameson. Luckily, Ellie agreed to it with very little questions asked.

"Are you sure you're okay? I feel like I'm doing a drug deal," Ellie commented, handing Tate a check for $3,000.

"I'm fine," Tate laughed.

"I saw the baby stuff, online. About Jameson. I'm sorry," Ellie said softly. Tate shrugged.

"No biggy. I mean, we're not really together, and we certainly weren't together then," she replied, but when she looked up from putting the check away, Ellie was frowning at her.

"It would be hard for me, if you suddenly said you were pregnant with Angier's baby," Ellie added. Tate laughed again.

"Who says I'm not?" she teased, winking at her sister. Ellie didn't laugh.

"What are you planning?" she suddenly asked. Tate sighed.

"Nothing you need to worry about. I'll talk to you later," Tate replied, getting up and kissing Ellie on the forehead. Her sister grabbed her hand.

"Be careful, Tate," she warned her. Tate chuckled, and it sounded vaguely evil.

"I always am."

She kissed her fingertip and pressed it to the baby's forehead, then waltzed out the door. She made a brief stop at her bank, cashing the check before she headed back to the house. Back home.

Well, back to *his* home.

Being sneaky around Jameson was difficult. He was very smart and very intuitive, and on top of all of that, he watched her like a hawk. She had to execute her plan in stages, usually when he was out of the house. Which wasn't often; he'd barely left at all since "*The Petrushka Incident*".

"*Baby girl,*" he whispered one night, sliding into bed beside her. Tate had been trying to act like she was asleep.

"Hmmm?" she mumbled, trying not to slither away when his arm went around her waist.

"I know what you've been thinking. And it's not true. You promised me, remember. You promised you wouldn't freak out," he reminded her. She sighed.

"I haven't freaked out at all."

"You're freaking out *right now*."

"Well, it's kinda freaky, you have to admit," she started. Saying something close to the truth had always worked well for her. She was a horrible liar. "And I said I wouldn't freak out *every ten seconds*. It's been a lot longer than that."

"Whatever you're thinking of doing, *don't*," Jameson urged, scooting her back so she was pressed to his chest. She closed her eyes.

"You said we'll deal with us later. Later, Jameson. *Later,*" she insisted, scratching her nails down his arm.

"Or we can deal with it *now*," he growled back. "I didn't sleep with her. That picture of me and her, in Spain ... remember the night we went to the club, when you saw her? The next day, when I was coming home, she was in the parking lot. I told her to stay the fuck away from you, and then I had the harbor master escort her out of the marina. *That was it*. I should have told you. I am now very sorry that I didn't."

Liar. Such a fucking liar.

Tate rolled over under his arm. Pressed against his chest, forced him onto his back.

How easy it is, to fall into old tricks. Distraction. Sex. Samesies.

"This is all *boring*," she replied, biting into his chest. He hissed and his hands flew into her hair.

"You don't want to do this," he whispered. She chuckled and reached down between their bodies, rubbing her hand against his growing erection.

"Oh, I *really* want to do this."

See? Truth that's close to a lie, or vice versa.

"God, you're so horrible to me," he groaned, putting his hand over her own. Wrapping his fingers around hers, working her hand faster. She laughed and managed to slide her hand free, leaving him stroking himself.

"I've *always* been good to you, Jameson," she whispered, kissing her way down his chest.

"So good," he whispered in agreement. She pulled the sheet away from him, watched him for a minute, admired his body.

"Say it again," she urged, tracing her tongue against his hip bone. His hand moved faster.

"You're so good to me, Tatum," he groaned. She kissed her way to his thigh.

"Mmm, maybe you should say it one more time," she suggested. Suddenly his free hand was in her hair.

"Maybe you need to shut the fuck up and get to work," he swore, then forced her down on his dick.

Sex was not an option for her. Tate couldn't, it was too much, she always got all chatty and honest during sex. Hard to be chatty when her mouth was busy. So she worked him good, and when his hand pulled at her hair again, tried to drag her away, she refused to budge. Just sucked harder and licked more and took him deeper. She had him coming in record time, and she swallowed everything.

"Work, work, work, I'm like Cinderella around here," she joked, kissing her way back up his chest.

"Goddamn, Tate, one of these days you're gonna give me a heart attack," Jameson panted. She laughed and stretched out next to him, laying on her stomach.

"I keep trying," she whispered.

"I'm not complaining," he chuckled, pressing a hand to her back.

See? Distraction. Works every time.

Tate knew it wouldn't last long, though. She had a couple days, at best. Jameson needed sex to function. He became unbearable if he didn't get it regularly. That's why she hadn't believed him, when he had claimed to have gone all fall without sex. *October to New Year's!?* She had doubted it. And now she knew she had been right.

Fucker.

"Sandy," she said the next afternoon, walking into the kitchen. Jameson was at his office, getting some paperwork he needed. Sanders glanced at her.

"Whatever it is, no," he replied. She made a face.

"I haven't even asked you anything," she pointed out.

"I know you. It's coming," he said. She swallowed thickly.

"I need a ride. I can take the Jag, but you'll just have to pick it up, anyway," she told him. He had been reading a newspaper, and he looked up at her.

"Why? Where are you going?" he asked. Tate smiled sadly at him, reached out and held his hand.

"It's time for me to go, Sandy," she said softly. He stood up, dropping the newspaper and pulling away from her.

"No. You promised. You cannot let this, this ... this *woman*, rip you apart. I have —," Sanders started babbling, backing out of the kitchen. She went after him and grabbed back onto his hand.

"It's not just her, I swear. I mean, yeah, I don't want to live life waiting for the next time Pet fucks something up, but it's other things, too. Maybe ... maybe I do want to get married someday, Sandy. Maybe I do want babies. Maybe I want to change the world, or maybe I want to live on a farm. Who knows? He won't compromise, for anything. He just *is*, he has made all this very clear, to all of us. And I just can't handle that," she explained. Sanders began swaying from side to side, foot to foot.

"No, that's not true. None of that is true. You ... you just won't see it. You won't listen to him. You're happy here. Why can't you just let yourself be happy?" Sanders insisted, staring over her head. She gripped onto his lapels.

"*Because I can't.* I just can't. Sanders, I bought a plane ticket. I *am* going," Tate informed him.

His face cracked then. He wouldn't look at her, kept staring at the wall as his perfect features folded into agony. He was so good at hiding his emotions, that it was shocking to see such a transformation. He closed his eyes, lifted a hand to the side of his head, pulled at a lock of hair. She wrapped her arms around him, pressed her face to his chest.

"He's going to be so upset. You're going to hurt him so badly. Please, *please,* don't go," Sanders begged.

"Come with me," she whispered, holding onto him as tightly as possible. He started to shake, his swaying getting a little chaotic.

"No. I can't. *I do* love him, *I am* happy here. Please, Tatum. Please, don't go. You forgave him. You promised. Please," he was crying. She started crying as well.

"You want me to stay? You want me to be unhappy? To always be questioning myself, questioning him? I'll do it. For you, Sanders, I would do it," she told him.

He slowly stopped swaying. Took a couple deep breaths. Then his arms came around her, hugged her tightly. Crushed her to his chest. She felt his face against her head, pressing into her hair.

"I'll take you. I'll take you anywhere you want to go," he whispered. She nodded.

"Thank you."

Sanders didn't look at her, just let go of her and walked out of the kitchen. Tate stood there, feeling like a small piece of her had died. She never wanted to hurt Sanders. Life wasn't fair. How come Jameson wasn't ever the one shaking and crying?

Sanders loaded her luggage up into the Bentley, then left the car parked across from the porch. She wasn't going to run away in the middle of the night, not again. She would say goodbye to the devil, see him face to face. If she didn't die of a heart attack, first.

Tate was collecting things out of the library when she heard the Jaguar pull up into the driveway, its tires spinning in the loose pebbles. She was holding onto the Cartier necklace, the one Jameson had secretly bought for her at Nick's auction. A sweet gesture, but just another way to buy her. Stupid man, he had gotten her for free, and he had never even realized it. She was looking over the pearls when the library door burst open with such force, she jumped as it banged off of a wall.

"Did you think I wouldn't find out!?" Jameson yelled at her.

"Excuse me?" she asked, a little shocked. Sure, she had seen him angry. He snapped at her on a regular basis, it was one of their things.

REPARATION

But rarely did he yell. He stalked towards her and she skittered away, got penned in between him and the back of the couch.

"You used *my* credit card. What the fuck were you thinking?" he growled, looming over her.

Oops. I thought I'd have more time. Does he check his online statements every day!?

"I paid you back. I already deposited the cash into your bank account. I don't have a card, I had to —," Tate started to explain.

"*I don't give a fuck about the money!*" he shouted, and she shrieked in surprise. "You could spend *all* my money, and I wouldn't give a fuck! All you have to do is ask! But you *cannot* use it to run away to *him!*"

"But I paid it back," she stressed. Jameson moved to get closer to her and she slid to the side, heading towards the door. He grabbed her hand, his fingers tangling in the necklace she was still clinging to.

"That you used it without my knowledge, that you used it to get away from me, that you used it to fly to *him* ... I don't even know where to start," he hissed. She tried to pull away.

"It's not a big deal, Jameson," she insisted. He yanked on her arm and she stumbled forward.

"Apparently it's a big fucking deal, if you feel like you have to lie to me! Sneaking around this house like a fucking shadow! I'm surprised you're even taking this!" he yelled, holding up her hand with the pearls in it. "Of course, you used me for my money. I suppose it's not a leap to assume you'd use my gifts. It is worth a lot of money, you could get far on it."

"I wasn't going to take them!" Tate shouted back, offended that he thought she would use him like that – he was the one who equated everything with a price, not her.

"Sure fucking looks like it! But by all means, go ahead, you certainly earned them!" he snapped. Tate gasped.

"*Fuck you, Kane!*" she hissed, then she gripped the necklace between both hands and yanked. Pearls flew around the room.

"Lost out on a lot of money, baby girl. Your boyfriend certainly won't be able to pay for you the way I have," Jameson said softly.

She was out on the porch before he caught up with her. Tate halfway expected him to grab her, to pick her up and carry her inside. But he didn't. He hurried down the steps alongside her, matching her step for step as she headed towards the cars.

"Just let me go," she insisted, walking next to the Jag. He finally grabbed her, pulled her to a stop.

"We are long past that. So what happened to promises, huh? You won't freak out, right? *Wrong.* I knew you'd fucking do this. The minute shit gets real, you fucking flip. Have you ever stuck anything out? Ever given anyone the benefit of the doubt?" he demanded. She slapped at his arm.

"Sure, when they're not the goddamn devil!" she yelled back.

"*I am not the devil!* If anyone here is the devil, it's *you!* You lied to me! *You goddamn liar!*" Jameson shouted. Tate got up in his face.

"You lied first! Such sweet words, '*only you, Tatum. It was only ever you,*'" she mocked him. "Hadn't slept with a soul, you were '*waiting for*' me. *Bullshit.*"

"I never lied, but what about you? You said Nick was nothing, that there was no relationship, yet you always call on him, don't you? Looks real fucking suspicious," he snapped. She steeled her nerves, willed away the tears.

"Your lies are worse," she hissed. "Why don't you just go be with her!? You obviously can't stay away from each other."

"I wasn't with her. I don't want her. I want *you,*" he replied through clenched teeth. She shook her head.

"Well, too bad, cause I don't want you," she told him.

"Don't lie to me, Tatum."

"I'm not. It was always just fun, wasn't it? It's not a big deal, we can just —,"

REPARATION

"Stop lying."

"It's just sex! You don't even give a fuck, you couldn't care if I —,"

Jameson let out a shout and slammed the side of his fist against the car window. It shattered and Tate shrieked, throwing her hands up. Blood ran down the side of his palm, dripping onto the ground, but he looked like he didn't even notice. He stared down at her, his eyes on fire.

"*Stop. Fucking. Lying,*" he growled. She glared up at him.

"Look. *It's over.* I'm going. This, whatever it is, is *over. Deal with it,*" she told him, then turned around and strode towards the Bentley.

"Does he know!?" Jameson called out, following her. "Did your boyfriend help you plan this? Or are you surprising him, too?" She managed a laugh, wiping at her eyes.

"Always about you, isn't it."

"You fucking make it that way, not me. Does he know you like I do? Does he know that at the first hint of trouble, you're going to flip the fuck out? Does he know that you'll use him, lie to him, then leave him?" he demanded, hurrying around and getting in front of her, stopping her mid-stride. She took a shuddering breath.

"He knows me *better* than you," she told him. Rage washed over his face.

"*Not possible.* So what kind of lie did you tell him? You said you loved me; what kind of lies does he get to hear?" Jameson said in a deadly soft voice.

"*They're not lies when I say them to him,*" Tate whispered back.

Both Jameson's hands were around her neck, shoving her back into the side of the Bentley. She grunted, his thumbs digging into the sensitive skin under her chin. She glared at him and he leaned in close, forcing her back over the hood, his forearms pressed against her chest.

"*Don't fucking say that to me,*" he hissed. She lifted her hands, slowly gripped onto his wrists.

"But you hate it when I lie," she pointed out. His fingers tightened on her neck.

"You weren't lying when you said those things to me," he said. She raised an eyebrow.

"You're so sure?" Tate whispered.

Jameson stared at her for a long time. His eyes seemed to wander over every inch of her skin. She didn't care. This would be the last time she saw him, the last time she got to touch him. Now that it was upon her, she didn't want it to end. A tear finally slipped out, sliding over her temple, into her hair.

"Sure enough," he whispered back. She took a shaky breath.

"*Liar.*"

He let her go then, and she stumbled forward. He backed away and stared down at her, shoving his hands into his front pockets. When she stood upright, he continued staring at her. His eyes were hard, and cold. They threw her back in time, back to that first night. Back to him forcing her out of his apartment, looking at her like she was insignificant. Like she was *nothing*. She gasped, choked on a sob. Her eyes filled up with tears at the same time Sanders hurried up to them.

"Is everything alright?" he breathed, standing next to Jameson. Tate couldn't answer. Just kept staring into her past.

"Perfectly fine, Sanders," Jameson's clipped voice rang out. "Tatum would like to leave. By all means, take her wherever she'd like to go."

"Sir, I think you should —,"

"*Goodbye*, Tatum. And good luck. Though somehow, I don't think you'll need it," Jameson finished, then strode off back into the house.

"Are you hurt?" Sanders asked. She shook her head.

"Just my heart," she whispered. He frowned down at her.

REPARATION

"Would you like me to —,"

"No. I just want to leave. Let's go," Tate replied, then turned and opened the car door.

As she slid into her seat, she couldn't help but remember the last time she had run away from him, from that house. She stared out the window. It was nighttime, again, and she was in the Bentley, again. But this time it was her choice, not his; and not a bottle of whiskey and xanax.

Sure it is, baby girl. But if it's your choice, how come you're leaving one very important piece of property in that house?

"What?" she breathed out loud, just before Sanders got into the car as well.

Your soul.

12

OF COURSE, SHE HADN'T PLANNED on just immediately flying off. Tate had booked a hotel room for three days. She went and saw her sister, said goodbye to her and the baby. She wouldn't be gone forever, just for a while. Long enough to get over him a little. She had never let herself do that before, it would be a hard road.

Ang thought she was being abso-fuckin-lutely stupid. When he had crossed over to the dark side, she didn't know. Ang hated Jameson – why was he calling her stupid for leaving him? She pointed this out to him.

"Because, you stupid bitch, you're in love with him. And in his own creepy, sadistic, satanic way, he sorta kinda loves you back. Why are you doing this!? Because some slutty model tells a lie about him!?" Ang demanded.

"She's probably not lying, but no, it's not just about that, there's a lot of other stuff I realized. Some things … just aren't meant to be," she told him.

"Tater tot, you two have been dancing around each other for seven years. I'd say it's pretty fuckin' meant to be."

REPARATION

Tate threatened to refuse to see him before she left, so he calmed down. Ang gave one last loud speech about how stupid she was being, and how it was the worst idea ever, and how Nick Castille was one of the most boring people he had ever met, and then he didn't say another word on the subject. Just held her and cuddled her while she cried.

And cried, and cried, and cried.

Surprisingly, Sanders stayed with her the whole time. Her hotel room had double beds, so he didn't even book another room, just laid down across from her. He never went home, and Jameson never even called. She would wake up at five in the morning to find Sanders ironing his suit. It would have been funny, if the idea of never seeing him do stuff like that again hadn't been so goddamn sad.

"You don't have to stay here," she told him on her last night. He was sitting in a chair, pulled up next to a bed, facing the TV. Tate was stretched out on the bed, staring at the ceiling. She could see him out of the corner of her eye. He shrugged.

"I know that. I would like to stay," he replied.

"To the bitter end?" she laughed.

"To the bitter end."

"You can't take me to the airport, I probably wouldn't be able to stop crying long enough to find my plane," she joked.

"Then I should definitely take you."

"Sandy," she warned.

"There is time to go back. Time to fix this," he assured her, his eyes trained on the TV. It was on mute.

"No. That time passed a long time ago," Tate told him. He shook his head.

"No. He's upset, but he would forgive you. He is very forgiving," he said.

"I don't want to be forgiven. I shouldn't need to be, for feeling a certain way. There is nothing wrong with not wanting to be with someone. It's horrible, and it's sad, and it hurts – but it's not *wrong*," she explained.

"It is when it's all a lie, though, and you're doing it just to hurt somebody," Sanders pointed out. She frowned.

"You think that's why I'm doing this? Just to hurt him? Sandy, he'd have to have a heart, first, before I could hurt it," she snapped.

"He has a heart. He has shown it to me many times. You, however, have been purposefully blind to it."

Ouch, okay, that kinda hurts.

"It was always more sex than anything. He said that a dozen times, maybe a hundred times. He just wanted me for sex, I was only supposed to be sex to him, just sex, sex, sex. Do you understand how that makes me feel?" she asked, tilting her head back to look at him.

He had taken off his jacket, and his arms were folded across his chest, bunching up his tie. She was wearing her underwear and a loose tank top. Normal evening wear for the pair.

"You wanted that relationship as well, in the beginning. You changed it, and he went along with it. It was never entirely about something as ridiculous as sex," Sanders told her. She laughed.

"Sandy, there was nothing ridiculous about the sex Jameson and I had," she snickered. He frowned.

"I shall take your word for it."

"That's another thing that sucks about this whole situation," she said, looking back up at the ceiling.

"What?"

"Sex. I think he's kinda ruined me for other men."

"*Good.*"

"Stop. How am I supposed to ever have a normal relationship? Hard to do that, when there's only one person I can think about having sex with," she sighed.

"You could just be having sex with *him*, problem solved."

"*Sandy.*"

REPARATION

"Not everything is about sex, Tatum. The world does not revolve around it."

"It kinda does."

"You make it that way. *He* makes it that way. But it doesn't have to be."

"It's hard with a person like him. He makes me feel like that's all I'm good for, all I'm worth to him, so I feel guilty, but then it's *so good*, I can't stop wanting it, so I feel even guiltier. Do you know what I mean? Have you ever had sex like that?" Tate asked, putting her hands behind her head.

"No," Sanders finally replied after a long pause.

"Well, okay, but like … you've had really good sex, and it's basically like that. Imagine the best sex you've ever had, and then imagine that person treating you like trash," she urged. He was silent for a long time.

"I can't do that."

"Why?"

"Because I can't."

It hit her like a lightening bolt. She sat straight upright. Turned her head to face him.

"Sandy … are you a *virgin!?*" she exclaimed. His neck turned bright pink, but he didn't look at her.

"There is nothing wrong with that," he said quickly.

Oh. My. God.

It made complete sense. If anything, the idea of Sanders having sex was actually weirder than the idea of a twenty year old virgin. But he was right, a large chunk of Tatum's world revolved around sex. She just assumed *everyone* had done it, including him. *Especially* him. He was wealthy and he was good looking; those two things alone would make women overlook his personality quirks and social oddities. She had *watched* women overlook them. Why had Sanders never taken the leap!? Tate was shocked that Jameson hadn't simply hired a hooker and locked the two of them in a room together.

Kinky.

She suddenly felt so guilty. For touching him inappropriately. For parading her body around in front of him, for flaunting her sexuality. *God*, all the times he had walked in on her and Jameson. She had thought it was funny. She had assumed that none of it was anything he hadn't seen and done before, himself. It must have made him so uncomfortable.

"No, no, of course there's nothing wrong with that," she agreed quickly. "I'm just surprised, that's all."

"Why?"

"Just ... because. I hate to tell you this, Sanders, but you're kinda hot. And the way you spend money —," Tate started.

"*Jameson's* money," Sanders corrected her.

"Doesn't matter to chicks, they love that shit. Sexy guy in an expensive suit dropping money, that's all they see. I just assumed ... I figured ... I mean, Jameson ..." she stammered. He cleared his throat.

"Jameson hasn't questioned me on the matter. Just because he is promiscuous does not mean I am going to be," he assured her.

'Going to be'. So he has plans to lose it someday.

"Why have you waited so long?" she pressed, swinging around and sitting cross-legged style, facing him. He still refused to look at her.

"I ... *am uncomfortable*. Around people, in general. Women, specifically. I am also a perfectionist. I don't like to rush into things," he explained. She laughed.

"I guess that's good," she chuckled.

"I am also strange. I am aware of this, I just don't care. But women do. I don't want it to be an issue, when the time comes. I want it to be ... perfect," he told her.

"Awww, that's kinda romantic," Tate sighed.

"You're wrong. I don't mean perfect as in waiting for true love to come along. I mean perfect as in as soon as I have studied everything on the issue and am confident in my abilities," Sanders clarified.

Oh my. He's going to study? For losing his virginity?

"You could hire somebody. I mean, I'm not saying that to be rude, just like … someone who has done it before, a lot. Someone who knows what they're doing," she suggested quickly.

"I have thought of this. It is a very viable option."

Someone who knows the ropes.

"Sandy," Tate suddenly breathed, pushing herself to the edge of the bed.

"Hmmm?"

She stood up and walked towards him.

"I was seventeen when I lost my virginity," she said softly.

"Yes, I know. Jameson has told me."

"Did he tell you it was awful? It was with my first boyfriend, and I didn't even really like him. He was horrible in bed, but I didn't know that then, and he was horrible for a first time. I didn't know what I was doing, he didn't know what he was doing, and he didn't care. It was over before I even knew what was happening," she told him. He frowned.

"See, that is what I am trying to avoid."

"Jameson was the second person I ever had sex with, and he knew *exactly* what he was doing. It was *so much* better. *The best thing ever,*" she said. Sanders nodded.

"I'm sure. Sounds like a much better experience."

"Sanders. *I* have a lot of experience."

His eyes snapped to hers.

"Excuse me?"

She stood in front of him.

"I have a lot of experience. I've been told I'm pretty good at it. I like you. I want you to feel good. I would want it to be special," she whispered. He held up a hand.

"No. *No*. The very idea is repug —,"

Tate put her hand on his mouth and straddled his legs. Sat down on his lap. Sanders stared at her, wide eyed. She almost laughed. He looked terrified. Sure, they were very close. They cuddled, slept next to each other, and he had seen her in many various stages of undress. But this was different. She was almost pressed against his chest, in a very intimate manner. She could feel, *see*, his breathing pick up.

"First of all, telling a woman she is '*repugnant*', is a definite turn off," she hold him. She let go of his mouth.

"*You're* not repugnant, the *idea* is. Please get off of me," he urged, his arms hanging rigidly at his sides. She ran her hands up his chest. He was very solid and firm.

"Second of all, you should never look a gift horse in the mouth. Women are very fickle. One minute, you think you're getting laid. The next minute, she's yanking those panties up and stomping off. You should take it where you can get it," she suggested. He squirmed under her weight.

"We can't do this."

"We can do anything we want."

"Jameson would kill me," Sanders stressed, his eyes looking past her, at the wall. She dug her fingers into his shoulders.

"No, he wouldn't. He would probably congratulate you. Pat you on the back. Then you could swap stories," Tate teased. Sanders shook his head.

"No. He would kill me. He loves me, but he loves you more," he whispered.

Tate couldn't handle that, handle those words. She yanked him forward and kissed him.

She had actually kissed Sanders quite a few times. Always in a silly manner, just to make him blush, or to make Jameson laugh. Now, knowing what she knew, she felt awful. God, what if she had been his first kiss!? Had she ruined that for him!? Selfish, thoughtless bitch. She would make up for it.

She moved her hands up to cup his jaw, holding him gently. He hadn't moved. Hadn't kissed her back. She gave a soft moan, pressing her lips to his once again. Twice. On the third time, she traced the seam of his lips with her tongue. Knowing that she was the only one to have ever done so sent a shiver down her spine.

Sanders cracked. His arms went around her waist and he leaned into her, his tongue diving into her mouth. She gasped at the intensity of his kiss, almost slid backwards off his legs. His hands were flat against the back of her hips and he yanked her forward, forcing her flush against him.

Strong. He's so strong. Why do I never remember that?

It was over almost as quickly as it started. He got control of his breathing, pulled his mouth away from hers. She pressed her forehead to his, her hands still holding onto him. His fingers were digging into her hips, almost painfully. She panted against him, watching him. He cleared his throat, but kept his eyes closed.

"That was very nice, I'm sure," he breathed. She chuckled.

"'*Very nice*'!? Sandy, I think you just ate my tonsils," she laughed.

"Yes. Just because I don't have sex, does not mean I am not *sexually frustrated*," he explained, and she burst out laughing harder. He finally laughed, as well.

"Sandy, if you have sex the way you kiss, then you have *nothing* to worry about," she laughed, fanning herself.

"Thank you. It was very lovely. But may I be honest?" he asked, finally opening his eyes. She smiled.

"Always."

"I do not have any siblings, that I know of," he started. "But if I did, I imagine that if I kissed one of them, it would feel very much like the kiss you and I just shared."

Tate laughed even harder and started to slide again. This time he let her go, and she fell onto her butt at his feet. She laughed so hard she cried a little, and he had to help her get to her feet.

"Sorry, Sandy, I don't think you're getting any nookie from me," she told him.

"Pardon me, but *thank god*."

Later that night, after they had gone to bed, Tate crawled out from under her covers and crawled under Sanders'. Scooted up next to him and wrapped his arm around her waist. She settled her back against his front.

"No hanky panky," she warned him, and he chuckled sleepily.

"Wouldn't dream of it."

"But you will find someone, someday. I promise," she whispered.

"You wouldn't have done it, you know," he told her.

"Excuse me?"

"You wouldn't have actually done that, with me. You wouldn't hurt him, that way. You couldn't," Sanders informed her. Tate sniffled. Nodded.

"*I know.*"

"Though I am flattered by the offer. And it was a very good kiss," he assured her.

"It was one of the best I've ever had. Are you going to tell him?" she asked. He hesitated.

"Probably. Would you like me not to?" he asked. She shrugged.

"Whatever you think is best. I don't want to hurt him. And I wasn't using you, I promise," she stressed. His arm got tighter around her.

"I know. You are confused. I understand. I thought maybe making a mistake with me, would help you realize the mistake you are making with Jameson," he told her in a soft voice.

"You would do that? Jeopardize your relationship with Jameson, for mine!?" she exclaimed.

"Yes, I would, but the fear is unnecessary. When Jameson and I say we love each other, it is unconditional."

REPARATION

She felt like such. Complete. Utter. *Shit*.

"Someday, Sandy," she cried, "I hope I can be as good a person as you."

"Someday, Tatum. Someday."

She was gone. She had really left.

Three days later, Jameson watched the Bentley pull up the driveway. Sanders got out of it, alone. They hadn't spoken the entire time. Jameson hadn't called – if he had, he probably would've lost his shit and demanded Sanders drag her home. And he didn't want to do that. Sanders probably hadn't called for the very same reason.

"Nice little vacation you had there," Jameson commented, taking in Sanders' rumpled suit. He had been wearing it for three days straight, obviously.

"I wouldn't say that," the younger man replied, heading into the house and straight into the kitchen. Jameson followed him.

"I almost thought you had left with her," he voiced his fear. Sanders stopped in front of a cupboard.

"I would never do that. I simply stayed with her till her flight left. Tried to reason with her," he said.

"Oh really. And how did that go?" Jameson snorted. Sanders snorted as well and pulled open the cupboard.

"Not well. She is severly unbalanced."

Jameson was a little shocked as he watched Sanders pull a bottle of Jack Daniel's out of the cupboard. He walked up next to him, watched as Sanders got a tumbler out of another cupboard and then poured about three-fingers worth of the amber liquid into the glass.

"She is also a bad influence. What are you doing?" Jameson demanded. Sanders handed the glass to him.

"This is for you," he replied. Jameson took the glass.

"Oh god, why?" he groaned, then knocked back the liquid.

"She offered to sleep with me."

Jameson started choking on the whiskey. Sanders pounded on his back, but Jameson waved him away. Stumbled over to the sink and turned on the faucet, stuck his mouth underneath it. He must have heard wrong. He couldn't believe it.

"I'm sorry," he gasped for air, leaning against the counter. "You'll have to repeat that. What happened?"

"Sex. She offered to have *sex* with me."

"I see. Did you take her up on this offer?"

Pause.

Oh my god. I have to kill Sanders. How am I going to do this!? That stupid bitch.

"I let her kiss me."

I think there is a shovel, in the pool house. I can bury him under the roses. He likes roses.

"Sounds nice."

"It was *very* nice."

Then I am going to fly to Arizona, and I am going to strangle her. Just a little.

"And the sex? She is pretty fantastic."

"She didn't actually want to do that. She discovered that I am a virgin. She wanted to do me a favor. The kiss was just calling her bluff. It worked. She was very upset at the idea of hurting you," Sanders explained.

Oh thank god, thank god, thank god, thank god. Even I can only handle so much.

"Somehow," Jameson started. "I highly doubt that."

"Regardless of what you believe, it's true. She said it. When are you going to go after her?" Sanders asked, pouring another drink. Jameson moved to stand by him.

REPARATION

"*I'm not.* Did you hear the things that were said between us? She doesn't want this, Sanders. She doesn't want *me*. I'm sorry. I gave it my best shot," he said. Sanders shook his head.

"No. She is *scared* of you. Do you see what your actions have done? One act of cruelty, and you have caused her to doubt you forever," he started. Jameson went to argue, and Sanders held up a hand and continued. "Her running away is not right. It is not fair. She made promises that she is going back on. I do not condone this. But *you know* that she wants to be here. That she wants to be *with you*."

"Sanders, she said it was all a lie. This was her plan, ever since Paris. I don't think she ever forgave me, ever stopped wanting to do this. She said she loved me," Jameson's voice fell into a whisper. "*And it was a lie.* All a lie. She got me. Finally won something."

"No. It wasn't a lie. You know that."

"I don't. I don't really wanna talk about this, I already feel like shit. I've got lawyers up my ass about this whole Pet thing, I've got clients I've been ignoring, and I feel like *shit*. Like *absolute fucking shit*. I'm so glad you spent the whole weekend making *her* feel better, while *I* had to stay in this goddamn house and wallow in my own self-loathing," Jameson snapped.

It was true. Paranoia and panic, for three long days, wondering if he had lost her forever. Wondering if Sanders had left him, too. By the third day he had somewhat come to peace with her being gone. He couldn't force her to love him. Couldn't force her to return any of his feelings. But Sanders. Sanders was family. He couldn't just walk away.

"Good. Sometimes I think you need a little of that. Pity it didn't help," Sanders said, and handed Jameson the glass with the Jack Daniel's in it.

"What the fuck are you talking about?" Jameson snapped.

"It sounds like you have given up on her. And the Jameson I know doesn't give up on something, not when he really wants it,"

Sanders stressed.

"Maybe I don't want it anymore."

"Now who is the liar?"

Jameson slammed the whiskey down in one shot.

"She doesn't want me, Sanders! Get that through your fucking head. She wants to pretend to have some nice, normal life, with her goddamn baseball player. I can't change that! What do you want me to do!?" Jameson demanded.

"I want you to go get her back."

Jameson slammed his hand down on the counter.

"*I can't do that!* You act like I'm some kind of god, like I can just snap my fingers and she'll come back! That's not how it works, Sanders, *believe me*. How often are we going to go through this!? How many times am I going to have to chase her down?" Jameson asked.

"As many times as it takes."

"Takes to what?"

"Takes for her to realize where she belongs."

Jameson poured his own shot that time around.

"Sanders," he breathed after swallowing the whiskey. "I know this may be hard to believe, but I do feel things on occasion. She said she loved me. I believed her. I have believed it for a long time. I have pretended not to care. But now that she has taken it back, I have discovered that I care very much. *And it hurts.*"

"Do you see where pretending has gotten you? *Alone*. Maybe if you spent half the amount of time being honest as you did pretending, we wouldn't always find ourselves in these predicaments," Sanders snapped. Jameson raised his eyebrows.

"Do you speak to Tatum this way, when you're trying to make her feel better?" he asked.

"No. She prefers cuddles."

"Maybe I'd like a cuddle."

"Forgive me, sir, but that is not going to happen."

Jameson laughed, and took another shot.

"I miss her, Sanders. It's been three days, and I already miss her. Was it all a lie? Tell the truth," Jameson said softly.

"Only what she said at the end; that was all a lie. Nothing else."

Jameson dropped his head to the counter.

"*Fucking bitch,*" he whispered.

"Excuse me?"

"It doesn't matter, Sanders. Lie, or truth. She doesn't want me. So much so, that she was willing to lie and run away. I'm not going to force someone to be in my presence. I am better than that; *we* are better than that," he gestured between him and Sanders. Sanders nodded and poured another shot. But this time, he didn't hand it to Jameson. He took the shot himself.

"One more question, sir," Sanders' voice was barely above a breath.

"What?"

"Why do you think you are incapable of love?"

Jameson blinked, caught off guard.

"Excuse me?" he asked for clarification.

"You pretended to not care that she loved you. You pretended not to love her back. Why can't you just let yourself love her?" Sanders pressed.

"Since when did you become a fucking couples therapist?" Jameson snapped. Sanders shrugged.

"I don't think I even necessarily understand what love is, but I understand that it is very important between the two of you. And I see that you won't allow yourself to do it. I don't understand. You love me, yes?" Sanders asked. Jameson made a growling sound.

"*Yes.*"

"Then why can't you love her?"

"It's not that I can't …"

"Why *don't* you?"

"Sanders," Jameson groaned, rubbing his hand over his face. "Can we get existential another day? I am so fucking tired."

But he thought about it, as he went to bed. Jameson laid in the middle of his bed, on purpose. Trying to erase the distinction of there being "*sides*"; her side, his side. She slept on the right side of him, most of the time. But it was *his* bed, so really, there shouldn't be sides.

Even you started calling it "our bed", as opposed to "my bed". You know what's going on.

Jameson didn't think he was incapable of love. He had loved his mother. He loved Sanders, very much. But he had never been *in love* with somebody. He certainly hadn't loved Pet, and he had never been with any other woman for too long, before her. Hadn't ever really liked any of the women he'd been with; he hadn't even been with Tate for that long, so he certainly couldn't love her.

Could he?

He loved her body. He loved fucking her. He loved her filthy mouth, and her sick mind. He loved how she would let him do *anything* he wanted to her. Loved that she was *never* scared of him. Loved that she had always allowed him to be himself, through and through. He loved that she was funny, and smart, and that sometimes she would look at him like she was so happy to see him, she couldn't even stand it.

He loved coming home to her, and he loved waking up next to her. He loved calling her names, and he *loved* that she loved it. When he had first talked with her, in his office so many months ago, he had never imagined it would go so far. Tatum O'Shea had looked like a good fuck, and that was all he had been looking for; she had been looking for the same thing. When had they gotten so lost in each other?

God, every piece of him was tired. Sometimes, even the devil needed to be cut a break.

13

ARIZONA WASN'T SO BAD.

Nick had picked her up at the airport. He didn't say anything, just wrapped her in a big hug and carted her home. Tate had called him, after Ellie had her baby. Gave him a brief overview of what had happened. Of course, he had instantly offered to take her in, which she had been counting on. Tate made it very clear that she wasn't coming to him for some sort of relationship. She just needed a break. If he wanted something more, then she would rather stay in Boston.

He promised to leave her alone.

It was sunny, and compared to Boston, it was warm. He had a nice, three bedroom house in a cul de sac. She stayed in a hotel, in downtown Tucson. He didn't even ask her to come stay with him. Smart man.

Tate was thinking of it as a vacation. As a way to clear her mind. Thinking while Jameson was nearby was impossible. She had to figure out what she wanted, what she *really* wanted in life. So far, all she knew was that she didn't want to be harassed by a psychotic supermodel, and she might want kids. Someday. Maybe.

Not a very big list.

She thought of what she had told him, once.

"... I want Prince Charming to ride up on a white horse, and carry me off to his castle. The only difference between me and other girls is once I get there, I want him to bend me over the throne and pull my hair while he fucks me hard and calls me names. But I know that'll never happen with you ..."

That wasn't asking for too much, she felt. And it was relatively normal. Lots of people had wild sex, she wasn't the only one. She could always dial back the sex, anyway. No one would ever be as good as Jameson, so she should probably just get over that right away.

She talked to Ang, every single day. He asked her to come home, every single day. But she didn't mind Arizona. She spent most of her time alone. It was peaceful. Quiet. *Still.* She had already put in applications for jobs.

Ang threatened to cry.

"Move out here with me."

He told her to go fuck herself.

Mostly he was worried that she was simply hiding. Sure, she was standing in one place, but she was effectively running away. He was scared she would eventually run straight into Nick's arms. Then there would be no going back.

"Don't settle for him," Ang hissed into the phone.

"He's a great guy!" she snapped.

"He is, he really is. I don't have a problem with him. It's *you*. You're fucking using him, Tate. That's fucked up."

"I'm not doing anything. I told him from the get go that I'm not doing this to be with him. I have repeated it, over and over. Threatened to cut his nuts off if he so much as looked at me wrong," she pointed out. Ang laughed.

REPARATION

"Why do these men want you so bad!? We've had it all wrong – *you've* been the devil, this whole time," he joked.

Too close to home.

Tate worried about Sanders. During the first week, he didn't call her. Didn't return her phone calls. If it was part of his tactic to get her to come home, it almost worked. She was beside herself with panic. Had Jameson killed him, when he found out what Tate had tried to do? Did Sanders hate her now? Or worse, was he embarrassed?

When she was almost to the point of hitchhiking back to Boston, Sanders answered her phone call. He had been busy, he explained. He chatted with her for a while, but he was very tight lipped. He didn't say one word about Jameson, or one word about asking her to come home. Obviously still upset with her. She vaguely referenced the idea of him maybe possibly sort of coming to visit, some day in the far off future. He got off the phone, almost immediately.

At night, Tate thought about Jameson. He hadn't tried to contact her at all. She wondered what he was doing. *Who* he was doing. He had been very upset when she had left. It shocked her a little. His face. Breaking the window. Bleeding. He had been angry. He had been upset. And, if she was completely honest with herself, he had been *hurt*. She wouldn't have thought it possible. When she had told him it was all a lie, wanting to be with him, loving him, he had looked ready to commit murder.

So, in Jameson-speak, his feelings were hurt.

Selfish. He wanted her to love him. He wanted her to live and breathe for him, but he would never return the favor. Tate didn't want that anymore. She wanted someone to live and breathe for her. Someone to begin and end with her. *Fuck real pearls*. She deserved *love*. He would never understand that. He could throw all the sex and money he wanted at her, but he could never give her what she really wanted.

Sometimes, it almost didn't sound like settling, giving in to

Nick. He was halfway to loving her, anyway.

Two weeks later, those thoughts were still in Tatum's head. Something had to give. She wanted to claw her face off. She was having dinner with Nick, zoning out. She hadn't spoken to Sanders or Ang in a couple days. She felt like a life line of sorts had been cut. She figured she should get used to it, if she wanted to start life over. She sighed and turned her attention back towards Nick.

"… but then Chet said he wants to drive over to San Diego, pick up some – hey!" he stopped, smiling at something behind her. She glanced over her shoulder. A small boy was being pushed towards them, a very eager looking father behind him.

"Go ahead, Hank. Tell him," the dad whispered. The little boy held out a pad and paper.

"Mr. Castille … I really loved your double-play … in the last world series," the boy said softly. Nick smiled and leaned down, ruffling the kid's hair.

"Thanks. It wasn't easy," he laughed. The kid held out the paper.

"Could I have your autograph?" he asked. Nick nodded.

As he signed the piece of paper, the dad began to blabber on and on. They were from Worcester, Massachusetts, and were huge Red Sox fans. Had been to every home game, loved the pitcher. Loved the team. Were so happy have run into him. Nick went along with it for a while, and then finally leaned back in his chair.

"Look, I'm really flattered, but I'm trying to have dinner with my lady friend," he explained, gesturing to Tate. She smiled down at the little boy.

"Sorry. Your girlfriend is really pretty," he whispered loudly. Nick laughed again.

REPARATION

"Thanks. But she's not my girlfriend. You should put in a good word for me," Nick stage whispered back, winking at Tate. She laughed and the little boy turned towards her.

"You should like Mr. Castille. He's real good at basbeall, so he'd probably be a good boyfriend," he assured her. Tate leaned down.

"Oh really? So being good at baseball is what makes a guy a good boyfriend?" she clarified.

"Sure. It's pretty much the best thing ever!" the kid exclaimed.

Everyone laughed at that, and the dad lead the kid away. Tate and Nick finished their meal, the mood lightened a little. The little scene had been pretty adorable. They walked back to her hotel after that, laughing about the kid.

"He's right, though," Nick started as they wandered into the lobby.

"About what?" Tate asked, digging around for her key.

"Being a baseball player does make me pretty good boyfriend material," he said. She glanced at him.

He had been very good about not mentioning his feelings for her. She had been in Arizona almost three weeks, and they had spent many days together, and he hadn't hit on her. Hadn't tried to touch her, or be inappropriate with her, or anything. She sighed.

"And why is that, Mr. Castille?" Tate asked, turning to face him once they had gotten on the elevator.

"Well, I'm good at working in a team. I'm strong. I make a lot of money. Some people say I'm nice, and a lot of people tell me I'm good looking," Nick laughed. She laughed as well.

"All good things, I'm sure. I just don't know if those are things *I* want," she told him.

"What *does* Tatum O'Shea want?" he asked. She chewed on her lip.

"I don't know, most of the time. Sometimes I wonder if I ever will."

"Then how can you be so positive you don't want me?" he pointed out, and the elevator came to a stop. They got out on her floor.

"Nick … okay. So we date. We have sex. We go out on lots of dates. And I still feel the same way. What then? I lose *another* friend?" she pointed out.

"I'm not that weak, Tate. You're stuck with me. I'm not gonna hate you, just because you don't like me. I'm just asking for a chance to change your mind," he explained. She snorted.

"You say that now, but most men wouldn't be so okay with it after the fact. '*So how was that, baby?*', '*Good, but I was picturing the last guy who fucked me, the whole time,*' — you okay with that?" Tate asked bluntly. Nick stepped up close to her, pressing her into her door.

"No. But I am very confident in my abilities to make you forget him," he said softly. She sighed, looking up at him.

"No offense, Nick, but I'm not," she whispered.

He leaned down and kissed her. She didn't want to, but she kissed him back. She had to do something. Sever a tie. Cut her losses. She was already heading in this direction – at least she had warned Nick that she most likely wouldn't like him. That she wouldn't be thinking of him. Because she certainly wasn't right at that moment

She fumbled to open her room door, and he pushed them through it, yanking her up against him. She pressed her hands to his chest, not knowing how far she wanted things to go between them. Kissing was fine. Sex? Hmmm … she didn't know if she was willing to test that theory quite yet.

How far down the rabbit hole are you going to go, baby girl?

"We're good together," Nick whispered, his lips wandering down her chin as he shrugged out of his jacket.

"That doesn't necessarily mean we'll make a good couple," Tate whispered back, as he pushed her jacket away from her shoulders.

"We were good together once before," he reminded her. She

laughed.

"That was a whole lifetime ago. A whole different girl," she warned him. His hands ran down her body.

"Then let me get to know *this* girl," he pressed, his hands sliding over her hips.

"She might not like you, either," she warned him.

"*She might love me.*"

"Nick, I don't want to hurt you," she whispered, wrapping her arms around his neck.

"No expectations, Tate. No pressure. Just give me a chance," he said softly, squeezing her butt and lifting her up, walking her backwards.

"You say that, but what about tomorrow? I don't want you to hate me," she told him, wrapping her legs around his waist.

I don't want to hate myself.

"I won't hate you, no matter what."

You need to do this. You need to get over him. You need to at least try.

He laid them on the bed, put his weight onto her. Tate always loved that, feeling a heavy frame pressing down on her own. He bit his teeth into her bottom lip, pulled on it, and she loved that, too; loved it when he nipped at her ear lobe. Loved his hands, running over her breasts, clenching, massaging.

Nick peeled her clothes off, kissed his way down her body. She lost herself in the feel of his skin, the movements of his muscles. He rolled them around on the bed. His arms were so strong, she felt like he could just throw her around. But of course, he didn't. His touch was gentle, his words kind. He worked above her, pressed his lips to her ears, whispered sweet things to her. His body felt amazing, his skin hot to the touch, and his hips were pounding her straight towards an orgasm. What wasn't there to like?

It feels wrong, and you know it. But get used to this, cause it's your future. Settling for not quite what you want, but definitely what you need.

Nick came right after she did, stiffening on top of her, then collapsing. Tate took deep breaths, staring up at the ceiling. She wondered if this was going to be forever. Wondered what Sanders would think if he knew. Wondered what Jameson would think. She felt like he was in the room, sitting in a dark corner, watching her.

"*Is that the best you could do, baby girl?*" he would've laughed.

I gave it all I got.

"*You gave me so much more,*" he would add.

I gave you everything.

"*Well, it's only fair – it all belongs to me,*" he would remind her.

I know. It always has.

"*Good. Remember that. And next time, ask him to talk dirty to you. It'll remind you of me.*"

Everything always does.

Tate apologized. Nick said it was okay. She told him that she liked him, and that she *really* wanted to be in love with him. Said she could try. He said he wasn't asking her for anything. She said she *would* try. He told her to calm down, then he carried her into the shower, left her alone with her thoughts.

She turned the water scalding hot, wanting to feel the burn and sting against her skin. Wanting to be punished. Wanting to be absolved.

The sex hadn't been bad. It had been great – Nick was no slouch. But Tate was no nice, normal girl. The whole time he'd been inside of her, she'd been thinking of someone else. Someone with sharp claws and sharper words.

This is it. This is your choice. I hope you're happy with it.

14

"*MR. HOLLINGSWORTH*," SANDERS' COOL VOICE cut through the din in the cafe.

Ang stood up, held out his hand to the quiet man. Sanders had always made Ang a little uncomfortable. He rarely made eye contact, and then when he did, it was a very direct stare. He was also a lot shorter than Ang, easily six or more inches, so that added to the awkward feeling. But he cared a great deal for Tatum, Ang knew, so he couldn't be a bad guy.

And after almost three weeks of Tatum playing house in Arizona, Ang figured it was time to cut the shit.

"Hey, thanks for meeting me," Ang said. Sanders barely shook his hand before taking a seat at the table. Then he stared at the wall behind Ang.

"It's no trouble. How have you been?" the other man asked. Tate had said Sanders had spent most of his life in London, but his accent sounded different to Ang. Sharper.

"Good. Okay. Working on a new movie. Helping Ellie with the baby," he replied.

"Are you and Mrs. Carmichael an item again?"

"No," Ang laughed. "That was a mistake."

"A pretty large mistake, if you don't mind my saying."

"Are you always this blunt?"

"Yes."

"Whatever. How is Satan?" Ang asked, leaning back in his chair and sipping at his coffee.

"If you are referring to Mr. Kane, he is well," Sanders replied, not touching the coffee Ang had ordered for him.

"Really? Moved onto the next woman already?" Ang pressed. Sanders finally looked at him.

"If you would like to talk about her, please, don't waste anymore time," he stated. Ang nodded.

"Alright. She hasn't mentioned him to me at all. How is he handling all this bullshit?" Ang asked. Sanders sighed and his eyes slid back to the wall.

"Not very well. He is very hurt by her. He thinks she lied to him. I think he is a little afraid of her now," Sanders explained.

"Those retards. All they've managed to do is scare each other, from *each other*. How do they function day to day?" Ang grumbled.

"Sometimes, I honestly wonder. Without us, I am pretty sure they wouldn't make it very far."

Ang actually laughed. Sanders could be funny. Who knew?

"Look, I wanted to talk to you cause I'm worried about her. She's been down there for like three weeks now. She's talking herself into staying. Nick is buzzing in her ear, telling her all that shit she thinks she wants to hear. She's going to do something stupid, like move in with him, or marry him, or something. She'll turn back into a Stepford-wife, and ten years from now, she'll be some pill popping alcoholic, just like her mother. I can't handle that," Ang stressed. Sanders nodded.

"All of this has occured to me."

"Well, what are we going to *do* about it!?" Ang demanded. Sand-

REPARATION

ers' eyes met his again.

"What can we do? It seems to Jameson and I that she has made her decision, and it is not us," Sanders replied.

"You don't mean that. I don't know you very well, or Satan, but I know you guys wouldn't just give up on her. Sanders, she is *going* to do it. You know her. How often does she make the *right* decision?" Ang asked. Sanders pressed his lips together.

"Not very often," he said in a soft voice.

"Please. Help her. She listens to you. She *needs* you. She's lost. *Find her,*" Ang replied, his voice low.

Sanders stood up abruptly, startling Ang. He glanced around the cafe, then down at Ang. Straightened his tie. Cleared his throat. Fiddled with his tie again.

"I will discuss these things with Jameson. I can't make any promises. He is very upset. If he won't go, I would be useless. She needs *him* to find her," Sanders said. Ang nodded and stood up as well.

"Yes."

Sanders didn't say anything, just walked away. Ang figured that was kind of typical behavior. He ran a hand through his hair, then pulled out his phone and glanced at it. The background screen was a picture of him, Tatum, and Ellie. Ellie was staring coolly at the camera, one perfectly sculpted brow lifted. Tate was turned towards him, her smile wide as she bit into his cheek. He was sticking his tongue out to the side, almost touching her with it. He sighed.

"Just come home, Tater tot. *Come home.*"

Sanders strode through the Kraven Brokerage office building. On his own, he knew he was not an intimidating man. But with the weight of Jameson's name and wealth carrying behind him, people respected Sanders. Made way for him. He knew this, and took advantage of it. He had picked up some tricks from Jameson along the way, and was very good at pretending like he was confident and in charge.

"Good afternoon, Mr. Sanders," a security guard tipped his hat.

"How are you, Mr. Sanders?" the new secretary downstairs breathed, looking up at him with big eyes. He glanced at her. She was very attractive. Blonde. Icy. Tatum's words rang through his head, "... *I hate to tell you this, Sanders, but you're kinda hot ...*". He usually brushed her words aside. Maybe it was time to stop. He nodded at the secretary and continued to the elevators. Went straight up to the top floor.

"Mr. Dashkevich," Jameson's secretary leapt out of her chair. "He wasn't expecting you. He's on a conference call."

"It's fine," Sanders said, walking across the outer room. She hurried around her desk.

"But you can't, it's with —," she started, and Sanders turned towards her. Stared at her.

"Is there a problem?" he asked, his voice frosty. She shook her head.

"N —no, Mr. Dashkevich. Would you like me to bring in any coffee?" she asked. He shook his head.

"No."

She calls me 'Mr. Dashkevich'. I am going to inform Jameson that she needs a raise.

He walked into the main office. Jameson was sitting at his desk, two computer screens set up in front of him. He raised his eyes at Sanders' entrance, but he didn't say anything to him. He was talking in German, running over some long term investment plans for a client. Sanders marched up to the desk.

"I need to speak to you," he said. Jameson's eyebrows went up, but he shook his head. "*Jetzt. Es ist wichtig,*" Sanders continued in German. Jameson shook his head again, glaring now. Sanders sighed

REPARATION

and switched tactics. "*Soy **muy** serio.*"

Spanish was actually Jameson's first language – he hadn't started speaking English till he was five. Sanders wasn't quite fluent in it, but sometimes when he had something very important he wanted to say to Jameson, he used Spanish. German for business. English for everything else.

"*Estoy trabajando en este momento, esto tiene que esperar,*" Jameson whispered, covering the computer mic with his hand. He was working. Sanders had to wait. Once again, Tatum's voice drifted through Sanders' head.

"*... Fuck this ...*"

"*Ahora,*" Sanders said loudly. *Now.* Jameson's glare got worse.

"*Me estas avergonzando en mi lugar de trabajo. Salte ya,*" he hissed. Oh, so Sanders was embarrassing him; Sanders needed to leave? Somewhere, in his mind, Tatum was laughing.

"*... you don't get to tell me what to do ...*"

Sanders strode around the desk. Jameson burst out loudly in Spanish, telling him to walk away. Sanders ignored him and knelt down, groping under the desk. Jameson wheeled out of the way, looking completely bewildered. Sanders' fingers came across the power strip and he yanked it forward. Pulled every single plug out of the sockets. Jameson jumped out of his chair.

"*Dije ahora,*" Sanders said in a soft voice as he stood up.

"*Que cono te crees que estas haciendo!?*" Jameson demanded. Sanders straightened his tie.

"Vulgar words are still vulgar, in *any* language," he pointed out.

"I don't give a fuck! Do you have any idea how much money you probably just cost us!?" Jameson shouted.

"You have enough money."

"What the fuck has gotten into you!? For three weeks, you have been moping around the house, and now —,"

"No more than you."

Jameson. Looked. *Pissed.*

"**Mi** *corazon es el mismo que se ha pisado,*" he growled. Sanders rolled his eyes.

"The way you behave, sir, most wouldn't know you even had a heart, let alone one to get stepped on. You have moped just as much as I have. We have both missed her. *It is time,*" Sanders snapped.

"Time for what?" Jameson snapped back.

"Time to go and get her."

"I am not —,"

"I was not asking, *sir.*"

Jameson. Looked. *Shocked.*

"Where on earth did you go for lunch, Sanders?" he asked, almost laughing.

"I met with Mr. Hollingsworth."

"*Mierda.*"

"He is … concerned. About Tatum," Sanders started.

"Big fucking shock. Need I remind you, Sanders, that *she* is not concerned about *us.* She didn't just leave me," he pointed out.

"No. But she did invite *me* to go with her."

Jameson fell back into his seat.

"I just can't win with her. She wants to get away from me? Maybe I need to get away from *her.* I used to be a nice, normal, borderline sociopath. I would like to get back to that," he groaned. Sanders moved to sit in a chair across from the desk.

"No you wouldn't. I have let you get your wind back. Now it is time to go," Sanders said.

"I don't want to go to goddamn Arizona. I want that bitch to rot in hell, and I want to stay as far away from her as I possibly fucking can," Jameson swore.

"*Do not speak of her like that.*"

"I'll speak of her anyway I want to. I'm the one who got treated like shit. I'm the one who got lied to. Walked out on. I can't just forget that, Sanders. Maybe you can, but I can't," Jameson snapped.

"Stop being overdramatic. You are upset because you care. The sooner you accept that, the sooner we can get over your insecurities and go get her," Sanders snapped back.

"She didn't trust me. After everything, she didn't trust me. Do you know what that fucking feels like!?" Jameson was almost shouting. Sanders nodded.

"Probably awfully similar to how she felt, when you brought Petrushka home to humiliate her," he replied.

Jameson closed his eyes. Took a deep breath. Sanders had hit a chord.

"Say we go there. Say I let you drag me all the way to fucking Arizona. What if she's *with* him? Did you ever think of that? What if it's too late, and she is already making a happy home with her *boyfriend?*" Jameson asked. Sanders shrugged.

"Then we will know, and we will leave. But we have to try," he urged.

"*You* have to try. I don't have to do sh —,"

"Mr. Hollingsworth thinks she is going to marry him," Sanders burst out. It was reaching. Most definitely stretching the truth. But Ang had definitely said all those words; just mostly at different times. Jameson's eyebrows shot up.

"Really. After three weeks. Quick operator," he said in a soft voice. Sanders cleared his throat.

"Someday. He thinks she is convincing herself that Mr. Castille is what she wants in life. I think she wants to feel loved and wanted. Mr. Castille gives her those things," Sanders explained.

"And I didn't?"

"No."

"*Siempre Tatum. Obligarme a hacer cosas que no quiero hacer,*" Jameson mumbled, staring off into space.

"It seems to me, sir, that she never once made you do something that you didn't want to do," Sanders countered.

"No. No, I suppose not. I'm going to be honest, Sanders. If we go there, and she can't be won over; if I find out that she really never loved me … I am *not* going to handle it too well," Jameson warned him.

"No, I wouldn't imagine you would. But would you rather continue on, not knowing?" Sanders asked.

"Sometimes, I think I would. I don't like being scared."

Jameson's voice was soft, almost like he was afraid to say it out loud. Sanders frowned and looked out a window. He didn't like hearing those things. It was one thing for him to assume them about Jameson, it was another for Jameson to admit them. Jameson was a powerful man. Not just in Sanders' mind, but in real life. In the world. A man not to be reckoned with – and Tatum O'Shea had managed to scare him.

"I will be right there with you, sir," Sanders assured him. Jameson snorted.

"Sometimes I don't know whose side you're on," he grumbled.

"When are we leaving?" Sanders asked.

"Do you really think she would stay with this man?"

"Yes."

"Do you really think I have a chance?"

"… um …"

"*Por que perder el tiempo con usted?*" Jameson groaned. Sanders stood up.

"If you are going to complain about me, I prefer it in German. I understand the subtleties better," he said.

"*Du mein Leben zur Holle zu machen, sollte ich dich verlassen habe, wo ich dich gefunden,*" Jameson spat out, but he stood up as well.

"A vast majority of the time, I make you're life better, so saying I make it hell is a gross overstatement. And yes, you could have left me on that street – but then you really would be the devil," Sanders said, heading towards the door. Jameson caught up with him. Wrapped his arm around the smaller man's shoulders.

"*Mein Sohn*," Jameson kissed the top of Sanders' head.

"*Ja. Jetzt, um unsere Familie zu beheben wollen wir,*" Sanders told him. Jameson nodded.

"We can try, Sanders. How often have you known her to be compliant? Hard to fix what she won't admit is broken," Jameson warned him as they walked out of the room. The secretary glanced at them, then went back to her paperwork.

"We won't know if we don't try."

"I've been thinking. Instead of flying —," Jameson started as they got on an elevator.

"Oh, so you have been thinking about this?" Sanders asked, glancing up at him.

"Of course. Constantly. You can't just forget a woman like Tatum O'Shea. Getting her back the last time was a battle. This time, it's going to take a war. We have some ground work to cover, before we reach her. I was thinking," Jameson began again.

"Now *I* am afraid."

"How about we drive?"

"I'm sorry, what did you say?"

"We take the Bentley, and we drive. It would take us a week, at most."

"Why do you want to drive?" Sanders asked.

"She doesn't do well with memories. There are a lot of them in the Bentley. I'd bring the goddamn house if I could. The car will have to do," Jameson explained.

"If we take turns," Sanders added, "we can get there in about three days." Jameson laughed.

"Three days. I was hoping for a little more time."

"It is plenty of time. You will use most of it to think of how you are going to say it."

"Say what?"

"It."

"*What?*"

"Love."

"You have completely fucking lost me," Jameson said, staring down at Sanders. "What are you talking about?"

"You will use the time it takes to drive out there to think of how best to tell her that you are in love with her," he spelled everything out. Jameson lifted his eyebrows.

"You just don't quit today, Sanders. Just because *you* believe everything is peachy keen, and just because *she* believes in fairy tales, does not mean I —," Jameson started to grumble. Sanders held up his hand.

"Then say you don't," he challenged.

"Huh?"

"You are such a man of honor, you claim. You '*never lie*', you say. Then say you don't."

Jameson pressed his lips together hard for a moment, glaring lightning bolts at Sanders. Finally, he took a deep breath and looked away. Stared at the elevator wall for a few moments. Then he cleared his throat.

"*Nunca miento,*" he said softly. *I never lie.*

"That's what I thought."

"Jesus. Maybe *you* should be calling *me* '*mein Sohn*'," Jameson grumbled, still not meeting Sanders' eyes.

"I have often had similar thoughts."

"This is all going to blow up in our faces. You realize that?" Jameson warned him. Sanders nodded.

"Probably. I am prepared to face that. Are you?"

"No. But let's get it over with. Like ripping off a band aid."

The two men walked out of the building, sucking all the air out

REPARATION

with them.

Tate hurried across a street, holding her hand up as a car honked at her. She held her phone to her ear with her other hand, listening to Ang bitch at her. She sighed, rolling her eyes.

"I'm sorry, all I'm hearing is *whomp wuh whomp*," she laughed at him.

"Seriously, Tate. Two weeks ago you called me, all crying and sobbing, and now this!?" he snapped at her.

"I've gotten over the crying," she assured him.

"Yeah, but do you still do it?" he asked.

"Only sometimes."

"*Tatum.* Why are you doing this?" Ang asked.

"I told you. I just want a normal life," she said.

"*You're using him,*" Ang hissed.

"No. He knows how I feel. I told him this is just a trial thing. It's *his* idea," Tate pointed out.

Nick had asked her to move in with him. She had resisted for a while. She hadn't had sex with him since that time in her hotel room, two weeks ago, but he had kissed her plenty. He was trying to win her heart. She warned him that there was a strong possibility that it would always belong to Jameson.

"*Then why don't you go be with him?*"

"Because he doesn't have a heart to give back."

"*So if you can't be with the man you want, you're going to settle for a man who wants you?*"

"No. I could just be alone. *Unfortunately, there is a certain man who won't leave me alone.*"

"Sorry. You're addicting. I have high hopes that I can change your mind."

"I have rational realizations that you most likely won't."

"When you talk like that, I think it's really **him** talking."

"I think so, too."

Conversations like that were what made Tate decide she was going to take Nick up on his offer. She had been living in a hotel room for over a month. Sanders hadn't answered her phone calls for the last two weeks. No word from Jameson, *at all*. It was really over. She needed somewhere to go, someone to be. Maybe it wouldn't work out with Nick, but he was okay with that, okay with trying. And she had to *at least* try.

She was staying at a Marriott hotel, near the University of Arizona. There was a huge function being thrown at the hotel that night, a ton of baseball teams were gathering together. Food, champagne, awards of some sort. Seemed a good time to tell him she would move in with him.

"You're in love with Jameson." Ang said it as a statement. She swallowed thickly.

"Maybe. But I'm done waiting for him to be in love with me. And he and his stupid girlfriend can go have their love child together and live —," she started to ramble, pacing outside the doors to the hotel.

"Don't you watch the fucking news!?" Ang interrupted.

"Huh?"

"You idiot. *It's not his*. The real father stepped foward, proved that it couldn't be Jameson. There was a paternity test and everything. Jameson's lawyers have been suing the shit out of her. Will you come home now!?" he whined. She stopped pacing.

"Not his?" she asked.

No. No, no, no, no.

REPARATION

"Not his. That fucker, from the party, who hit you," Ang told her.

"*You are shitting me,*" Tate gasped.

"Not at all. Apparently she didn't go straight back to Berlin after Jameson kicked her ass out. She hung around with that Dunn guy. It's *his* baby," Ang explained.

She was blown away. She started laughing. She was fully aware that she looked completely crazy, cackling into the phone like a hyena. Well, Petrushka had wanted an American financier. She got one, and one who was almost as big an asshole as she was; *winning.*

"This is amazing. Ang, you have made my day," Tate gasped for air.

"Good. Will you come home?" he demanded. She sighed.

"Ang. Do you love me?"

"What?"

"Do you love me?"

"Right now? Not very much," he snapped.

"Just let me figure shit out, alright. I tried it with Jameson. It didn't work. Let me try it with Nick. If it doesn't work, I'll run home," she promised.

"Or somewhere else. Tate ... please. *I'll* sleep with you. *I'll* love you. Don't just give up," he urged.

"A lot of women would kill to be in my position, moving in with Nick," she pointed out.

"Exactly – and you're robbing them of that. I'm worried for you, worried you'll end up like your mom," Ang said softly. She stiffened up.

"That won't happen. I'm not giving up. I'm testing the waters," she replied.

"Last time you '*tested the waters*', I had to pull you out, and baby girl, I'm not there this time around."

Tate hung up on him. Stared at the phone like she was holding a snake. Ang had never called her '*baby girl*' before, *ever*. He had called her just about every other name under the sun, but not that one. No, that was Jameson's name for her. What he had been calling her since she was eighteen. And to bring up the pool, that was *low*. Even for Ang.

She sighed and looked out onto the street, trying not to cry. Tate had made a deal with herself. No more tears. She focused on different things, tried to distract herself. There were a lot of really nice cars everywhere, a lot of rich baseball players were checking into the hotel. She saw a Porsche. A couple Escalades. A Ferrari. She smiled sadly when her eyes landed on a black Bentley.

At least someone at this hotel has classy tastes.

She walked through the lobby, glancing around. The hotel was buzzing with people. Lots of new people checking in, bell service people running around. A cart whizzed past her, filled with Louis Vuitton luggage. She frowned. Something didn't feel right.

Tate stood in front of an elevator, frowning at her feet. It was just Ang. His phone call was weighing on her soul. That's why she felt weird. And the Bentley. She would probably never be able to look at a Bentley the same again. Good thing she didn't know anyone else who owned one.

She took a deep breath as she heard a ding announcing the elevator's arrival. She walked forward, starting to lift her head, but something caught her attention out of the corner of her eye. A man, striding towards the front desk. Impeccable suit. Styled hair. Trim frame. Tate gasped, turning even as she stepped into the elevator, ignoring the people inside.

"Sanders?" she whispered, craning her neck to see. There was shuffling behind her, and someone brushed against her elbow as they reached for the floor buttons. Fire spread up her arm.

"Going up, baby girl?"

She felt like the elevator was falling out from underneath her. She slowly turned, the doors sliding shut. Satan was in the elevator, smiling down at her. Taking up every square inch of space. She stared up at him, her jaw hanging open.

"How … how …" Tate breathed. He put a finger under her chin, shut her mouth for her.

"You have a whole network of people trying to do what they think is best for you. Ang talked to Sanders. Sanders wouldn't calm down till I agreed to come out here," Jameson explained in a soft voice. She swallowed thickly.

"Sanders brought you here," she whispered. He shook his head.

"*You* brought me here."

She turned her back to him, trying to remember how to breathe. How come every time she felt like she was gaining a grip on life, Jameson fucking Kane had to pop back up!? She kept trying to let go. Why wouldn't he? Tate reached out, pressed the button for floor seven.

"Sorry," she managed to choke out as the elevator started to lift. "Were you getting out at the lobby?"

"I was. I don't mind the ride."

She nearly fell over.

"What are you doing here?" she asked. She felt his hand on her shoulder, forcing her to turn around to face him.

"We have unfinished business," he informed her.

Tate would have done anything, at that moment, to get out of that elevator. So many thoughts were pinging around in her head. She wanted to scream. She wanted to cry. She wanted to slap him across the face. She wanted to throw herself at him, *so badly*. She wanted Jameson to erase every single one of Nick's touches. She wanted to tell him that she had slept with Nick, see if it would scare him off for good. See if it wouldn't bother him at all. Luckily, she didn't have to say or do any of that – the elevator lurched to a stop and the doors slid open.

"I thought we said everything we had to say," she told him,

breezing out into the hallway. He followed her.

"I thought so, too. I was wrong," he replied.

"Really? You seemed pretty satisfied, last time I saw you," she reminded him.

"I was *angry*. You have a tendency to make me that way. I was hoping we could talk," he said.

"When have we *ever 'just talked'*?" she laughed.

"We could start. Right now," he suggested. She stopped in front of her door, her hands shaking so badly she couldn't get her key card in the slot. He took it from her, opened her door. She glared at him.

"Too late. I said everything *I* wanted to say, so I'm sorry if you —,"

"You said you loved me. That doesn't just go away," he told her. She blinked at him in surprise.

"Yeah, and I also told you it was a lie."

"*That's* a lie. You loved me. You love me *right now*. Why can't you just admit it?" he asked.

He was so calm, it was making her uncomfortable. Jameson was never calm. He was a walking ball of energy, full of spice and vinegar. Always scratching, always lashing. Never calm. Tate didn't know what to do with this Jameson.

"Because," she breathed, then cleared her throat. "It doesn't matter."

"It matters to *me*."

"Well, not to me. Not anymore. You told me to figure shit out. I did. I don't want this," she told him, feeling bold. He laughed.

"That baby isn't mine. It was wrong of you not to trust me, but I'm willing to forgive that," he told her. She felt enraged.

"How magnanimous of you. I *know* the baby isn't yours, and that *still* doesn't change how I feel about you," she snapped at him.

"Good, because you're in love with me."

"Stop saying that!" she yelled at him.

REPARATION

"Why? Because it's true?"

"*Stop it!*" Tate was almost shrieking.

"Tate, Sanders and I *drove* here. Do you have any idea what that's like? I thought I was going to have to kill him and dump his body in Oklahoma," Jameson told her. She was stunned.

"Why on earth would you drive here!?" she exclaimed.

"Because. I had to see you, but I needed time, to work some stuff out. And when we go home, I wanted more time with you, so *we* could work some stuff out," he explained. Her rage level went to Defcon Four.

"I am not going *anywhere* with you, let alone driving across America. Fuck that. I'd dump my *own* body in Oklahoma," she snorted. Jameson laughed.

"I missed you, Tatum," he chuckled. She glared.

"Oh really? On a scale of one to ten, how much —,"

"*Eleven.*"

Her breath caught in her throat.

"Stop being cute. You're never cute. It's weird," she told him. He laughed again.

"I'm flattered that you think I'm cute, Tate. What do you want from me? I asked you once, a long time ago. What can I do, to fix this? What do you need from me?" he asked, his voice simple. Sweet. *Calm*. Her eyes welled up with tears.

"What if I want babies, Jameson?" she whispered. He looked equal parts shocked and sick.

"*Excuse me?* You just had a fucking fit over the idea of Pet having my baby, and now *you* want to have it?" he demanded. She took a deep breath, shaking her head.

"No. I don't know if I ever want kids. But what if I did? What if I want to get married? What if I want a big wedding, a white fucking dress, and all my friends and family to sit in a church and watch me become Mrs. Kane?" Tate asked.

Sick. He definitely looks more sick than shocked.

"You have never mentioned *any of this* before," he pointed out. She nodded.

"I know. Petrushka, and then Ellie .., it all made me think. I always thought you were too much for me. Turned out you weren't quite enough," she managed a laugh.

"So. You want to get married. You want kids. Any sort of time frame for me to work with?" Jameson asked, clearing his throat nervously. Tate had never really seen him look nervous.

"Jameson, you won't *ever* want those things. And that's okay. It's just not okay *with me*," she stressed. "I don't want to waste any more of my time."

"*I'm* a waste of time?" he said softly. She shook her head.

"No. You were the *best* time, of my whole life."

Suddenly there was a shrill ringing sound, shattering the mood. They stared at each other for a moment, and then she headed over to the phone. Tate knew who it would be – talk about fucking awkward. She glanced at Jameson, then lifted the receiver out of the cradle.

"Hi," she said in a soft voice, keeping her back to the room. She couldn't look at Jameson, not while she was talking to Nick.

"Hey, so I was thinking, wanna get dinner somewhere else? We can go to the hotel shindig afterwards," Nick's voice was excited.

"I was looking forward to dinner here. It's … it's been a long day. I'm tired," she sighed into the phone.

"We don't have to do this, you know. We can just do room service, picnic on your floor," he laughed. Suddenly, she felt Jameson right behind her. He always radiated heat. Like he was the sun.

Just the center of your universe, that's all.

"No, you should be there. I've got a dress ready," she told Nick. Jameson's hands crept onto her shoulders.

"Are you sure? You sound kinda weird," Nick pointed out. She managed a laugh.

REPARATION

"I'm always weird, don't you know that about me yet?" she asked.

"*He'll never know you the way I do,*" the devil whispered in her ear. She shivered.

"Alright, I'll pick you up at your room," Nick said.

"*Tell him you won't be here,*" Jameson hissed.

"I'll be ready," Tate assured Nick.

"*Ready for **me**,*" Jameson breathed. She started to shiver.

"See you later."

"Later."

She hung up the phone and Jameson's fingers dug into her shoulders. She closed her eyelids. Sighed. He massaged her, though it was more pain than release. Just like she liked. She opened her eyes, shook him off. Stepped away from him.

"You have to go," she said, her voice thick.

"*No.*"

"No, you really do. I have to get ready, and get changed. I have plans for tonight," Tate told him, striding to the door and yanking it open. Jameson didn't move from his spot, just turned to face her.

"I don't give a fuck. I'm not leaving," he replied.

"Jameson! Get the fuck out of my room!" she commanded him. He shook his head.

"*Make me*, baby girl," he taunted. She gaped at him.

"You don't get to do this! You're like a fucking stalker! *Get out!*" she yelled. He slowly walked forward, but stopped in front of her. Leaned down close to her face.

"You can get as loud as you want. I'm not going *anywhere.*"

Tate screamed. As loud and as long as she could. Jameson raised his eyebrows in surprise, but he didn't budge. When she finished screaming, she gasped for air, watching him. She could hear doors opening along the hallway. Footsteps running down the hall.

"Loud enough?" she panted. He smiled.

"I've made you scream louder," he replied. She opened her

mouth to scream again, but then there were more footsteps. Someone stood in her doorway.

"I'm sorry, is everything okay?" A security guard asked. Tate cleared her throat.

"He was just leaving," she said, gesturing to Jameson. He didn't even acknowledge the guard.

"Sir, are you a guest of this hotel?" the guard demanded. Jameson nodded.

"Yes. Under the name Kane," he replied. The other man stepped back and mumbled something into his radio. A second later, it squawked back. The guard did a double take at Jameson.

"Yes, Mr. Kane. So sorry to disturb you, Mr. Kane. Is there anything I can do for you, while I'm here?" he offered. Tate groaned and Jameson smiled.

"You can leave, thank you," he replied. The guard tipped his head and then hustled away.

"Sometimes, I really fucking hate you," Tate grumbled.

"The fact that I am even staying in this piece of shit hotel, shows how much I care. I would like you to make a note," Jameson told her. She gasped.

"This is a nice hotel!" she snapped.

"Tatum. Please. Remember who you're talking to," he laughed.

"Get the fuck out! Just get out of my life!" she shouted, shoving at his chest. He let her push him into the hallway.

"We're not done," he warned her.

"We're *done*, Kane. You don't want a girlfriend. I don't want to be a fuck toy. It's *over*," she informed him.

"Why do you think that's all you're good for?" he asked, cocking his head to the side.

"Because *somebody* told me that," she snapped.

"You really shouldn't listen to everything you hear, baby girl."

She slammed the door in his face.

15

IT HADN'T EXACTLY GONE AS well as Jameson had hoped. He hadn't gotten to say anything he'd wanted to say. She hadn't fallen into his arms and begged him to take her home. She hadn't cried as much as he would've liked. But she had said a lot of things that had *really* messed with his mind.

Marriage!? *Kids!?* Was she fucking with him? When he had met Tatum, she had been sex on legs, screwing just about anything with a dick. She had turned him inside out – still had the ability to; was the only woman he had ever slept with that was truly okay with him sleeping with other women. The only woman who always kept him wanting more. The only woman who let him put his hands on her any goddamn way he pleased.

Hmmm, if that's not marriage material, I don't know what is.

It was ridiculous. They couldn't go two minutes without fighting. They had probably been "together" for a grand total of … two months? Three months? What was she saying, she wanted him to *propose?* Jameson fucking hated titles, he refused to even think of her as his girlfriend. She was just Tatum. He was just Jameson. Why couldn't that be enough!?

As it got later, he had to get out of the hotel. Knowing she was downstairs, probably looking sexy as fuck, and hanging on some other guy's arm ... he couldn't handle it. Not even a little bit. He felt like he was going to kill someone. Most likely a baseball player.

Maybe Sanders, as well. Just for dragging him there.

He strolled down the street, walked a couple blocks. There were lots of restaurants and pubs, little shops full of stupid shit that no one ever needs. They were basically in U of A's backyard. He would never have chosen to stay in a hotel like that; he had wanted to stay somewhere else. Sanders insisted it would be easier. Jameson caved.

Only for you, Tatum.

She had acted strange. He was nervous. Scared. She hadn't been as angry as he would've liked. Anger meant she cared. Sure, she'd gotten mad. But in Spain, she had fought against him, almost killed him. That was passion, in his mind. In that hotel room, she had looked ... detached. That was the *worst*.

Sanders had said to work out how he felt, and what he was going say. Well, he felt like he wanted to be with Tatum, for as long as possible. For as long as both of them could stand. He wanted to tell her things, things he had never said to anyone ever before, but she wouldn't listen. He had to find another way to talk to her. A way she would hear him.

He didn't see the store on his way up the street, but after he'd wandered for about twenty minutes and then made his way back, he noticed it. Stared in the window. So much silver and gold glittered back at him. Jameson was accustomed to nice things, had been his whole life. He didn't see anything wrong with buying them if he could afford them. Tatum always thought he was trying to buy her – she never realized, it was just his way. He bought nice things for Sanders, because he wanted to do nice things. He bought nice things for her, because that was the way he showed that he cared.

She couldn't just let him be him. She was always trying to twist him into her stupid fairy tale Prince Charming. It seemed to him that his choices were to either walk away, or wear the crown.

He frowned and pushed his way into the little shop. Several young women looked up at his entrance. Perked up. They were all young, maybe early twenties. Or younger. Babies. He ignored their smiles – he could eat them for breakfast, and still be hungry. No, he was on a mission for one last meal.

She broke the last necklace. She will not break this one.

―――

Jameson felt better when he got back to his hotel room. He ignored all the rabble downstairs, the crowds of people everywhere. He took a long shower, almost forty-five minutes. Laughed to himself as he stood under the spray. Tatum always made fun of how long he spent in the shower. He had never really thought about it before – he just liked to be warm. That's why he liked his fireplace. That's why he liked *her*.

He changed into a t-shirt and a pair of jeans. His hair had reached ridiculous lengths, and when it was wet, it curled down his forehead, almost into his eyes. He grabbed a U of A hat that had come with the room, shoved it on his head. Made a drink, stood in front of the windows and looked out over the city. He almost felt at peace. So he was actually waiting for the interruption. It came on cue.

"*You have to stop her!*" Sanders shouted, bursting through the door. Jameson closed his eyes for a second, took a deep breath.

"Life was so much simpler before her," he sighed. Sanders stomped across the room.

"Excuse me?" he asked. Jameson finally looked at him.

"Nothing. What's wrong now? What do I have to do for her now?" Jameson asked.

"Mr. Hollingsworth called me. He talked to her earlier today," Sanders said quickly.

"Yes. So did I."

"You did!?"

"Yes."

"When? What did she say? Is she here?" Sanders asked, glancing around the hotel room.

Sweet Sanders, always believing in that happily ever after.

"No. I bumped into her on the elevator. We talked. She is not happy. She wants all sorts of fairy tale promises, and she doesn't think I can give them to her," Jameson explained.

"Can you?"

"I'm not sure. I'm not that kind of man, Sanders. I never asked her to change," Jameson pointed out.

"No. But you will change, for her."

"Probably."

"Well," Sanders took a deep breath, "you should probably start, right now."

"Why? Where's the fire?" Jameson asked.

"Downstairs."

"Excuse me?"

"She is downstairs, with Mr. Castille, at some event," Sanders clarified. Jameson rolled his eyes.

"I know this, Sanders. I told you, I saw —,"

"He is going to ask her to live with him," Sanders stressed. Jameson frowned.

"Well, she can't live in a hotel forever, I'm sure there will be time to —,"

"As his *girlfriend*. And she is going to say *yes*," Sanders hissed. Jameson's eyebrows shot up.

"How do you know this? How can you be sure?" he demanded.

"She told Mr. Hollingsworth. Mr. Castille has been asking her for a while. Something happened a couple weeks ago. He has been trying to get her to move in with him ever since," Sanders said. Jameson glared.

"*What* happened?" his voice was low and threatening.

"I don't know. Mr. Hollingsworth wouldn't say – just said that when she first got here, there was an understanding between her and Mr. Castille that she was not coming here to be his girlfriend. Something happened two weeks ago to change that," Sanders told him.

"What are you telling me!? She's *already* his girlfriend!?" he snapped, disdain dripping from that word that he hated.

"I don't know. I think so," Sanders said slowly.

"*Goddammit!*" Jameson yelled, and he stomped across the room. Grabbed a plastic bag that was sitting near the door. "So when the fuck is this momentous fucking occasion happening!?"

"They're in a conference room downstairs. Mr. Hollingsworth said they're going to be talking about it over dinner. Which was served, twenty minutes ago," Sanders told him. Jameson groaned.

"*Goddamn Tatum,* always making me do things I don't want to fucking do," he growled, and hurried out the door.

Tatum stared at herself in the bathroom mirror. She looked good. She had on a heavy red lipstick. Light eyeliner. Her hair was down, but in soft waves. It had grown pretty long – she wondered if the sun had positive effects on it. It curled down almost past her breasts. When she swished it over her shoulder, she could feel it against her bare back.

She was wearing the dress Jameson had bought for her, the one she had worn to her parents' house. It was the only nice one she had brought with her to Arizona. It felt strange wearing it again.

It felt even stranger knowing Jameson was upstairs. He had been so different. Staring at her, so calm. Not angry. Not demanding. Almost laughing. Flirting. He hadn't run away. He hadn't dragged her down to hell. He had wanted to ... *just talk.*

She couldn't handle it. She felt like she was going to throw up. When Nick had met her at her hotel room, he had kissed her thoroughly, and that made her feel like she was going to throw up, too. She had hurried out of the hotel room ahead of him, laughing nervously. He thought he made her giddy. He had no idea it was *Jameson* making her giddy.

She'd made it through the meet and greet. Managed to laugh. What had Jameson said once? She could be cordial. She could be fucking polite. She had been raised in polite society, after all; she was good at faking it.

As Nick could tell anyo —, SHUT UP! SHUT UP SHUT UP SHUT UP!

When dinner was served, though, she didn't have the protection of the crowd. Of other people. Nick sat close to her, rested his hand on her thigh as food was brought out. As they tucked into their dinners, he started bringing up how glad he was that she was there. How happy she made him. How much easier it would be if ...

She had jumped out of her seat. Practically out of her skin. This was the moment Tate had been waiting for, for him to ask her to move in with him. But now that it was there, she couldn't handle it. She laughed and asked where the bathroom was, and one of the players' wives pointed her in the right direction. She then spent ten minutes on a toilet seat, her head between her knees. When she felt like she wasn't going to pass out, she finally made her way to the sinks. Patted her cheeks with cold water.

What the fuck is wrong with you? You leave a path of destruction. Not Jameson. You. **You** *are the devil.*

She took a deep breath. If she could just get through dinner. Get through the next couple hours. Jameson would fade away, when he saw that she was serious about her wants and demands. He would never give them to her, she just had to be strong.

Even if that meant doing something she *really* didn't want to do.

She took another deep breath, then squared her shoulders. Looked herself over, and didn't find herself wanting for anything. She walked out of the bathroom. She was holding herself so stiffly, she had a very distinct impression of how Sanders probably felt when he walked around. Roughly like she had a stick shoved up her ass. She tried to ignore everyone, the hum of the people in the hall, the din in the lobby, the sound of someone calling her name.

Huh?

Tate turned around and was shocked to see Jameson practically barreling through people. He was hurrying away from the bank of elevators, shouting her name. She was stunned into a standstill. He finally caught up to her, grabbed her by the shoulders.

"What are you doing? Are you drunk!?" she exclaimed, her eyes sweeping over him.

Her mind was blown. He was wearing a baseball hat. *A hat.* Crazier than him wearing sandals in Marbella. Was he trying to be incognito? She almost hadn't recognized him. He was wearing a plain grey t-shirt and jeans, and no shoes. A plastic grocery bag swung from his wrist.

He's gone crazy.

"No. What the fuck do you think you're doing!?" he demanded. It was weird, instead of hiding his eyes, the bill of the hat almost amplified them. Like a telescope, focusing all of her vision onto his blue, blue eyes.

"What are you talking about?" she asked.

"You can't be with him, Tate. You're a part of me, you belong with me," Jameson all but shouted. She was stunned.

"What has gotten into you?" she hissed, shrugging out of his hold. She grabbed his bicep and yanked him out of the flow of people, to the inside of a hall.

"*You*. Don't do this. Don't go be with somebody, *some guy*, just to not be with me," he growled. She rolled her eyes.

"He's not *'some guy'*, and he likes me, Jameson! *Really* likes me!" she snapped at him.

"*I* really like you! Why aren't *I* good enough?" he asked. She groaned.

"You don't like me, Jameson. You like having someone around that you can feel superior to," she told him.

"No. Since Spain, I have *never* made you feel that way – if that's how you felt, then it's something *you* did. Stop blaming all your shit on other people!" he yelled.

"I don't have to listen to —,"

"Yes, you do. I want to be with you. I want you to be with me. What else do you want!? Do you want me to beg? Is that the fucking problem?" he pressed.

"Oh, yes, I would love that. Jameson Kane, begging —,"

"*Please*. Please, don't do this," he whispered, grabbing her arms and yanking her close. "Please. I'm *begging* you. *Don't do this.*"

The shocking just did not stop.

"Jameson, stop, you're making a scene," she hissed at him. He shook his head.

"Do you think I give a fuck? Goddammit, Tatum, just listen to me, *for once*. You're willing to try out all this happy-home bullshit with him? Well, let *me* try it out *with you*," he urged.

"You don't mean these things," she breathed, shaking her head.

"*Please*. You haven't given me my chance, and I was here first. You want all these things, let me try to give them to you. You said you wanted a prince – I'm as close as you can get," he told her.

"I said I wanted Prince Charming; *you're* the Prince of Darkness."

REPARATION

"Still a prince, baby girl."

Too much. This man is so much.

"Jameson …" she breathed, closing her eyes.

"Here. I bought you something. Today," he was suddenly saying, letting her go. She opened her eyes to see him digging something out of the plastic bag. He pulled out a large, square, velvet box. She glared.

"Is this a joke?" she demanded, yanking it out of his hands as he held it out to her.

"No. Just open it. You'll —," he started. She smacked him in the arm with the box.

"*You just don't fucking get it!* For such a smart fucking person, you don't fucking get anything! *You can't buy me!*" she shrieked the last part, hitting him over and over with the box. He grabbed her wrist and the box fell out of her grasp, clattering to the ground at her feet.

"I'm not trying to buy you, you stupid bitch! Just fucking open it!" he yelled back. People were starting to stop and stare at them.

"Go fuck yourself. This is why I didn't want you here, why I don't want to see you. You ruin *everything*," she growled at him. He glared back at her.

"You know what? Fine. *Fine.* I can't make you be with me, you're right. You wanna be fucking stupid, then go be fucking stupid. *But don't be with him.* Don't go be with him, just to not be with me. *That's* stupid. I can bear the thought of you being out there alone, without me. What I can't bear is the thought of you being out there with *the wrong man.*"

Tate didn't know what to say to that – Jameson, willing to let her go. Jameson, simply begging her to not be with the wrong person. She was at a loss. It didn't matter anyway. She still hadn't found her voice when she felt an arm slide around her waist.

"Are you okay? Excuse me, mister, you can't just —, *oh.*"

Nick and Jameson stared at each other. She felt like she was going to melt into the floor. The two had never met. She had never wanted them to meet. They were from different spectrum's of her life. Jameson was the dark. Nick was the light. The two weren't ever meant to meet.

"*Tatum,*" Jameson's voice was full of warning, but he kept his eyes on Nick.

"I didn't realize you were here," Nick started, glancing at Tate briefly before going back to Jameson. "I'm Nick Castille." He held out his hand. Jameson *did not* shake it.

"I know who you are. The question is, do you know who *I* am?" Jameson asked, his voice full of steel. Nick nodded.

"I am very aware of who you are. Is he bothering you?" Nick asked her, his arm getting tighter around her waist. She pulled away from him, moving to the side of them both.

"No, just give us a minute, he was about to leave," she said quickly. Jameson snorted.

"I'm not fucking going anywhere," he replied.

"She asked you to leave. You need to leave," Nick stressed. Jameson moved his stare to Tate.

"*Unfinished business, Tatum,*" he told her in a soft voice. She shivered.

"Not anymore, *Kane,*" she whispered. Nick glanced between them and stepped forward.

"Alright, enough. You're obviously upsetting her. Time to go," he told him. Jameson barked out a laugh and stood to his full height, a good two inches over Nick.

"I'm not going anywhere. Didn't she tell you? The whole point of my existence is just to *upset her,*" Jameson informed him. Tate actually laughed at that one. Nick just got angry.

He never did quite get my sense of humor.

"That's it. You need to leave, or I'll get security to kick you out of the hotel," Nick warned him. Jameson laughed again.

"Try it. I'll buy *this hotel*, then redecorate the interior with your small intestines," Jameson threatened.

"Stop it," Tate finally piped up.

"Wanna say that again? I didn't quite hear you," Nick growled, stepping closer to him.

"I don't repeat myself to people *like you*," Jameson growled right back.

"Probably because people *like me* are too far above you."

"Yet not far enough above me that I couldn't make you regret ever touching her."

"*Stop it!*" Tate shouted, pushing her way between them. She put a hand on each chest and shoved. Nick took a step back. Jameson didn't move a muscle.

"Tate," Nick said, his tone no-nonsense. She glanced at him.

"Give us a minute," she urged. Nick's eyebrows almost went into his hairline.

"Are you kidding me? After everything he's done!? Tate, don't let this guy ruin what we —," Nick started to argue, when Jameson stepped foward, pushing into Tate so she was trapped between the two of them.

"*Stop!*" she hissed, trying to push them away from each other again.

"'*This guy*' was here long before you ever were, and he'll be here long after you're gone," Jameson warned him. Nick glared and stepped forward as well. Tate was officially squished, her shoulders pressing against a chest on either side of her.

"Yeah, well, I'm the guy who's with her right now, *not you*," Nick snarled. Jameson laughed demonically.

"You so sure about that?" he challenged.

"I was sure last night."

It happened so fast, Tate didn't even see it coming. For a big guy,

Jameson was pretty quick. He gave a sharp jab with his right arm, slamming his fist into Nick's nose. Tate shrieked as Nick stumbled backwards into a wall. She turned and hurried to his side.

"I didn't even see you yesterday! Why would you say that!?" she demanded, grabbing his head and forcing him to look up. Blood was coming out of both nostrils, and from his teeth, but nothing looked broken. He managed a chuckle.

"I wanted to piss him off," he sighed.

"Mission fucking accomplished," Jameson swore behind them. Tate glared over her shoulder at him.

"Just go away. You've already ruined my evening – did you have to ruin his!?" she snapped.

"*Yes*. I came down here to say something, and I'm not fucking leaving till I say it," Jameson snapped back.

"Well I don't wanna fucking hear it. I've heard enough, so just go fuck yourself," she said through clenched teeth. He smiled.

"I believe that's your job."

Nick lurched off the wall, almost knocking her down. She pressed her hands against his front, trying to stop him, but he surged forward. She yelped, lost her footing, and had to wrap her arms around his chest to hold herself upright.

He thinks that's an insult? That's everyday-polite-conversation for Jameson Kane.

"Talk to her like that again, and we'll see who —," Nick started to shout.

"*Shut up!*" Tate finally shrieked. Everyone paused. She pushed herself upright and stared at Nick. "Stop trying to defend my honor – there isn't much there to defend. He's not going anywhere, so let's just go back inside." She heard footsteps and then Jameson was right behind her. She didn't look, but held out an arm, putting her hand on his chest again to force him to keep his distance.

"*Tatum*," Jameson's voice was right near her head. Almost pleading sounding. "*Hear me.* Just this once. Do what *you* want, not what you think is going to piss me off." She turned her head back to face him.

"You need to *go*," she urged.

He stared at her for a long moment. One of his hands went to his chest and covered her own. His palm was warm. Almost hot. He clenched his fingers around hers, and it was like he was transmitting images and memories straight to her brain. The places his hands had been, the places they had taken her to, if she would just remember. Just listen to him.

"Aright. Alright, baby girl, I'll go. If that's what you want. That's all I came here to do, all I *ever* wanted to do for you; just give you whatever you want," he said in a soft voice.

Tate swallowed thickly, but before she could even think about what he had said, he was walking away. Striding towards the elevators, barefoot and in a ball cap. Looking as unlike Jameson Kane as he ever could, as she would probably ever see.

Too much.

"Tatum, are you okay? I'm sorry, about all that, what I said. I didn't know he was here, I was caught off guard," Nick said from behind her, his hand cupping her elbow. She nodded.

"Yeah. Yeah, I think he got here today," she said softly.

"You knew?"

"I bumped into him earlier. Just for a couple minutes."

"Why didn't you say something?" he asked. She shrugged.

"I didn't think it mattered," she whispered, still staring after *him*.

Nick pulled her into a hug. She leaned into him, trying to hear his heart beat. Trying to let it ground her. Tried to concentrate on his arms around her. But all she heard was words. So many words, running around her head.

"*... You're part of me, you belong with me ... I want to be with you. I want you to be with me ... I can bear the thought of you being* *out there alone, without me. What I can't bear is the thought of you being out there with* **the wrong man** *..."*

"Do you want to leave?" Nick asked. She shook her head and pulled away.

"No, I'm fine. Let's just go sit down," she told him, and started walking back towards the conference room.

"Wait. What is this?" Nick asked. She turned back to see him scooping up the velvet jewelry box from the ground.

"Nothing. Just ... nothing. Here, it's mine," she said, taking it from him.

She sat at the table and fidgeted. She felt like her heart was going to beat out of her chest. She felt like was going to puke. She smiled and laughed at all the appropriate times, but she wasn't listening. She was thinking about blue eyes and strong fingers.

Wrong. He's wrong for you. He's never understood what you want, what you really want.

By the time dessert was brought out, she felt like she was calming down. She was laughing at something an outfielder's wife was saying. Nick had even lightened up a little. He had cleaned himself and his nose had stopped bleeding, which was a plus. Now his hand was back on her knee. She ignored the way her skin felt so ... *normal*, under his touch.

"Doing okay?" he asked, leaning close to her ear. She nodded.

"Yeah. Just tired," she replied. He smiled at her.

"Why don't we go upstairs, and I can —," he started, when he was interrupted by one of the coaches. Tate let out sigh of relief. The last thing she wanted to do was *"go upstairs"* with Nick.

While he chattered away to the coach, her eyes fell on the black velvet box. She glared at it. Stupid Jameson. Stupid fucking pearls. Fitting though, pearls the first time they came together. Pearls the last time they parted. She wondered how much they cost, wondered if she could leave them at the front desk for him to pick up. Won-

REPARATION

dered if she could strangle him with them. She drummed her fingers against the box.

"Awww, did Nicky get that for you?" the same wife from earlier drawled in a thick Southern accent. Tate smiled.

"Oh no, it's from … an admirer," Tate joked.

"Ooohhh, may I ask what it is?" the lady continued. Tate shrugged.

"I'm not really sure, I haven't opened it."

"Well, honey, what are you waiting for!? That's a big box! Open it!" the woman insisted. Tate sighed and dragged the box forward. Braced herself to see what her price was this time around. $50,000, $60,000, hell, maybe he'd gone all out — $75,000. She flipped open the lid.

She gasped, and her hand flew to her mouth. She couldn't believe it. Couldn't fucking believe it. Tears filled her eyes, and she managed a laugh. She was vaguely aware of the woman asking her what was wrong, asking what was in the box, but she ignored her. A long ago conversation floated into her mind.

"It's knowing the worth of what you have. Fake pearls are just as good as real pearls, if they're given with good intentions and love. If Ang gave me the gaudiest, ugliest, tackiest, strand of fake pearls ever, I would love them more than any set of real pearls my parents ever gave me. Ang loves me."

*"If **Ang** gave you pearls, huh. And what if I gave you pearls? What would they mean to you?"*

"You don't love me, so to be impressed, that price tag better be huge."

Sitting inside the fancy velvet box, a box that had a *Cartier* logo on the inside of it, was the guadiest, ugliest, tackiest strand of fake pearls, *ever*. Fake was too generous a word. The necklace was basically costume jewelry. It was like he had walked into one of those Claire's boutiques, then looked through the clearance bin for the cheapest piece of shit necklace he could possibly find. It even had the price tag still stuck to it. The actual cost had been crossed out with a black marker, but it had been marked down and the original price was still visible.

$4.99.

She could not stop laughing.

Oh, Satan. Got me again.

"What's so funny?" Nick suddenly asked.

"He … it's … I can't," she laughed. He glanced into the box.

"Jameson Kane got you that?" he asked, surprise obvious in his voice. She nodded.

"You see, we … it's a long story," she sighed, sitting the box on the table, leaving it open.

"So strange. Look, what I was saying was, maybe we could go upstairs, and continue our discussion," Nick said, leaning his elbow on her chair.

"Hmmm?" she asked absent-mindedly, staring at the pearls.

You thought he was trying to buy you. He asked you to listen. Are you listening now?

"You know, what we've been talking about," Nick pressed, trailing his fingertip in a circle on her arm.

"What?" she asked, not able to tear her eyes away from the box.

He's hearing you. Really hearing you. He didn't run away. You ran away. **Hear him.**

"What we've been talking about. You, me," Nick lead her along.

"I don't … know what …" she couldn't form coherent thoughts. Jameson was in her head, taking up all the space, forcing everything out.

"… *you're willing to try it all out with him? Let me try it out with you …*"

REPARATION

"You and me, moving in together," Nick finally spelled it out. She lifted her eyes to his. Really looked at him.

"… That's all I came here to do … to give you whatever you want …"

All I ever wanted was for him to love me.

Hear him.

"I'm sorry," Tate breathed.

Nick blinked in surprise, clearly confused for a moment. Then he looked at the box. Back at her. Then the box. Realization dawned across his face and his smile fell away. His eyes found hers, and she started to cry again.

"I see," he whispered back.

"I'm so sorry," Tate babbled. "I'm so, so sorry. I tried. I really tried. You are one of the best people I've ever known. You're smart and funny and sexy, and everything. You're *everything*. I don't know what's wrong with me, I'm just this horrible, demon, person, thing—"

"Hey, hey, it's okay. Stop," Nick urged, cupping her face in his hands.

"No, it's not okay. This is what I was so scared of, I didn't want to use you. I didn't want to hurt you," she cried. The people around them were starting to look uncomfortable, but she didn't care.

"I'm okay. I mean, I'm not gonna lie, it kinda hurts to come in second," he managed a laugh, and her heart broke a little for the beautiful, amazing man in front of her. "But somehow, I don't think I was ever really in the running."

"I tried," she whispered.

"I know," he whispered back.

"Please, don't hate me. I can't stand the thought of you hating me," she begged, and he outright laughed.

"Tatum O'Shea, I could never hate you. I just hope that while you're jet setting, or vacationing in Monaco, or lounging in the

Hamptons, that sometimes you'll think of me," he told her.

"Nick, I could never forget you," she laughed as well.

"You sure about that? I'm not a mutli-millionaire, or an aspiring porn star," he teased.

"No. You're better."

"Don't you forget it. Now, get out of here. You're cramping my style. I was very set on not going home alone tonight, and the girl I had my eye on is taken," he told her, playfully shoving her head away. She laughed.

"The girl you had your eye on is stupid," she sniffled, wiping at her nose with a napkin.

"Sometimes. But sometimes, she's pretty great."

She leaned forward and kissed him, just softly, on the lips. She felt his hand on the back of her neck, for the briefest moment, then he pulled away. He smiled at her, wiped at the edge of her bottom lip with his thumb, then nodded. He grabbed her jewelry box, snapping it closed before handing it over.

"Alright. Make sure he works for it – that guy's an asshole," he warned her. She stood up and nodded, wiping at her eyes.

"I know. Haven't you learned yet? That's exactly my type," she joked.

"Jesus, I really never stood a chance."

"Is it okay if I call you?" she asked.

"You had better. Now *go*."

She walked out of the conference room. Dashed across the lobby. Ran up to the elevators. She hopped from foot to foot, struggling to take off her heels. The elevator doors finally opened and she hopped inside, managing to get one shoe off. A little girl, clearly straight from the pool, walked onto the elevator as well, hugging a huge towel around her body. The doors slid shut and Tate hit the button for the second to highest floor.

"Hey," Tate asked, bending down to take off her other shoe. "Do you have a hair tie I could borrow?"

"What?" the girl asked.

"A hair tie. I'll give you my shoes," Tate laughed. The little girl pulled an elastic band off her wrist and handed it over.

"They won't fit me. Don't you need your shoes?" the girl asked, eyeballing Tate like she was insane.

"No, not where I'm going," Tate replied, yanking her hair up into a high, messy ponytail.

"Where are you going?"

"To chase down a guy."

"Your boyfriend?"

Tate laughed.

"No, not my boyfriend," she replied.

"Then why are you chasing him?" the girl asked. Tate looked at her reflection in the shiny walls, straightened out her dress.

"Because I think I want him to be my boyfriend," she said. The girl scrunched up her nose.

"Oh. I thought boys asked girls out," she said in a matter-o-fact voice. Tate snorted and lowered herself so she was eye to eye with the girl.

"No way, girls can do *anything* boys can do, including ask people out. You know what I say? If you really like somebody, *just go for it*," Tate explained. The girl smiled.

"I think you'll get him," she assured her. Tate stood up.

"You think so?" she asked, holding out her arms like she was under inspection.

"Yes. You look really pretty," she told her. Tate nodded.

"Good. He likes pretty," Tate said, turning to stare at the floor numbers.

"Is he cute?" the girl asked. Tate glanced down at her.

"The truth? He is the cutest boy I have ever met, in my entire life," she told the girl.

"Wow. Cuter than Justin Bieber?"

"Yes. Cuter than Justin Bieber."

"*Wow.*"

The elevator stopped and the doors dinged open. Tate squealed and kicked her shoes out onto the floor in front of her. She glanced up and down the hall, then turned back to the elevator. The little girl was giving her the thumbs up. Tate gave it back.

"Wish me luck!" she said. The girl laughed.

"Good luck!"

And then the elevator doors slid shut.

Tate realized in her romance-movie-style rush to see Jameson, she had forgotten that she didn't have a fucking clue what room he was in, let alone what floor. He was staying in a suite, that was for sure. The suites were on the top floors. She dug her fingers underneath the side of her dress, at the side of her waist. She made contact with something hard and she pinched it between her fingers, yanking her cell phone out. She called the front desk.

"Hi!" she shouted when someone picked up. "Hi, yeah, sorry, I need to speak with a guest."

"Alright, who are you looking for?" a sweet sounding woman asked.

"I need Jameson Kane's room," she told her.

"Please hold."

The phone rang and rang and rang. Tate let out a frustrated yell and kicked a wall, then promptly regretted it, as she was painfully reminded that she wasn't wearing shoes. She hopped around on one foot and the line finally picked up.

"I'm sorry, ma'am, the guest you are trying to reach is not available. Would you like to leave a voicemail?"

"No. No, uh, what is his room number?" Tate asked, pacing up and down the hall.

"I'm sorry, but I am not allowed to give out that information."

REPARATION

"Uuuggg, c'mon! I already know he's staying here! Just tell me the room!" Tate demanded.

"Mr. Kane is a preferential guest. I cannot give out that information. Thank you for calling, good night."

And the line was dead.

Tate let out a shriek. What was she supposed to do now!? In a fit of passion, right after she had gotten to Arizona, she had deleted Jameson's cell phone number. She didn't have it memorized – who did that anymore!? And she didn't want to call Sanders to ask for it, in case he was with Jameson. Talk about a mood killer.

She marched to one end of the hall and began knocking on the door. No one answered. She began banging. She realized she was acting crazy, but she was long past the point of caring. She'd moved on into acceptance. Jameson Kane made her crazy. She should probably start getting used it.

When no one answered at the third door, she began yelling. Calling out for both Sanders and Jameson, hoping that they were behind one of the doors, and just not answering because they thought it was housekeeping or something. At the fourth door, she got a disgruntled elderly man. At the fifth door, she got a teenage boy who invited her inside. The eighth had a half dressed baseball player, telling her to shut the fuck up. She told him he could suck her dick. That shut *him* up.

She was prancing around from foot to foot in front of the elevator, waiting for it to open so it could take her to the top floor. She felt like she had taken speed. And coke. Or crack. Some lethal combination of all three. She couldn't stop moving, she had so much adrenaline pumping. She hopped around, hugging the jewelry box to her chest. Finally, the elevator opened up.

But it wasn't empty.

"What the fuck are you doing!? We can hear you all the way upstairs!" Jameson snapped. She glared at him.

"Then what the fuck took you so long to come down here!?" she snapped back.

"Are you fucking serious right now!?" he exclaimed.

"Are *you* fucking serious!?"

"You're fucking crazy, you know that, right!? *Goddamn psychotic!*" he yelled at her. The elevator started to close and he slammed his palm against a door, causing it to open again.

"Oh yeah!?" she yelled back. "Well if I'm *fucking psychotic*, it's because *you made me this way!*"

"Tatum!" he snapped her name through clenched teeth.

"What!?"

"*Shut the fuck up.*"

She fell on him, throwing her arms around his neck. He moved backwards with her weight, and they fell against the back wall of the elevator. The jewelry box fell between them, smacking her on the foot as it hit the floor. The elevator doors slid shut behind them.

"Sorry, sorry," she breathed, resting against him at an awkward angle. He yanked her upright, standing her on her feet. She pushed away from his chest, straightening out her dress.

"Where the fuck are your shoes?" he asked, staring down at her feet. She stared down, too, taking in both their barefeet. She smiled. Just like that first time, in his house.

"In the hall," she replied. "Where's your hat?"

"In my hotel room. Tatum. What *the fuck* are you doing?" he asked.

"I opened your present," she told him. He raised his eyebrows.

"Oh really. How – what did you say? – *magnanimous* of you," he said snidely. She snorted.

"I know, right? What a fuckin' ugly necklace, Kane. I came up here to give it back. Can you hit the floor for the lobby? I'm in the middle of a party," she told him.

"Noooo, I think you're done with your party," he replied.

REPARATION

"Oh really? What makes you think that?" she asked.

"That look in your eye."

"What look?"

"That look that says you *really* want to be fucked," he told her. She laughed.

"And you think you can do something about that?" she asked. He nodded and leaned around her, but he didn't hit the lobby button. He hit the button for his floor.

"I think I'm the *only one* who can do someting about it," he replied.

"I don't know how my date would feel about that," she wondered out loud.

"*I don't give a fuck.*"

She grabbed him by his shirt and yanked him forward. They stumbled backwards, her back ramming into the elevator doors. She moaned against his lips, their tongues swirling around each other. His fingers dug into her hips, holding her against him, and then he wrapped his arms around her, squeezing her so tightly she could barely breathe.

"Don't leave me again," he whispered, tracing his tongue along her bottom lip. She shook her head.

"I won't. I promise," she whispered back, combing her fingers through his thick hair.

"Your promises haven't worked out so well for me," he growled, his mouth against her neck.

"We'll have to work on that," she replied.

"I thought I had lost you."

"Me, too."

"You never listen to me."

"I'm trying. I heard you down there. It just took me a while."

"I swear to Christ," he growled, his lips moving across her face. "If you come back only to run away again … I won't do this forever,

Tate."

"Yes, you would."

"*Yes.* Are you fucking around? Am I gonna wake up tomorrow and you'll have run away again? Am I gonna have to chase you to New Jersey? South Dakota? Maybe give me a heads up so I can know what to pack."

"You're such a dick."

"At least I'm consistent."

She sighed. She had missed him, *so much.*

"*I'm so sorry I left you.*"

"I'm going to make —,"

She hadn't even realized the elevator had come to a stop, but suddenly the doors were sliding open. She shrieked and fell backwards. Jameson stumbled with her. He managed to keep her upright, but they tripped across the hall, slamming into the far wall, all his weight ramming into her. She grunted and then his mouth was on hers again.

He grabbed her ass hard, yanking her up against him. Her dress was too tight for her to lift her legs, and he carried her like that down the hall. She raked her fingers across his shoulders and he let go of her, her body sliding down the length of his. When her feet touched the floor, he shoved her against a wall.

"Off, you need to get this off," he breathed, yanking her slim belt apart.

"Yes," she agreed, her fingers joining his as she whipped the belt away from her body.

"*All of it,*" he insisted, his fingers going to the zipper that ran down the seam over her butt.

She slid to the side, pulling him with her, until she landed against a door. She braced her hands against the frame while he worked the zipper all the way down. Then his hands slid heavily up her body, over her breasts, to her shoulders. He pulled at the material there,

REPARATION

yanked her arms free. The moment the top of the dress slid away from her breasts, he pressed himself against her, covering her up with his body.

"We either do this in the hall, or we go inside," she whispered to him.

"Okay," he replied, and his hands flew to his own belt.

"*Jameson.*"

He stepped away from her and she almost fell forward. He grabbed her upper arm and dragged her down the hall. She held the front of her dress to her chest, trailing behind him. He stopped in front of the last door, fought with the key card, finally got it in, and kicked open the door. Sanders leapt up from a couch.

"Oh, good, I'm so glad you —," Sanders started to gush.

"*Out. Now,*" Jameson barked, yanking Tate up against his chest.

Sanders hurried out of the suite, closing the door behind him.

"*Wait, wait, wait,*" she rushed out, pressing against Jameson's chest. He shook his head, pulling her dress away from her hands.

"I've waited long enough," he said, one of his hands covering her breast and squeezing. She shook her head.

"I have to tell you something," she whispered, covering his hand with her own. His lips worked their way down her shoulder.

"I don't care."

"I think you will."

"I don't want to hear."

"I want you to."

"*Stop.*"

"I had sex with him."

Bomb. Dropped. Time stood still. He stopped moving. She stopped breathing. His hand slid away from her skin, and any breath she had, flew out of her body. He stood back from her and she grabbed at the material of her dress, pressed it to her bare chest. He rubbed a hand over his mouth.

"I told you I didn't want to hear," he sighed. She nodded and sat on a couch, pressing her hands flat against her chest.

"I know. I just couldn't ... not without saying anything. Later would have been so much worse," she whispered. He nodded.

"Yes, I suppose."

"Do you hate me?" she asked, looking up at him. He chuckled and squatted down low, putting his head in his hands.

"I have tried very hard to hate you, Tatum. At various times, throughout a large chunk of my life, I have tried to hate you. I haven't been very good at it," he told her. She sniffled.

"I was so angry at you," she said. "I wanted to get over you. The Pet thing, and then Ellie ... I just ... he was there. I told him that I didn't want to be with him, that it probably wouldn't mean anything."

"And what? He wanted his shot?"

Well, it sounds dirty, when you say it like that, Mr. Kane.

"I wanted to forget you. Get over you. He offered to help."

"Did it work?" Jameson asked, lifting his eyes to hers.

"What?"

"Did he make you forget?" Jameson asked. She chuckled.

"Jameson. No one will ever be able to make me forget you."

He stood back up and stalked towards her. Grabbed her wrists and pulled her up. He kept staring at her, didn't look away as he worked the dress over her hips and pushed it to the floor. When it pooled at her feet, he pulled her forward, away from it.

"I remember buying you that dress," he said, pulling her against him. "I remember the first time you wore it. I remember you coming into my room after taking it off, only wearing your underwear and those shoes."

"Happy times," she laughed. His arms wrapped around her.

"Hmmm. Was he any good?" he asked, pressing his hands flat against her shoulder blades. She swallowed thickly, staring at him.

"Good enough."

REPARATION

His hands slid down her back. Worked their way inside the sides of her underwear. Kept moving, pulling her panties down over her hips. Past her thighs. He let them go, and they fell to her feet. She was completely naked, pressed against his completely clothed form.

"Did you follow the rules?" he asked, and it took her a second to figure out what he was actually saying.

"Yes," she nodded. "I thought of you the whole time."

"Does he know this?"

"I didn't say it. But I think he did."

"*Pussy.*"

"Stop it."

"How many times?" Jameson asked, his hands moving back to her butt. He picked her up, forced her legs around his waist.

"Just one night. I couldn't do it again," she assured him. He carried her to the couch, and then he sat down with her straddling him.

"You have been very naughty, Ms. O'Shea," he sighed. She nodded, rubbing her hands down his chest.

"I know," she agreed.

"And trying to corrupt Sanders? That was especially low," he added, his voice evil sounding. She winced.

"Would you rather him be with a stranger? At least you know I would take care of him. I would treat him right," she pointed out. His fingers dug into her waist and she winced again.

"Tatum. I am giving you *a lot* of get out of jail free cards. If you *ever* touch Sanders – inappropriately – *ever* again, I will kill *him* and maim *you*," he warned her. She chuckled.

"You want to keep him in a box forever. You need to stop treating him like some thirteen year old street urchin. He's a man," she whispered, undoing his belt buckle.

"You need to stop noticing that he's a man," Jameson growled, leaning back from her as she undid his pants.

"And you may hate Nick, but you should know that he knows

I'm up here, right now. He knows, and wished me luck. That man downstairs is better than you or I will ever be," she told him. He snorted and worked his jeans down his hips from underneath her.

"We'll reassess that in about fifteen minutes," he told her.

"Fifteen minutes? You've gotten soft in the last month."

"*Shut your fucking mouth, Tate.*"

His hands were on her hips, guiding her down on him. She moaned and shuddered, scratching at his t-shirt. She was completely naked, and he was still almost completely dressed. It was a bizarre, different sensation. She worked her hips against his, gasping.

"I don't want that life with him," she suddenly moaned.

"I know."

"But I don't want what we had," she pressed her forehead to his. One of his arms wrapped around her waist.

"I know, Tatum."

"I want you."

"Yes."

"I want to be with you."

"You're with me."

"Only me."

"*Only you.*"

She gasped, all of her muscles contracting. His arm got tight around her, holding her down to his thrusts. She let her head drop back, abandoning herself to him. Not that she'd ever had a choice.

"I just want to be like this, all the time," she sighed, dropping her head to his shoulder.

"You can be."

"I lied to you. I lied so much to you," she gasped for air. He groaned and she felt his fingers in her hair, pressed against the back of her head.

"I know," he replied, his voice straining.

"It was all a lie," she whispered, her whole body starting to shake.

REPARATION

"Every word I said. I loved you. I didn't love him. I've never loved anyone else, ever."

"*I know.*"

If you always know everything before me, why don't you clue me in and save us some time?

She came hard, shuddering and shaking on top of him. He stopped moving, just held her close against him. His touch was gentle. If he had been rough, it would have been too much, too soon. He always knew exactly what she needed. She pressed her face into his shoulder. Sucked in air. Cried a little.

"Are you alright?" he breathed. She nodded.

"Yes. For the first time, in a long time, I think I am," she managed with a laugh.

"See? A good fuck always makes you feel better. Remember that, next time you get upset," he told her, and she laughed harder.

"Maybe you should just remind me."

"Is it my turn now?" he asked. She lifted her head and looked down at him.

"What do you mean?" she asked. He lifted his hands to her face and ran his thumbs underneath her eyes, wiping away tears and mascara.

"I mean, that one was for you, baby girl. To reassure you, I'm not going anywhere, no matter what you do. You're feeling upset. You feel bad. That one was to make you feel better," he told her. She smiled.

"Very generous, sir."

"I know. Now, I think it's my turn."

"And what exactly are you feeling?"

"*Angry.*"

"*Ooohhh*, and what would you like to do about that?"

"*Anything I want.*"

"Sounds fun."

"You up for that?"

"*Always.*"

The hand in her hair clenched and yanked, forcing her head back. She gasped, and then moaned when she felt his teeth on her nipple. The arm around her waist held her tight against him and he stood up. She wrapped herself around him, digging her fingernails into his shirt. He let his pants fall to the floor and stepped out of them as he walked across the room, carrying her into the bedroom.

"I'm gonna treat you so bad," he warned her.

"Exciting."

"I'm gonna fuck you so hard," he added.

"*Even better.*"

"You are *never* going to want to fuck anybody else, ever again," he continued, dropping her on the bed and then yanking his t-shirt off.

"Too late for that." She scrambled onto her knees.

"You are *never* going to want to leave me, ever again," he finished, his hand gripping her high on her throat, fingers and thumb pressing underneath her jaw. She managed to nod.

"Never again."

"Now, you are going to shut the fuck up, and you are going to *show me* just how much you love me," he informed her. She smiled.

"That could take a long time," she warned him.

"Good thing we've got all the time in the world."

Oh, Satan, still so clever.

16

"**D**O I HAVE TO PROPOSE now?"

"No, Jameson."

"Good. The words make me physically ill."

Tate rolled onto her back, turned her heads towards Jameson.

"Do you want to propose to me?"

"Do you want the truth?"

"Always."

"No. Jesus, Tate, I barely know you. I don't even know your full name. What's your middle name?"

"Elliot."

Jameson turned his head towards Tate.

"Serious?"

"Yes. Not all of us are as blessed as you, Santiago."

"Shut up."

"Alright."

"I missed you, baby girl. So goddamn much."

"Good. I missed you, too."

"You always miss me. Why do you keep trying to get away?"

"Because you scare me."

"You scare me, too, but you don't see me running."

"I know. You're braver than me."

"Sometimes I wonder."

Tate reached over and pressed her hand against his arm.

"Jameson."

"Hmmm?"

"You asked me to be willing to try. You said you were willing to try. That's what this is. I just want to be with you, and once in a while, know that you want to be with me, too."

"I always want to be with you, Tatum."

"Really?"

"Yes."

"I know how you hate titles."

"Because we transcend titles."

"That was really beautiful, Jameson."

"Thank you."

"We transcend …"

Jameson grabbed Tate's hand, brought it to his chest and placed it over his heart.

"We just work. Let it be, Tate. Seven years, a bottle of xanax, Pet, Nick, several countries, and a lot of miles – yet we're still here. Time to stop running, baby girl."

"Yes."

"Tell me you love me."

"I love you."

"Will you ever fuck anyone else?"

"Not without telling you first."

"Brat."

"Fair is fair."

"Will I always be your favorite?"

"Unfortunately, yes. Yes, Jameson, you will always be the best."

"Good."

REPARATION

Tate cleared her throat, drummed her fingers on his chest.

"And what about me?"

"Don't be fucking stupid."

"You're stupid."

"Watch it."

"What about me?"

"What about you?"

"Jameson."

Jameson pressed his hand flat over her fingers, stilling them.

"I'm not the one who has trouble admitting what we are to each other. I shouldn't have to tell you what I think of you, or how I feel, because I've made it perfectly clear."

"Your idea of perfectly clear and mine are two very different things."

"Tatum Elliot O'Shea, sometimes I think you are the stupidest goddamn person I have ever met. Sometimes I think you're crazy. Sometimes I think I hate you. Sometimes I think you're a psychotic bitch, sent from hell to drag me back. But always, ALWAYS, I think you are the best thing that has ever happened to me."

Tate smiled up at him, her eyes filling up with tears.

"See?"

"What? Jesus, are you crying again?"

"Almost sweet."

"Say you love me again, that usually cheers you up."

"Get fucked, Kane."

"Close enough."

17

Tatum leaned between the front seats of the Bentley, staring out the windshield. Why they had chosen to drive to Arizona was beyond her, and Jameson refused to fly back with her and leave Sanders to make the drive. So there they were, driving across the country. She reached out to fiddle with the GPS and Sanders slapped her hand away.

"Please stop. Last time you touched it, we wound up lost in Albuquerque for hours."

"Honest mistake."

They had stayed in Tucson for a week. She saw Nick every day. He wasn't exactly happy, but he wasn't exactly mourning her, either. She was glad. Even Jameson came down and shook his hand once. She hadn't even asked him to, he had just done it. When she asked him why, he explained that even though he was Satan, he could recognize and appreciate a gentleman when he saw one.

Ang was beyond excited when she said she was coming home, and he got even more hyped up when she informed him that she had made up with Jameson. She pointed out that there had been a time, not too long ago, when he had been trying to drive them apart. He

REPARATION

pointed out that she never bothered listening to him, anyway, so why was she bothering now? Satan obviously made her happy, and Ang only ever wanted that for her.

They pulled into an underground parking garage for a Hilton hotel. She stretched across the back seat and made herself comfortable. They were all driving in shifts, in order to get back to Boston as quickly as possible. But Sanders refused to go a day without showering. He was renting a hotel room for a day, just so he could spend a couple hours showering and getting cleaned up.

"Sandy?" she called out. He twisted in the front seat.

"Yes?" he asked.

"Think of me, while you're up there," she winked at him.

"Always."

She didn't stop laughing till he was halfway across the garage.

Nobody had been happier than Sanders about Tate's change of heart. He had almost cried. That first night, she had fallen asleep halfway on top of Jameson, but she woke up in the middle of the night and snuck into Sanders' room. He needed an apology as well, so she spooned up behind him and wrapped her arms around him. Whispered to him, promised him, that she would never leave him again. No matter what the future held for her and Jameson, she and Sanders were forever.

"You're my soulmate," she whispered, and he had nodded, holding her hands.

"Yes."

So even though the stop was unnecessary, and added several hours to their trip, she didn't give him too much trouble. Her departure had been hard on him, she could tell. Harder than he had let on, during their phone calls. She had a lot of ground to cover, trust to build. She sighed and propped her feet up against the passenger side door.

"Maybe the real reason you came back was for Sanders," Jameson snorted from the front seat. Tate laughed.

"Maybe."

"How long are you going to wear that thing for?" Jameson asked, turning around in the front seat and looking down at her.

"What, this?" she asked, pressing her hand to the necklace he had gotten her. The first time she had tried it on, the cheap clasp had broken. She'd had to tape it closed, and hadn't taken it off since. Made showering interesting.

"Yes. It's ugly," he told her.

"I love it. I'm going to wear it on my wedding day," she informed him. He barked out a laugh and turned forward.

"Good thing that's very, very, *very* far away. I pity the groom, whoever he may be," he grumbled.

"Shut up!" She pushed herself up enough to slap him across the back of the head.

"Keeping pushing me, baby girl. See what happens," he growled, rubbing the back of his head while she laid back down.

She moved her leg and pushed the back of his head with her foot.

"*Push,*" she laughed. He batted at her foot.

"I am not above fucking you in a garage."

"Promises, promises," she sang, and pushed him in the head again.

"I'm serious, Tate. I'm still mad at you, for this whole little escapade. I haven't even begun to get back at you for your little fling," he warned her.

"Ooohhh, '*get back at me*', he says. Game?" she asked, and pushed his head again.

"No, no games. *Stop it,*" he growled. She went to push him again and his hand grabbed her ankle.

"Make me," she pursed her lips at him, blowing a kiss. He sighed and let go of her leg. Began pulling off his jacket.

REPARATION

"I don't know if you've noticed, but I'm not a small man," he told her. She laughed, stretching her legs back out.

"Yes, I have noticed," she replied. He lifted his hips and undid his pants.

"I have to fold myself into a piece of origami to fuck you in these cars," he complained, clumsily crawling between the two front seats and falling on top of her.

"Get bigger cars," she suggested, then choked on her words when his fingers ended up between her legs.

"Are you telling me what to do, Tate?" he asked, roughly yanking her legs around, rearranging her so he was kneeling between them.

"I wouldn't dream of it, Mr. Kane," she breathed

"I like that, you know. *Mr. Kane*. Makes me feel like you've finally learned your place. *Say it again*," he ordered.

"Fuck me, *Mr. Kane*," she begged, biting back a laugh.

"And why should I do that? You have been a very, *very* bad girl," he told her, pulling her shorts away from her hips.

"Then you should fuck me very, *very* hard," she suggested. He leaned foward, pressing his weight against her.

"Hmm, still sounds like you're getting rewarded. I was thinking more along the lines of a punishment," he whispered.

"Whichever, whatever, just get on with it," she growled, wiggling her hips around underneath him.

"Commanding me?" he asked, pushing himself up so he hovered over her.

"*Begging you*," she whispered. He smiled, then moved his hand across her forehead, brushing hair away.

"I like that, too. Maybe do that some more," he suggested. She laughed.

"You're only allowed so much begging. You've reached your quota for the week," she joked, but his hand moved into her hair and pulled sharply.

"*I* tell *you* what you're allowed to do, not vice versa. *Now fucking beg,*" he snapped at her.

"*Please,* Jameson. Please, I'm begging you. Please, do whatever you want to me. Do anything. Do *everything,*" she begged in a sexy, breathy voice.

"God, that sounds good. You're so good at that," he said with a groan.

"Really? I thought I was getting better at it," she agreed in a serious voice that cut the mood. Jameson laughed and playfully slapped her on the cheek. A mockery. An inside joke. *A promise.*

"You could stand to get better."

"Only for you, Jameson."

"Only for me."

"I do love you, you know," she said softly. He nodded.

"I know, baby girl. I know," he assured her.

"That doesn't scare you?" she asked, chewing on her bottom lip. He still had the ability to make her so nervous. She figured she should just get used to it – she wasn't going anywhere.

"No," he shook his head. "That doesn't scare me at all, not anymore."

"What changed?" she asked, looking away from his soul-stealing stare and smoothing her hands across his chest.

"The game. You, me. Everything," he told her. She cleared her throat.

"Jameson," she started, then lost her nerve. She had been working up the courage to ask him something since their first night back together.

"Hmmm?" he replied, one of his fingers tracing along her bottom lip.

"What does the necklace mean, to you?" she squeaked out, feeling all of two inches tall.

"Excuse me?"

REPARATION

"The necklace. I mean, I know what it means. To me, I mean. But what does it mean, you know, to you," she stammered.

"I'm not even sure what you just said, let alone what you're asking me," he teased her. She rolled her eyes.

"It's okay, you know. You said you were willing to try, and that's all I'm asking for. I promise, this time. I really promise. It's more than I could have hoped for, really. We're together, and you don't need to —," she babbled.

"Tatum. Are you asking me if I'm in love with you?" he asked, his voice serious. She swallowed thickly, staring at the collar of his shirt like it was hypnotizing her.

"Maybe," she whispered.

"Don't be fucking stupid," he snapped. She finally looked up at him, snorting.

"*You're* fucking stupid! I'm trying to be nice and tell you it's okay that you don't, that you don't have to feel bad, and you're such a dick, you always have to —," she started telling him off, trying to wiggle out from underneath him. He put his hand over her mouth.

"Tatum."

She blinked her eyes up at him.

"*Hmmfff?*" she mumbled.

"Shut the fuck up."

"*Ho hmuck hurr helf,*" she tried to swear through his palm.

"I have loved you since you were eighteen, you idiot."

Her eyeballs nearly fell out of her head.

"*Hreary!?*"

"I can't understand what you're saying."

She slapped at his chest. By the time he moved his hand, she had started crying.

"You're shitting me," she sniffled.

"I never lie, Tatum," he assured her. She pressed her hands against her face.

"You can't. You haven't … everything. So much time. Why didn't you say anything?" she cried. He pulled at her wrists.

"Because I didn't know," he replied.

"How could you not know something like that!?" she demanded.

"Hey, look who's talking. You've probably been in love with me for even longer, and you still don't realize it," he pointed out, finally peeling a hand away. She kept her eyes shut tight.

"God, sometimes I hate you," she cried. He laughed.

"I finally say the words, and this is the response I get," he chuckled, pulling at her other hand.

"Well you can't just spring it on me like this!" she yelled at him, finally looking up at him. He looked down at her like she was nuts.

"You asked me, you crazy bitch," he laughed.

"Well, I didn't expect that answer, *you crazy bitch!*" she yelled back.

"Would you like me to take it back?" he offered.

She wrapped her arms around his shoulders and yanked him close. She needed him to breathe. To exist. So much. She struggled with him, wrestled around till she was able to roll him underneath her, then she straddled his hips, pulling him to sit upright with her.

"I *never* want you take it back," she whispered, pulling her shirt over her head.

"Good. Because I'm not in the habit of taking things back," he replied, unbuttoning his own shirt and tossing it into the front seat.

"I want you to say it again," she breathed, leaning forward and kissing his jaw. His ear. His shoulder.

"Hmmm, can't have you getting accustomed to such things. You have to work for praise, baby girl," he teased.

"*Please*," she pleaded.

"Begging again. I'm on a roll today."

"Please."

REPARATION

"I don't know. I *am* Satan. Saying those sweet words actually burns me," he warned her. She shook her head.

"You love to burn. You've already burned me. *Do it again,*" she whispered. He pushed her away. Smoothed his hands over her hair, then rested them against the sides of her neck. Looked at her. Really looked at her.

"Tatum O'Shea, there is a very distinct possibility that I have been in love with you since the first time I saw you," he told her, his voice quiet. She laughed, wiped at her nose, and then laughed again.

"God, how awkward for Ellie. Better leave that out of the wedding vows," she joked. He groaned.

"Jesus. I'm just getting used to the *L-word*, don't go throwing around the *M-word*," he warned her. She leaned close, tracing the shell of his ear with her tongue.

"Hmmm, I think when you say '*M-word*', we both have two very different words in mind," she whispered huskily, siding her hand down his chest.

"I'm thinking the marriage-word. What the fuck are you thinking?" he demanded.

"*Menage.*"

He burst out laughing.

"Fuck, Tatum, I think I will marry you."

"You're so easy."

"Not as easy as you."

"No, probably not."

"Tatum?"

"Hmmm?"

"Will you please shut the fuck up now?" he groaned. She thought about it for a second.

"Maybe. If you say it just one more time," she told him. He growled, and suddenly her panties were ripped away.

"Prove to me how bad you can be, then maybe I'll say it again," he snapped. She sighed, scratching her nails down his arms.

"Anything for you, Satan."

"*Good answer.*"

Acknowledgments

Hmmm. Where do I start? I'm going to make this quick, stop it before the tears start. As always, for Sue. If you read the book, and you're reading this part, and you enjoyed that last chapter, you have Sue to thank – it didn't exist before her feedback.

Thank you to all the blogs, to EVERY blog that read, that reviewed, that posted, that showed promos. Big and small, interactive or not. You have changed my life.

To everyone who loves to read so much, they take time out of their day to seek out authors and reach out to them. I don't know about other authors, but I appreciate it immensely and I always ALWAYS welcome it.

Thank you to my husband. You put up with me. You support me. You allow me to be me.

Thank you to Becs, formerly of Sinfully Sexy Book Reviews. Despite stepping away from the blogging world, you were still willing to read and review.

Thank you to SueBee, Goodreads reviewer extraordinaire, who took a chance on an ARC and then read the whole series – the following Epilogue would never have seen the light of day without your encouragement.

To a naughty, dirty website that shall remain nameless, for inspiring me to write what was in me to write, and to not be afraid of it.

To Najla Qamber, the best graphic designer in the business, as far as I'm concerned. You have done all my covers, and all have been great. You deal with my changing mind and millions of e-mails. You make sense out of my non-sense. You translate my vision when I can't even figure out how to spell it. People, need a cover? Need a logo? Need something pretty? http://www.najlaqamberdesigns.com — you won't be sorry. She is amazing.

To the person reading this right now. When I wrote Jameson's story, I really didn't imagine it ever finding you, but I'm very glad it did.

There, and I didn't even cry.

Well, not too much.

About the Author

Crazy woman living in an undisclosed location in Alaska (where the need for a creative mind is a necessity!), I have been writing since ..., forever? Yeah, that sounds about right. I have been told that I remind people of Lucille Ball — I also see shades of Jennifer Saunders, and Denis Leary. So basically, I laugh a lot, I'm clumsy a lot, and I say the F-word A LOT.

I like dogs more than I like most people, and I don't trust anyone who doesn't drink. No, I do not live in an igloo, and no, the sun does not set for six months out of the year, there's your Alaska lesson for the day. I have mermaid hair — both a curse and a blessing — and most of the time I talk so fast, even I can't understand me.

Yeah. I think that about sums me up.

Printed in Great Britain
by Amazon